---- ★ ----

To Rafferty, it was looking more and more like the work of a copycat killer.

Keeping a careful distance between himself and the body on the autopsy table, Rafferty asked, "How much effort would it have taken to hold her down and suffocate her at the same time? Or do you think she was knocked out first? That bruise on her temple—"

"Might have stunned her, made her less able to fight back. But there are several indications she was conscious before she died. And if you left that wall to hold itself up and came a bit closer, you'd not only be able to see the pinpoint hemorrhages in the eyes, consistent with suffocation, you'd also be able to see the grazes on the backs of her legs. As if she'd scratched them on the rough grasses, as she tried to drag her legs up to remove a heavy weight."

Rafferty took Sam's word for it and stayed where he was.

---- ★ ----

Also available from Worldwide Mystery by
GERALDINE EVANS

DEAD BEFORE MORNING

Geraldine EVANS

Down Among The DEAD Men

WORLDWIDE.®

TORONTO • NEW YORK • LONDON
AMSTERDAM • PARIS • SYDNEY • HAMBURG
STOCKHOLM • ATHENS • TOKYO • MILAN
MADRID • WARSAW • BUDAPEST • AUCKLAND

To George, with love

DOWN AMONG THE DEAD MEN

A Worldwide Mystery/July 1996

First published by St. Martin's Press, Incorporated.

ISBN 0-373-26208-6

Printed in U.S.A.

ACKNOWLEDGMENTS

With thanks to Mr. Fred Feather, Public Relations Officer
of Essex Police, both for his helpful responses to my
questions about the Essex force and for supplying me
with so much informative literature on same.
Thanks also to Mrs. Gillian M. Goudge of the
Royal Horticultural Society for her advice
on research sources.

ONE

As THOUGH LULLED BY the heavy September air and the fluting whisper of the River Tiffey half a field away, the woman lay sprawled on the parched earth, her limbs in the abandoned posture of a sleeping child. The sun, emerging from behind a solitary cloud, turned her cap of flaxen hair into spangled silk against the dry dross of the meadow. It bestowed such an appearance of sparkling, vibrant life that Inspector Rafferty took several steps back, his usual good sense overtaken by an illogical fear that she would waken and discover him looming over her.

Feeling foolish as he sensed Llewellyn's startled glance, he ignored his sergeant and continued to study the figure more circumspectly. Dressed in some leaf-green gauzy stuff that bunched around her slender thighs, she had the other-worldly appearance of a woodland nymph; in her hand a single bloom, its crushed petals faded to an indistinguishable straw colour. A fairy-like bower of wild meadow flowers scattered around her body completed the illusion that they had somehow stumbled into a secret, fairy-tale world where princesses slumbered and frogs turned into princes.

Just then a faint breeze sprang up and wafted a malodorous whiff of the River Tiffey towards them. The tainted breeze brought reality back with a rush, effectively killing any lingering heat-induced fancies. The miracle was that they had sprung into being at all, Rafferty reflected. For, even at nine o'clock on a bright September morning, the Essex meadow had a desolate air. Twenty yards from the body, and tumbled around a stained and long-abandoned royal-blue mattress, lay a pile of worn-out tyres. This was the real world, not never-never land. Regretfully, Rafferty accepted that the woman was just another poor victim in an increasingly violent society, as mortal as the rest of humanity and as dead as it was possible to be. The tell-tale reddish-purple discoloration on the back of her limbs would have told him that sooner, if he'd bothered to look, and, judging by the extent of the after-death hypostasis, she'd been dead some hours. Feeling foolish again, but thankful he hadn't blurted out his nonsense to Llewellyn, Rafferty wondered how he could have forgotten that the only sleep the Sniffy Tiffey would encourage would be the permanent sort?

The smelly breeze dropped and, with the return of the dead heat, the day seemed even more stifling, almost as if some heavenly vacuum cleaner had sucked all the oxygen out of the atmosphere, starving his brain and leaving his thought processes sluggish. But, however sluggish his brain, there was no escaping the inevitable conclusions. She'd been murdered all right, smothered, he suspected, just like the other two victims over the border in Suffolk, where it was beginning to look as if a serial killer might have enlarged his area of operations. The thought was a chilling one, and Rafferty made a mental note to contact the Suffolk CID as soon as they got back to the office, in order to check out the murderer's MO for any similarities to this latest killing. With a nod of his head, he drew Llewellyn away from the body for a brief consultation, leaving more room for the photographer to do his work.

After unzipping his protective overalls a few inches, Rafferty sighed with relief as he loosened his grass-green tie and eased the creased shirt collar away from his clammy skin. His mouth turned down as he glanced at Llewellyn, who unlike himself, looked cool and untroubled by the heat. How did the man manage to look so spruce, so sweat-free? Rafferty wondered. Swallowing his irritation, he muttered, with a dispirited attempt at his usual whimsical speculation, 'What do you reckon we have here, Dafyd? The work of the Suffolk cyclepath, as my old ma calls him?'

Not given to either whimsy or speculation, the Welshman stated matter-of-factly, 'I've no idea, sir.' Apparently, his usual efficiency was as unaffected by the heat as the rest of him for he continued briskly, 'I'll get on to Missing Persons. See what the computer can tell us.'

Rafferty watched sourly as his bandbox-fresh sergeant turned and made for the car. He was twenty yards away before Rafferty thought to stop him. 'Don't bother,' he called. 'I reckon I know who this one is.' He should, he acknowledged belatedly, as her disappearance had only been reported to him yesterday, personally—by Charles Shore, her sort of brother-in-law, and the description he had furnished fitted this woman perfectly, even down to the colour of the dress.

Liven up, Rafferty, he ordered. As he forced his mind into something approaching a policeman-like alertness, he realized that the registration number of the red hatchback behind which they'd parked in the narrow tarmac lane matched hers too, and he dispatched two of the SOCO team to check it over.

Zipping his overalls back up, he returned to the scene. A small shoulderbag, already dusted for prints by the scene of crime team, lay close to the body, and after checking that it was OK to touch it, he opened it. Its contents confirmed his suspicions. 'Mrs Barbara Longman, wife of Henry Longman—or second wife, I should say, as I gather he's divorced from the first one. Wife number one is another member of the Shore family. I suppose you've heard of them?'

'One of the most prominent families in the county.'

Rafferty nodded gloomily. He had a vague recollection of an earlier tragedy involving the Shores, but as his mind refused to be cudgelled into throwing it up, he left it to come to him of its own accord. Just my luck, he groaned silently, as Llewellyn's comment echoed in his brain. Why was it he seemed to get lumbered with murders that involved important families? His last case had been the same. For some reason, Superintendent Bradley seemed to think this qualified Rafferty for mixing in exalted circles. Rafferty wished he could agree with him. Grim humour forced his lips into a semblance of a smile as another more likely explanation occurred to him.

Shore must have spoken to Bradley after he had reported Mrs Longman missing and, with the early reports of the victim's appearance, Bradley had put two and two together a bit quicker than Rafferty had managed. With typical Yorkshire caution, old Bradley had considered all the options. Just in case the murderer turned out to be more intimately connected with the Shore family than was so far indicated, he had decided Rafferty should take the case, presumably in the belief that the Shores would be less guarded with him than with a more sophisticated copper. The British Columbo, thought Rafferty, with a wry grimace, that's me. He turned to Llewellyn. 'Who found her?'

Llewellyn nodded in the direction of two teenage boys waiting at the edge of the meadow, well beyond the police cordons. Dark haired, and attractively tousled by the heat, WPC Green was with them, struggling to keep a comforting arm around each boy's shoulder, as they towered half a head above her.

'They were exercising their dogs,' Llewellyn explained, 'and one of the animals found her.'

Rafferty nodded. 'I'll just have a quick word with them.' However, the two youngsters could tell him little more than what Llewellyn had already learned and, after making sure they had a note of their names and addresses, he told WPC Green to drive them home.

He stood for a moment in mute admiration of the scene of crime team. Like a well-oiled machine, in anticipation of the many comings and goings, they had already checked and cleared a narrow path to the body, so as to ensure that the rest of the murder scene remained untouched till they could examine it. And when they did, the search would be thorough and painstaking. If the murderer had left any clues to his identity behind him, the team would find them.

Wishing he exuded a similar air of smooth competence, Rafferty's mood brightened as he watched the rounded figure of Dr Sam Dally approach the cordon. He stopped, in order to give his name to the young clipboard-clutching constable, and, after a struggle in which he finally persuaded his body into his protective gear, Dally followed the path indicated by the officer.

Like the two detectives, he'd had to leave his car a field away and walk; sweating and cursing with equal profusion, he looked ready to perform a premature post-mortem on anyone who provoked him. He bestowed a scowl on Rafferty, his unpredictable early morning temper evidently not improved by the knowledge that the usually tardy inspector had managed to beat him to the scene.

'I'm too old for all this gambolling about the countryside,' he complained, when he'd finally forced his way through nature's wonders. 'What happened to you, Rafferty?' he demanded in an irascible tone. 'Did your bed collapse? Or has Sergeant Llewellyn succeeded in recruiting you to his early morning jogging routine?'

'Neither.' Rafferty's teasing, lopsided grin earned him another scowl. 'It's not me that's early, Dilly Dally. It's you that's late. You said yourself you're getting too long in the tooth for this game.'

Sam grunted. 'And for that you can blame my dentist.' He bared gleaming dentures. 'New set—could have bought a house when I was a young man for what that bloodsucker charged me. Bloody uncomfortable they are, too. Gums are red raw.'' He stopped blinding him with his magnificent new molars and put his bag down. 'Right. What have we got?'

'Been smothered like the women in Suffolk, I reckon,' Rafferty confided incautiously. 'Though it's funny...'

'Oh, *Dr* Rafferty now, is it?' jeered Sam. 'Sure you need me?' He elbowed Rafferty aside and, after studying the woman's body, he opened his bag and got to work.

'Reported missing last night,' Rafferty addressed Sam's bald spot. 'About nine. She'd hardly been gone any time at all and I was going to advise them to wait and see if she turned up, but the chap who spoke to me was very insistent. I must admit, I thought it a bit odd that a grown woman should be reported missing quite so quickly.' He frowned. 'Makes you wonder if he knew something I didn't. When do you reckon she died?'

Sam muttered cryptically, 'You mean you don't know?' before adding. 'Give me a chance, Rafferty. As you pointed out, *I've* only just got here, and a magician I'm not. Now, if you wouldn't mind getting out of my light...'

Feeling, like a spare groom at a wedding, sadly superfluous to the requirements of both Dally, the virgin-clothed bride and the forensic congregation, Rafferty took the hint and left him to it. With, for the moment, nothing else to occupy him but the twin irritations of dive-bombing gnats and sweaty flesh, he sought oblivion from his torment by letting his mind wander where it would. Fortunately, it didn't need to wander far.

As his gaze rose above the bustling murder scene, Rafferty's expression visibly softened, and he almost managed to forget the gnats and the heat, as his gaze settled on the horizon and the roof-line of Elmhurst, a mile and a half to the northwest. He sighed happily, as he remembered the envy he'd instilled in London friends, who had escaped the rat race for a blissful June fortnight. Proudly, he'd pointed out Elmhurst's Roman remains, the small bricks they had

favoured pillaged for later additions, and clearly evident in every building with any claim to historical
significance.

From here, as well as the prominent ruins of the
priory, in the oldest part of the town, he could see the
spire—unusual in East Anglia—of St Boniface Catholic church soaring above its pygmy neighbours.
Briefly, he wondered if his ma was attending morning mass?

Rafferty loved the place; the rich red blood of history seeped over its driest bones; timber-frame, flint
and weatherboard jostled for space, and within a
short drive he could choose between the pleasures of
coast and countryside. Most of all, Elmhurst had
character and he liked that. The knowledge that he
had the best of all worlds gave Rafferty a feeling of
contentment he'd never experienced anywhere else. It
was a feeling that had grown on him gradually, since
he and his two brothers and three sisters had been
unwillingly uprooted from London by his widowed
mother. That was why, although it amused him to say
he earned his living from crime, he hated it when the
murder of a fellow human being tarnished the place.

He sighed again, less happily this time, and wiped
his sweating face on the sleeve of his disposable
overalls, conscious once more of the furnace heat
caused by the high pressure that had lain punishingly
over the southern half of England for the past two
weeks. The horizon began to shimmer in dizzying
fashion and he lowered his gaze and prayed for rain,
daunted at the uncomfortable prospect of conducting a murder inquiry in a heatwave. With a wry smile,
he sacrilegiously paraphrased one of Llewellyn's more
edifying quotations, murmuring, 'Oh for the return

of the green and sceptered isle by a bloody good thunderstorm.'

The meadow was a haven for wild flowers; hazy blues, corn-ripe yellows and regal purples nestled among the dry grass. There were masses of them, and, of course, he couldn't put a name to any of them. But as his sergeant, equally at a loose end, materialized beside him, he guessed he wouldn't need to. Llewellyn, his personal oracle, would be sure to know.

He did. 'There's spiked speedwell, and there's corn-cockle.' The Welshman pointed them out with a long, fine finger. 'Do you know, I haven't seen those for years? The *Elmhurst Echo* carried an article by the local Conservation Society about these last week. Apparently, there are several rare species in this meadow.'

'Miracle they've survived then, with the tyre-dumping fraternity round,' Rafferty remarked dampingly. Perhaps it was the effect of the weather, but, for whatever reason, his sergeant's encyclopaedia-like knowledge irritated him more than usual this morning. Glancing back at the activity concealed behind the screens, he was thankful to see Sam Dally rise from his labours and beckon them over. 'Come on, looks like Sam's finished.'

Conscious of his sergeant's critical gaze, Rafferty was careful to avoid stepping on any of the wild flowers, but the scattering of rare meadow flowers around the body, combined with his sergeant's serious countenance, encouraged Rafferty to a moment's wild speculation. What if the woman hadn't been murdered by the Suffolk serial killer at all? he mused. Perhaps she had been killed by one of the local 'Green' community, outraged by her destructive flower-gathering? He let his mind go so far as to picture screaming KILLER CONSERVATIONIST headlines, before he regretfully dismissed the idea. It *was* pretty unlikely.

Sam, his face shocking pink from his exertions, nodded at the corpse. 'She can be taken away now. I can't do any more here.'

The victim's head, hands and feet had already been encased in plastic in order to protect any forensic evidence and as they watched, the entire cadaver was placed in a body bag, before it was carried in a fibreglass coffin to the waiting mortuary van.

'I'd say she died sometime yesterday afternoon,' Sam informed them. Briskly, he began gathering up his equipment. 'I'll have to wait till I've done the PM to be more definite, of course.' He glanced irritably at the innocent azure sky. 'This infernal heat doesn't help matters.'

Like a true-born son of the Scottish Highlands, Sam Dally preferred his mornings crisp and even, and he had no liking for 'these damned unnatural Mediterranean heatwaves', as he called the current weather.

'Cheer up, Sam. The weathermen say it'll break in a day or two.' As Dally snorted his derision of the entire meteorological breed and their promises, Rafferty added hopefully, 'I'd appreciate it if you could pin the time of death a bit closer.'

Sam scowled. 'I wish you'd get it into that thick Irish skull of yours that pathology is a bit more demanding than the average British Rail timetable. *They* don't have to get up in a court of law and defend their claimed departure times; I do.' Having vented his irritation, Sam relented a bit. 'All I'll say is that I'd plump more towards the time you're enjoying your second cup of tea of the afternoon. Satisfied?'

Rafferty nodded. It narrowed the time down nicely. If Sam was right, the time of death had probably been between three and five o'clock yesterday afternoon. According to her sort-of brother-in-law, the victim had last been seen alive at 3.00 p.m. Rafferty tried his luck further. 'Can you confirm the cause of death, Sam? Was she suffocated?'

'Probably.' He picked up his bag, and, smiling for the first time that morning, he added before he walked away, 'But you'll not make me commit myself till I've done the PM.'

Rafferty hadn't expected anything more, but he was satisfied. To get a 'probably' out of Sam was akin to a definite confirmation from anyone else.

Before he followed Dally, Rafferty had a word with the most senior member of the SOCO team. He wasn't surprised when he was told that they had, as yet, discovered nothing of obvious interest. It was early days, and their painstaking work would go on for some time yet, both at the scene of the crime and back at the laboratory. Still, he was hopeful, more so because it very much looked as if she had died where she had been found. The dry grasses under her heels had been reduced to tiny broken stalks, as if her shoes had pummelled the ground as she had struggled with her killer.

The countryside just here was sparsely populated; apart from some farm buildings several hundred yards away across the fields, there were few houses, just the tiny village of St Botolphe further along the main road, towards Elmhurst.

He got in the passenger seat. Llewellyn started the car and turned its nose in the direction of the Shores' house as Rafferty got on the radio to the station. As the meadow was in such a lonely spot, he doubted much would come of the house-to-house. He hoped they would manage to turn up more information from a second team, arranged to question the motorists using the main road adjacent to the meadow.

Radioing done, he sat back and thought about the victim. Had she been younger, he'd have thought it likely she had arranged to meet a lover, and had gathered the flowers while waiting for him. But this woman was in her late twenties, according to Charles Shore, and likely to prefer her clandestine couplings on soft sheets rather than dry grass shucks and hard-baked soil. So what had she been doing here? Surely, in this violent age, she hadn't just come to gather flowers, no matter how rare and enticing the local flora? Especially in the flimsy get-up *she* had on. It was asking for trouble in normal times, but with a known killer just a few miles over the county border . . .

THE ONLY ROUTE from the meadow to the Shores' house was via a road full of meandering curves. Occasionally, as the highway wound lazily eastwards, back upon itself, and the hedgerows parted, they caught a glimpse of the river to their right, straight as a Roman road, the sun making a tarnished sheet of glass of its sluggish green surface. It shadowed as a flock of black and brown brent-geese rose from the nearby mud flats, swooped low over the water and headed north, their plaintive *rott, rott, rott* cry echoing across the still countryside, as if mocking Rafferty and his habit of constructing theories before he had any facts to back them up.

After about ten minutes, tall grey chimneys reared up above the river's west bank. The Shores' place, thought Rafferty. From this distance, it had a touch of Victorian workhouse Gothic. The gloomy drive, edged with dusty dark-green graveyard yews, bearing a miserly scattering of scarlet fruit, disappeared behind the house. The house itself echoed the sombre theme. It was grotesque. There was no other word to describe it. So ugly, it had a peculiar fascination of its own, like an over-the-top first-prize winner in a bad-taste contest.

Constructed in grey stone, at a distance, it had looked merely drably institutional. It was only as they got nearer that the appalling decorative reminders of death—the great modern-day unmentionable—became visible. The roof-line was broken up with the most fantastic gargoyles: satyrs and devils with evil, grinning faces clutched three-pronged forks and stabbed with undisguised relish the eternally damned human wretches sharing their strange eyrie.

Of course, to the Victorians who had built the place, *sex* was the great unmentionable, he reminded himself. They had been only too familiar with death, in its many guises. As he stared again at the high-rise etchings, some details of the earlier tragedy in the Shore family came filtering back. Maximillian Shore, Charles Shore's father, had been murdered years earlier, blown to bits in his booby-trapped car. The old man had been a hard bastard, by all accounts, and although the case had never been solved, there had been a suspicion that one of his business rivals had been responsible.

Maximillian Shore—or Schurr as he'd been then, before he'd Anglicized it—had had a tragic beginning. His parents, his entire family, had died at the hands of the Nazis. The only survivor, he had arrived in England with just the clothes he stood up in; penniless, parentless and homeless. Yet he had thrived. Today, the Shore family empire was international and encompassed the wide arena of newspapers, chemicals and finance. It wasn't difficult to imagine the difficulties that the traumatized orphan must have had to overcome in order to acquire the wealth that had begun it all. The grinning devils dancing on the roof must have appealed to old Maximillian when he bought the place, Rafferty reflected, as he recalled the stories the papers had dredged up after the old man's murder. With his early experiences, he would have known more about the evil core of humanity than most. After telling Llewellyn about the earlier tragedy in the family, he remarked, 'Not a lucky family, despite their wealth.'

'Every man is the architect of his own fortune,' was Llewellyn's murmured response. 'Sallust, sir,' he explained to Rafferty's blank face. 'He was a Roman historian at the time of Julius Caesar and he...'

'Yes, yes. Thanks for another piece of useless information.' Llewellyn lapsed into silence and Rafferty, noting the glint in the Welshman's dark eye, wondered, not for the first time, if Llewellyn paraded his erudition out of sheer mischief. It was impossible to deduce much from that impassive poker face. 'I mightn't know much about this Sallust johnny,' Rafferty admitted briskly, 'but one thing I *do* know is that the super will hang me out to dry if I make a mess of the case, so perhaps we can get on?'

However, before he could carry out his good intentions, as they got closer to the house, the sound of youthful voices distracted him.

'Stupid, stupid. Mini Maxie's stupid.'

'I'm *not* stupid.' The old boy's deeper voice broke through the piping taunts. 'I'm not stupid,' the boy repeated. 'I'll prove it, just you wait and see.' But his boasts only brought more jeering laughter.

'You?' The younger boy's voice was shrill with spite. 'You can't even get basic grades without my father paying for extra holiday tuition.' In the precocious manner of modern children, he sneered, 'I heard him telling Mother that if *your* mother had been his sister-in-law instead of his sister, he'd suspect you were the result of some affair and had no Shore blood at all.'

The sound of a blow broke into the stillness of the morning, and the older boy's voice, its triumphant note unmistakable, echoed towards them. 'You said it! At least I can be sure I belong here, as you'll realize before you're much older, which is more than can be said for you; with *your* mother.'

'You hit me!' Rafferty wondered why the younger boy should sound so surprised. He had certainly asked for it.

'Yes, and I'll hit you again, you little rat. It's about time somebody taught you some manners. Come back here!'

The next second, a well-built and weasely-faced boy of about ten raced around the side of the house, pursued by a tall, wiry youth of about fifteen. The smaller boy easily avoided Rafferty, but the older one, probably because his eyes had that glazed, unseeing look brought on by anger, cannoned into him. He was panting heavily and, as his vision cleared, he looked wildly from Rafferty to Llewellyn and back again, before he tore himself out of Rafferty's grasp and continued his pursuit round the far side of the house.

'They must be old Max's grandchildren,' Rafferty remarked. As he wondered what relation the dead woman was to them, he spared them a moment's pity. The years of childhood were all too brief; if the relationship was a close one, it was likely that the dark, adult passions that had brought the woman's violent death would shatter their childhood for ever. The thought depressed him.

He gave the gargoyles one final glance, tightened his tie and made for the front door. Depressing or not, you've got a job to do, Rafferty, he reminded himself. Just climb out of the slough of despond and get on with it.

TWO

A WOMAN OF about fifty opened the door to their ring. The housekeeper, Rafferty guessed. Deep lines were scored from her nostrils to her mouth and her lips were puckered, as if life had sapped her dry. Her eyes, though, were sharp and bright with curiosity.

Her appearance only served to increase Rafferty's sense of foreboding. For, in an attempt to bridge the intellectual divide between Llewellyn and himself, he had recently embarked on some self-education, starting with what he chose to regard as the lighter classics, and the grim housekeeper reminded him strongly of Mrs Danvers.

In case the resemblance to the Manderley housekeeper should extend to the personality as well, Rafferty was at his most formal as he introduced himself and Llewellyn. 'We'd like to see Mr Henry Longman, please,' he requested, putting away his warrant card. 'It's about his wife. We have some news for him.'

'I see.' Her gaze flickered over him, and although she didn't question him, Rafferty got the impression she guessed they didn't bring good tidings. Silently, she ushered them inside.

'You're Mrs...?'

'Mrs Griffiths. I'm the housekeeper here.'

Rafferty nodded. Been here for years, he imagined. She had that air about her that suggested she would know all the family secrets.

They followed her down the hallway. On the walls on either side were what appeared to be hand-painted flower pictures. The hallways was too dark for Rafferty to read the inscriptions under the flowers, but the paintings were exquisitely executed, and even Rafferty, whose knowledge of flowers was scanty, had little difficulty in recognizing several of the more distinctive flowers: pansies and marigolds and delphiniums.

As they passed the last of the paintings, the perfume from a massed arrangement of late roses greeted them and Rafferty paused to admire the display. Palest pink, each petal was touched with yellow, and their spicy fragrance provided much more of a welcome than had the housekeeper. The flowers looked fresh, as though they had only been picked the day before, yet already several bright petals lay scattered like fallen tears on the polished mahogany table and, in a return to the fanciful earlier mood, Rafferty imagined they wept for the dead fairy nymph in the meadow. He gave an appreciative sniff and murmured, 'Beautiful.'

Obviously Mrs Griffiths wasn't a nature lover, for her lips tightened and she observed tartly, 'Beautiful maybe, for those who haven't got to keep clearing up petals from all over the floor.' She met Rafferty's glance with a censorious stare and said no more.

The old mahogany panelling that looked as if it had been there since the house was built made the hall depressingly dark, and the flowers provided a delightful and much needed splash of colour and scent. Rafferty was surprised that such a high flier as Charles Shore hadn't torn out all the morbid panelling years ago, or at least stripped off the old varnish. Perhaps, he mused, he was fostering a lord of the manor image, but if so, the ugly Victorian mansion was hardly appropriate.

'Mr Henry's upstairs,' Mrs Griffiths informed them. She opened a door to the left of the hallway. 'Perhaps you'll wait in the library while I tell him you're here?' Unsmilingly, she shut the door on them.

There were more roses in the equally gloomy library. By way of contrast, these were yellow, flushed with pink, and had the sweet soapy scent of a freshly scrubbed infant. The room should have been bright and airy with its high ceilings and large windows, but, like the hall, the panelling defeated other architectural merits. Perhaps in the winter, with a fire crackling merrily in the grate, the room would shed its melancholy atmosphere, but somehow Rafferty doubted it and now the oppressive heat, the heavy old-fashioned furniture and the dark wood walls all combined to give him the sensation of being enclosed in a king-sized coffin. Striding over to the windows, he flung one open to its full extent before gazing around the rest of the room.

As a bit of light relief from the panelling, floor-to-ceiling bookshelves covered one entire wall and part of a second. He'd never seen so many books outside a public library. There were literally hundreds of them, all with rich dark green leather bindings and gold lettering that echoed the geometrical patterns of the crimson rug that covered the middle of the floor.

'Keshan,' Llewellyn commented, as he followed Rafferty's gaze. 'Persian,' he enlarged, when Rafferty still looked blank. 'Made of silk. Much sought after now, I believe. There's an old Persian saying, "The richer the man the thinner the carpet."'

'Prefer a nice Wilton myself,' Rafferty retorted. Aware he had uttered a heresy, he turned away and studied the stacks of books. The dismal thought occurred to him that he could match Llewellyn knowledge for knowledge and quote for quote.

More books were scattered on assorted tables. Whoever had stocked the library had certainly had a lively interest in other people's business, he realized, because as he roamed around the shelves he noticed that there were a great many histories and biographies of well-known people: Chaplin, Abraham Lincoln, Tolstoy, Mark Twain, all the greats from every sphere were represented here, politicians, sportsmen, industrialists, writers. Unsurprisingly, given that the Shore family's entrepreneurial skills had gained them the bulk of their wealth, biographies of businessmen seemed to dominate.

School-books were strewn on the long table under the windows; an open exercise-book showed no more than half a dozen badly spelled and ungrammatical lines, scrawled in an immature fist. The older boy's extra holiday work, Rafferty guessed. Poor little sod, he thought wryly, reminded of his own extra-curricular reading tasks, he didn't seem to have got very far with it. It appeared that, like himself, the boy wasn't much of a scholar.

Suddenly becoming conscious of eyes staring at him, Rafferty raised his head to the portrait which hung between the windows. It was a magnificent piece of work. It dominated the room and although, like the house, the oil colours were sombre—workhouse grey and mourning purple—the personality of the subject fairly leapt out of the canvas.

There was no mistaking the family patriarch; it was old Maximillian Shore to the life. Rafferty guessed that it must have been done not long before his murder, because he remembered exactly the same uncompromising features staring out from newspapers after his death. Almost biblical in appearance, his was the sort of uncomfortable face that caused a lapsed Catholic like Rafferty to seriously consider his sins. Under black brows fairly bristling with Old Testament fervour, the fierce grey eyes that had demanded his attention stared contemptuously back at him, as if taking in every detail of his unruly auburn hair, his carelessly tightened grass-green tie, and scuffed down-at-heel black shoes.

Feeling censured, Rafferty looked down at the inscription beneath the portrait, but was irritated to discover that this was in Latin and he was unable to read it. As he remembered that the old man's background was no more grand than his own, he raised his eyes to Shore's disdainful countenance and exclaimed cuttingly, 'Latin! You're a pretentious old twat, that's what you are.'

Llewellyn came to stand beside him and—naturally—read the inscription on the portrait with ease. ' "*Hoc volo, sic iubeo, sit pro ratione voluntas*"— "The fact that I wish it is reason enough for doing it",' he translated, 'from Juvenal's *Satires*. A more literal translation might go something like, "This I will, thus I command; let my will serve as reason". Pretty apt choice for Maximillian Shore, wouldn't you say, sir? From what you told me about him, I gather he was something of a tyrant.'

'Oh, yes,' Rafferty snapped. 'It's exactly what I'd have chosen myself.' It was ironic, he reflected, that,

although he was a Catholic, the only Latin *he* knew
was from the assorted hymns he used to sing as a
schoolboy, at Benediction on Friday afternoons. Like
a gathering of parrots, he and his classmates had
chirruped away, without the least idea what they were
singing about. The religious classes had been mostly
conducted on similar lines, and he recalled the rows
he'd had with his mother because he refused to believe something was true just because a humourless
man in a black frock told him so. Such independence
of mind was probably the reason he'd ended up a policeman instead of a builder, like the rest of his family, he concluded. Though, of course, his ma had had
something to do with the choice. He still wasn't sure
whether to be pleased or sorry, but when his *sergeant*
insisted on putting his Latin prose through its paces,
the thought of a building site, even on a freezing
winter's morning, appeared surprisingly attractive. At
least there, the only impressive gift for language he'd
be exposed to would be the crew's rich and un-
abashed fluency in Anglo-Saxon.

Scowling at the portrait and its inscription, Rafferty, more to shut Llewellyn up than from any great
interest, picked up a novel about Lloyd George from
the table and flicked through it, only to shut it hastily as he heard a hesitant throat-clearing from the
doorway. Expecting a thrusting executive type, he was
surprised to see some kind of handyman hovering
there instead, clad in an old shirt, covered in a colour
kaleidoscope of what looked like paint stains. It gave
him a raffish, bohemian air which was at odds with
his anxious, unbohemian expression. As the man just
stood there, saying nothing, Rafferty, made impa-

tient by the heat and his anxieties about the case, demanded gruffly, 'Yes? Can I help you?'

The man started and glanced nervously from one
to the other, before confiding, 'M-Mrs Griffiths told
me you wanted to see me.'

Rafferty's mouth dropped open and he shut it
hastily. With his tattered shirt and grey flannel trousers that conjured up memories of a thousand kneel-
ing masses, Henry Longman looked more like a
jobbing gardener than a side-shoot of the phenomenally wealthy Shore family. Even the way he sidled
into the room, as though unsure of his welcome, re-
inforced the impression of the employee fearfully
anticipating the sack. 'You *are* Mr Longman?' he
questioned doubtfully. 'Mr Henry Longman?'

The man nodded. 'I-I'm sorry. I thought... Mrs
Griffiths said you had news for me.'

Rafferty, recovered from his surprise, suggested
Longman sit down and Henry complied in a manner
that suggested he was used to obeying orders.

'I'm afraid we don't have good news for you, sir,'
Rafferty said, as gently as he could. 'Your wife...Mrs
Longman...' he cleared his throat and began again.
'I'm sorry to have to tell you this, but your wife's
dead. Her body was found a short time ago at Tiffey
Meadow.'

Henry blinked rapidly and stared at Rafferty with
a look of incomprehension tinged with shock, as
though his subconscious had understood Rafferty's
words only too well, but his conscious mind was less
willing to face facts and trailed reluctantly some way
behind.

'Barbara? Dead?' He shook his head, vehemently
at first and then more slowly, almost as if convinced

that as long as he continued to deny his wife's death it couldn't have happened. 'But that's not possible.' He raised a long, bony face on which puzzlement was the chief expression. 'She only went to that meadow because of those wild flowers she's so keen on. Mrs Griffiths told me. How could she possibly be dead?'

Rafferty felt at a loss as to how to deal with him. Bemusedly, he glanced again at the intimidating face of the portrait, before turning again to Longman. Slumped in his chair, Henry resembled nothing so much as an inadequately stuffed Bonfire Night guy. How on earth had the unworldly looking Longman managed to marry into a family as high-profiled and successful as the Shores? he wondered. He must be braver than he looked, Rafferty concluded. *He* certainly wouldn't have fancied old Maximillian as a father-in-law.

The silence lengthened, became uncomfortable. Suddenly, Henry Longman confided, 'Barbara was going to have a baby. She only found out yesterday morning when she telephoned the surgery and got the results of the tests. She was so pleased that she rang me at work straight away.'

Henry's face was bleak, his voice curiously flat as he revealed that the death had been a double tragedy. But Rafferty got the impression that Henry hadn't been as pleased about the pregnancy as his wife and guessed that remorse for his selfishness was adding to his pain. Probably, like a lot of men in a similar situation, he had been jealous and hadn't wanted to share his wife's love even with a baby.

'No one else in the family knows,' Henry went on. 'Barbara wanted to keep it a secret.' His eyes as they

finally met Rafferty's looked empty. 'In the circumstances, I'd rather you didn't mention it.'

Rafferty nodded and hoped it didn't become necessary to break Henry's confidence during the investigation. Of course, the victim's pregnancy would
probably come out during any trial, but that was a
long way in the future. It was the present that Henry
had to get through and his request was understand-
able. He could imagine that the revelation of the
double nature of the tragedy would bring an ava-
lanche of sympathy that would cause Henry even
more anguish and—if he *hadn't* wanted the baby—
even more guilt.

Unsure how to proceed, Rafferty glanced at Llewellyn, but the Welshman wouldn't meet his eye. Not
that he'd really expected any help from *that* quarter.
Llewellyn might be a smart-arse when it came to
Latin, he thought, but he was hopeless in situations
like this.

Still smarting from his own inability to understand
the Latin inscription, Rafferty decided that Master-
mind could at least make himself useful. Jerking his
head sharply at Llewellyn, he mouthed, 'Fetch the
housekeeper.'

Rafferty pulled up a chair beside Henry's crum-
pled-looking figure. Briefly, he gave him the few
facts. Henry didn't respond, just sat rocking his lanky
body backwards and forwards, as if the movement
gave him comfort.

Before Rafferty could break it to Henry that they
had good reason for suspecting that his wife's death
hadn't been a natural one, the housekeeper, who must
have been hovering like the Grim Reaper outside the
library, appeared at his elbow and instantly took over.

It was apparent that Henry Longman was the sort of man who brought out protective instincts in the most unlikely women, as the otherwise formidable housekeeper patted Henry's hand and clucked at him soothingly.

'What you need after such a shock is a hot drink and a lie down.' Glaring at Rafferty, as if Barbara Longman's death was all *his* doing, she clasped Henry to her thin bosom and marched him to the door. Before Rafferty thought of stopping her, she had shut it firmly behind them, leaving the two bemused policemen staring at it.

Rafferty had hoped to get the body formally identified, but he supposed it would wait. He was about to suggest they return to the station, when the front door slammed, and a loud voice informed the house at large, 'I'm home, Mrs Griffiths. Any news?' Presumably Mrs Griffiths had failed to appear quickly enough, for the voice boomed out again, more impatiently, 'Mrs Griffiths? Where the devil are you?'

Rafferty was ashamed of the momentary relief he felt that it had been Henry's wife who had been murdered, rather than the new arrival's. He guessed the impatient voice must belong to Charles Shore, old Maximillian's only son. He certainly *sounded* a chip off the old block, he thought uneasily. As he gave the portrait another glance, he hoped it was the only part of him that resembled the Shore patriarch.

THREE

MRS GRIFFITHS must have abandoned Henry for long enough to explain what had happened because, ten seconds later, the door to the library was flung open and a vigorous-looking man of about thirty burst into the room. He made the kind of impact that Rafferty, who had undeniably lost face to the housekeeper, could only admire.

He shut the door and came forward with outstretched hand. 'Inspector? Charles Shore. My housekeeper's just told me the news about Barbara.'

The white lines around Shore's mouth were the only things that betrayed his shock for his voice was clipped, as if directed by an iron self-control. Rafferty's hand was pumped vigorously and he wondered if Shore approached everything in life with the same competitive intensity.

'Henry knows, of course? You've told him?'

Rafferty nodded. Although it was apparent that Shore wasn't the type to attempt to run away from reality like Henry, Rafferty sensed that Barbara Longman's death had affected him profoundly, and it surprised him. Although people's reactions to sudden death were often unexpected, he knew the dead woman wasn't a relative; Shore had explained on the phone the previous evening that he hadn't even known her for more than a few years.

Charles Shore was a fleshily handsome man, his jaw-line just beginning to acquire the jowls from good living that usually came far later in life. But, for now, his excess weight was easily balanced by his height and vitality. Physically, he had little of his father in him; Maximillian Shore, to judge from his portrait, hadn't over-indulged in the pleasures of the flesh in any form. He had the gaunt features of a religious fanatic, though his religion had been the amassing of wealth rather than zealous disciples. The only touch of that formidable man that Rafferty could see in his son was in the eyes, which, like Maximillian Shore's, were a light and piercing grey; sharp and calculating, they gave the impression they would miss little and that little would be irrelevant.

Burying whatever grief he felt under a businesslike exterior, Shore went to the door and bellowed again. 'Mrs Griffiths? Bring some coffee, will you? I'm sure you'd like a cup, Inspector,' he remarked as he shut the door. He glanced at Llewellyn and frowned as if someone had just reminded him of his manners. With a quick, disarming smile, he added, 'And your sergeant, of course.'

Llewellyn's mouth set in a thin line as Shore unerringly identified him as the junior, and his face took on the bland expression of a waxwork dummy. Rafferty, recognizing the rarely apparent signs of displeasure, felt a fleeting amusement. His sergeant so often gave the impression that he considered *himself* the superior that Rafferty took a very human pleasure in seeing him set down.

When the housekeeper hadn't brought the coffee two minutes later, Shore, as impatient at home as he must be in the office, excused himself and strode out of the room, his demanding tones fading as he disappeared in what Rafferty assumed was the direction of the kitchen.

With a quick glance at Llewellyn's still shuttered face, Rafferty let his mind dwell on Charles Shore. Although he gave the impression of being an autocrat like his father, Rafferty didn't feel that Shore had been intentionally patronizing—it was more that, as the top man, he was used to dealing with other top men. It amused Rafferty to be bracketed, even temporarily, with such an elevated crew. To a man as successful as Shore, lowly assistants like Llewellyn were there merely to do what they were told. Apart from their duties, he would rarely consider them or their needs.

It wasn't the first time Rafferty had been granted such an insight into the rarefied world of the powerful. Such men seemed to share a single-minded outlook that was alien to his own easygoing nature. Their drive for profit made them less like fellow human beings and more like computer-controlled machines that calculated everything in percentage points.

He was surprised to discover that he'd taken to Shore; there was something disarming about the man. Of course, he hadn't done anything yet to make him *dis*like him, he reminded himself, at least not in person. But on bored Sunday afternoons Rafferty occasionally browsed through the city pages, and because Shore was the local tycoon he'd taken the trouble to read about him.

Although it had mostly been above his head, he'd learned something about Shore's exploits in the world of corporate take-overs, international deals and behind the scenes fixing. He'd grasped enough of it to understand that the columnist, with his oblique references to insider dealing, had implied that Shore skated close to the line that separated the just legal from the downright criminal, and did it very skilfully. There had been a hint of admiration in the way the article had been slanted. Rafferty couldn't see what there was to admire. In his book, cheating was cheating, whatever fancy name you might give it, and the more successfully you cheated, the more despicable a human being you were likely to be. Warily, he reminded himself that Charles Shore was *very* successful, and he hadn't achieved his current position by being understanding or forgiving of others' failures. Rafferty could only hope he succeeded in solving the case with a more impressive speed than he usually managed.

'Mrs Griffiths didn't know how Barbara died,' Shore remarked casually as he returned, slamming the library door to behind him. Llewellyn winced and glanced upwards, as though implying that Shore should have a care for the new widower. Apparently unconcerned that his remark revealed he'd been pumping the housekeeper, and oblivious to Llewellyn's silent reproach, Shore turned away to pour himself a large Scotch from the supply neatly concealed behind one of the bookshelves. Although his voice was firm as he enquired over his shoulder whether Barbara Longman had had a car accident, his hands were less obedient. They had a slight tremor, Rafferty noticed, and his entire body seemed to tense as he waited for Rafferty's reply.

'No, sir. It wasn't a car accident.' Rafferty cleared his throat, and told him quietly, 'Although the postmortem has yet to be carried out, I'm afraid there's little doubt that Mrs Longman was murdered.'

Shore turned sharply towards them, either unaware or uncaring that he had slopped some of the
Scotch from his glass on to the expensive rug. 'Murdered?' he repeated.

Rafferty nodded. 'She was found dead about ten
minutes' drive from here in Tiffey Meadow. We believe she was suffocated. The pathologist thinks she
died sometime yesterday afternoon, possibly shortly
after she left here.'

'Suffocated? But...' He broke off and stared at
them from eyes darkened to a smoky charcoal, shaking his head, as if, like Henry, he would prefer to deny
what he had heard. But Shore was a much stronger
character and it took him only a few moments to force
out the words Rafferty could see forming behind his
intelligent eyes. In a choked voice, he asked, 'Like the
women in Suffolk, you mean?'

Rafferty gave a reluctant nod, wishing he could tell
him otherwise. He did his best to minimize the news.
'Though we can't, of course, be sure at this stage, sir.
We'll know more when we've spoken to the Suffolk
CID.'

Shore frowned. 'But surely you can tell? Weren't
the women in Suffolk beaten and...and...' He seemed
to find the word 'raped' difficult to get out.

'The pathologist is fairly certain she wasn't raped,'
he quickly reassured him. 'But, of course, we'll have
to wait till the post-mortem for that to be confirmed.' As Rafferty recalled the single mark on the
dead woman's temple and the peaceful expression on
her face, he felt able to offer more definite words of
comfort. 'She certainly didn't suffer a beating.'

He had hoped the news would provide some so-
lace. Instead, Shore's face tightened, his eyes nar-

rowed to slits of chilly grey that evoked memories of
the Channel in February, before he turned abruptly
away. His voice, when he next spoke, was formally
polite, whatever passion he felt ruthlessly extin-
guished. 'Thank you for coming so promptly to break
the news to me—and Henry. I appreciate it.' He
turned back. 'You've told Henry what you suspect?'

Rafferty admitted he hadn't. 'I'm afraid your
housekeeper took him away before I could tell him
any more than that his wife was dead. But I'm not
sure he would have taken it in in any case.'

'You're probably right. Henry has always favoured the head in the sand approach to unpleasant-
ness. God knows how he'll face up to this when he
finally surfaces.' His expression a curious mixture of
exasperation and empathy, Shore added, 'If you like,
I'll break it to him.'

Relieved to be rid of one burden, Rafferty nodded
gratefully. 'Thank you, sir. I appreciate it.'

'Though it'll have to wait till later today.' Briskly
businesslike once more, he glanced at his watch and
told them, 'It's unfortunate, but I'm due at a very
important meeting in an hour. Can't miss it, I'm
afraid. I only came home to pick up some papers and
check if my mobile phone had turned up. It went
missing yesterday—my family tends to forget who
owns the damn thing.' Shore put down his glass and
came to an instant decision. 'I'll ring Henry's GP.
Get him to come over and give him a shot of something till I've got time to deal with him.'

For all the world as if he was talking about some
dumb animal, thought Rafferty, half-appalled. But,
perhaps he wronged the man. Shore seemed the type
who would take practical measures to deal with grief,

whether it was his own or anyone else's. And, from what he'd seen of Henry, escape from reality, however brief, would be welcomed.

Shore picked up the phone and dialled. Without breaking the even tenor of his breathing, he fielded an obstructive receptionist and was put through to the doctor. Luckily, Henry's GP seemed only too happy to obey Shore's command that he come over right away.

'When do you expect the post-mortem to be carried out?' Shore enquired, as he hung up. With a grim smile, and to Rafferty's relief, he supplied his own answer. 'Knowing public servants, I don't suppose it'll be before tomorrow.'

Rafferty didn't bother to contradict him. How was Shore to know that Sam Dally tended to set his own priorities and they didn't always coincide with his? Still, in view of the case's similarities with the Suffolk murders, he was reasonably hopeful that this time Dally wouldn't feel it necessary to live up to his name.

'Now then, Mr Shore,' Rafferty began, anxious to make some headway. 'Perhaps I could just get a few details from you?' Persuasively, he added what he felt certain would appeal. 'Just to save time, you understand?' Shore nodded. This was obviously an argument he couldn't fault. Time was money. 'You called me last night to report Mrs Longman missing. Did you do that as soon as you arrived home?'

'No. When Henry—perhaps I should explain that Henry is my ex-brother-in-law. Anne, my elder sister, was his first wife. They divorced several years ago and Henry married Barbara soon after.'

Shore seemed to have forgotten that he had already explained all that on the telephone, and Rafferty decided to use Shore's lapse of memory to indulge his own curiosity. 'And you were happy to let him live here with his new wife?'

Shore's reply was light and Rafferty thought he detected a tinge of irony. 'Oh yes. It suited me admirably.' He went on, more briskly, 'I'm afraid my wife, although she's the mother of two children, isn't exactly the maternal type. But Barbara was and the children very quickly came to love her.' He blinked and gave them a weak smile. 'So you see, Henry isn't the only one who'll miss her.' After a taut pause, he went on, 'Anyway, I came home at eight-thirty yesterday evening. Barbara was supposed to be at the hall in Elmhurst, rehearsing a play with my young daughter, but when my daughter came in shortly after, we discovered that Barbara had never arrived at the hall.

'Naturally, I made a few enquiries myself, before I contacted you, but Barbara was a reliable woman and wouldn't go missing for hours without letting someone know where she was. After trying the hospitals with no joy, I rang you.'

Rafferty nodded. 'I see. Mr Longman said something about his wife going to the meadow because of the wild flowers. I take him to mean she had gone there to pick them?'

This seemed to provide Shore with a grim amusement. 'I hardly think so, Inspector. Barbara was a dedicated conservationist. From what I understand, she had gone there, on her way to the rehearsal, in order to stop someone else from destroying them. According to my housekeeper, she took a telephone message from Barbara about three o'clock yesterday afternoon from one of Barbara's conservationist friends. She went rushing off immediately after that. From what I was able to glean from Mrs Griffiths, the message was that the farmer down the road was about to plough up a meadow full of rare wild flowers, this—Tiffey Meadow. Barbara was furious, apparently. Not much gets'—his lips turned upwards in a peculiarly bitter smile as he corrected himself—'got Barbara upset, but she was a staunch conservationist. Kind, but firm, in all areas of her life bar that one. She even worked in the offices part-time for a small salary.'

Shore's words not only explained why Mrs Longman had been at Tiffey Meadow, thought Rafferty, but they also signalled the first suggestion in his mind that someone other than the Suffolk serial killer had murdered her. Could it be just a tragic coincidence that in attempting to save the rare flowers she loved from destruction she had been destroyed herself? It was certainly an odd business, and one which he intended to look into at the earliest opportunity.

'You'll want someone to identify the body, I imagine?' At Rafferty's confirmation, Shore remarked, 'In the circumstances, I think I owe it to Henry to relieve him of that unpleasant duty. If I hadn't persuaded them to come and live here, Barbara would still be alive.' Shore seemed to give himself a shake, before he went on, 'I can come now if it won't take long.'

'Thank you, sir.'

'Charles?' A woman's voice wafted along the hall. 'Mrs Griffiths has just told me the news about Barbara. Why didn't *you* tell . . . Oh,' she excused her interruption. 'I didn't realize you had company.'

To Rafferty's amazement, as soon as she set eyes on Llewellyn and himself, the sharp, complaining manner vanished, and, like a chrysalis shedding its outer casing, the woman was transformed into a butterfly, whose automatic response to men—any men— was to flutter and flirt. Even her slim body seemed to develop more curves as she posed automatically in the doorway, mobile phone in one hand, while she smoothed her expensively tousled blonde hair with the other. Her reaction might have been appealing in a teenager, but in a mature woman it was ridiculous, as if she had never grown beyond the coquette's tricks to gain male attention. As he glanced at Charles Shore, Rafferty found himself pitying her. Didn't she realize that her husband found her behaviour irritating rather than appealing? Or didn't she care?

She raised the mobile phone carelessly, as though to explain what she was doing with it. 'I found it in Carlotta's room, though when I asked her if she'd had it, she denied it. That girl's such a liar . . .'

'This is my wife, Hilary.' Briefly he introduced them. The introduction was clipped, as if its necessity annoyed him. Once it was done, he didn't spare her another glance; nor did he bother to spare her feelings. 'As Mrs Griffiths has told you that Barbara's dead, you might as well know the rest.' Bluntly, he added, 'The police think she was murdered.'

She gasped, and as if to signal her distress, she dropped with easy grace into a convenient armchair. Shocked or not, she still managed to display her figure to best advantage, leaning forward so her cleavage could be admired, and, after making sure she had got their attention, she directed eyes huge, moist and appealing, at the two policemen. 'Murdered! I can hardly believe it. Poor Barbara. I do hope she didn't suffer?'

As she murmured the words of horror and grief while rearranging the hem of her skirt to show more of her tanned legs, Rafferty was struck by their insincerity. Like a less than grief-stricken mourner at a funeral, he felt she was merely uttering what the conventions demanded. Her eyes, too, betrayed her, because, in the brief fraction before she lowered her glasses over them, they showed her real feelings—she was glad Barbara Longman was dead, very glad.

Had she been jealous of the victim? Rafferty wondered. He remembered that Shore hadn't bothered to conceal his admiration when speaking about Henry's wife, so perhaps she had cause? Rafferty studied her with an interest that would have delighted her, if he hadn't taken the trouble to make his inventory both speedy and covert.

Although Hilary Shore was tall, slim, and so elegantly put together that Rafferty imagined it must take her half the morning to assemble herself, he knew she must be around the thirty mark, as he guessed that the younger boy he had encountered outside was hers and Shore's. And, although her make-up was skilfully applied, it couldn't quite restore the dewy complexion of a twenty-year-old. Nor could it disguise the fine petulant lines around her mouth. From the cream linen suit and soft leather pumps, she looked sleek and sly, expensive and dissatisfied—a dangerous combination in a woman with plenty of time on her hands. But then Rafferty was certain Shore would be well able to make her sheathe her carmine-painted claws. Probably all he would have to do to pull her into line would be to cancel a few charge accounts.

Hilary Shore looked up, her eyes ingenuous, with no trace of jealousy. 'Who can have done such a thing?' she asked, in a voice soft with appeal. 'Everyone thought the world of Barbara, didn't they, Charles?'

Shore didn't trouble to reply and her gaze fixed on Rafferty. He noticed she was beginning to get some crow's feet under her eyes and his pity increased. Life was cruel to beautiful but ageing women, and Charles Shore didn't strike him as a husband given to kindness. Was he planning to buy her off and replace her with the latest bimbo model? Rafferty wondered.

Unaware of his pity, her eyes fastened on him, their eager expression displaying a penchant for vicarious excitement that, for Rafferty, held even less appeal than her cloying flirtatiousness. 'Who do you think did it, Inspector? Might it have been that maniac up in Suffolk?'

Rafferty, unwilling to indulge her ghoulish curiosity, left it to Shore to tell her the details and merely commented, 'It's a possibility we're considering, Mrs Shore, but at this stage, we know little more than you.'

She frowned, obviously disappointed that he hadn't been able to satisfy her curiosity. Rafferty marvelled at the speed with which his private suspicions had become public property. The body hadn't even been identified yet, he reminded himself. 'At the moment, we're trying to piece together her movements. Perhaps you can tell me if you saw her at all yesterday?'

'Me?' She blinked rapidly and, before lowering her eyelashes defensively, directed a worried glance towards her husband. 'No. I was in London all day yesterday. I'd gone up the previous evening and only returned late last night.'

'My wife spends little time here,' Shore told them. 'What was it yesterday, my dear?' Despite the endearment, his sarcasm was biting. 'Shopping? Having your hair restyled—again? Or perhaps it was that expensive oil woman?'

With a sulky pout, she corrected him. 'Mrs Armadi is an aromatherapist, Charles.' Uncoiling her long golden legs in a gesture designed to be provocative, a tinge of complaint returned to her voice as she went on. 'You know how depressing I find this mausoleum. You're never here and I must have *some* lively company. The children, no matter how much I love them, are simply not enough. My nerves couldn't stand the isolation if I didn't see some bright lights occasionally.'

She cast a look of appeal at Rafferty and, in an explanation that was a subtle thrust at her husband, she added, 'Mrs Armadi is marvellously soothing. I don't know what I'd do without her.' Her voice sharpened as she addressed Shore. 'And why shouldn't I buy nice clothes? As your *wife* I do have a certain standard to maintain.'

Rafferty wondered if he'd imagined the slight stress on the word 'wife'? Was she letting Shore know that she suspected he spread his conjugal duties with other less *official* wives?

'I spent most of the morning at a fashion show at Harvey Nichols,' she continued, her voice softening as she returned her attention to Rafferty, 'and then went on to Mrs Armadi, so I had no idea Barbara was missing until I arrived home yesterday evening. Frankly, I thought Charles over-reacted when he called you so soon. After all,' she cast a spiteful glance at her husband, 'Barbara was a grown woman...she might have arranged to meet someone.'

Charles Shore's reaction to this was explosive and pointed. 'Don't you dare suggest such a thing,' he shouted at her. Incredibly, as soon as the words were out, his temper vanished, and, apparently with little effort, he regained control of himself and added more reasonably, 'Do you want Henry to hear you tarnishing her memory now she's gone? And perhaps if you spent more time at home, looking after the children, and supervising the household staff, instead of leaving it all to Barbara, *she* wouldn't have been murdered.'

Hilary Shore's eyes narrowed and she glared at him. Beside him, Rafferty felt Llewellyn shift uneasily, as if he sensed a row brewing. Rafferty sensed it too, and he wanted to get out before it erupted. He'd heard enough quarrels to last him a lifetime. First between his large, boisterous argumentative family and then with Angie, his dead wife. 'Er, if you're ready, Mr Shore, perhaps we ought to make a move and get the identification over with?' he suggested, drily adding as an inducement, 'I wouldn't want you to miss that meeting.'

His ironic tone was lost on Charles Shore, who obviously not only took his business meetings seriously, but expected everyone else to do the same. He simply nodded, picked up the mobile phone his wife had carelessly discarded and led the way to the door without a backward glance, ignoring Hilary's waspish enquiry as to when she could expect him back.

FOUR

'NOT YOUR AVERAGE Essex man,' Rafferty pronounced after Shore had positively identified the body as that of Barbara Longman and driven off to his meeting in the turbo-charged BMW in which he'd followed them to the mortuary.

Llewellyn nodded. 'Not your average family either,' he commented. 'Didn't you think it strange that Shore didn't even trouble to go upstairs to offer Henry his condolences? It would have been the normal thing to do.'

Reminded of his earlier pity for the children of the household, Rafferty nodded. 'But that household doesn't strike me as exactly normal.'

'Perhaps Mrs Shore will break the news?'

Rafferty gave him an oblique glance. 'You think so? I'd say it would be more likely that she'd take off back to London to get away from the general gloom. She didn't look as if she would be likely to join in any breast-beating. Besides, from what Shore said, the dead woman seems to have acted as a stand-in mother to all of them. Poor little sods. I suppose the job of breaking the news to them will fall to that sour-faced housekeeper.' Rafferty unlocked the car door. 'Oh, well, it's none of our business. Come on, let's get back to the station. I want to talk to the Suffolk CID—find out if their murderer's MO has any more similarities with ours than we've so far discovered.'

ONCE BACK at the station, and before he got on to Ellis, the Suffolk DI in charge of the other investigation, Rafferty had a word with those of the house-to-house team who had returned, though he had little hope that any witnesses would emerge. And so it proved. As young Hanks remarked, what would anyone but an ardent conservationist be doing, hanging around an overgrown meadow? Particularly one within sniffing range of the River Tiffey.

Though he didn't say so to the young constable, Rafferty shared his opinion, and Hanks's remarks deepened his doubts about the killer's identity. The bodies of the two victims in Suffolk had been found in alleyways. Why would a rapist like the killer over the border change his pattern and hang around a lonely meadow? Surely he would realize that potential victims were likely to be few and far between? Even the two boys who had found the body had only been exercising their dogs because they'd been at a loose end after being thrown out of their local soccer team for fighting, and were intent on proving to each other that they didn't care.

Dismissing the team for a quick cup of tea in the canteen before they went out again to resume their questioning, Rafferty was disappointed to discover that the early results of the team questioning the motorists on the main road by the meadow were equally disappointing. Reminding himself, again, that it was early days yet, Rafferty picked up the telephone once more. He hoped DI Ellis at Suffolk would have a bit more information for him.

But Frank Ellis, the officer in charge of the Suffolk investigation, wasn't available. His sergeant told Rafferty that Ellis was over at Ipswich, checking out a possible suspect of their serial killings. 'Perhaps I can help, Inspector?'

'I hope so,' said Rafferty. 'We've had a murder here that looks like it might be the work of your killer. Can you give me the details of his MO?'

'Sure.' The sergeant gave a tired laugh. 'To tell you the truth, Inspector, we won't be sorry if your killing turns out to have been done by our boy. We'd be glad of someone to share the work and the blame. I've had six hours' sleep in the last two days, and the way things are going, I'll be lucky to get that much in the next two.'

'I'd sympathize,' Rafferty remarked drily, 'only I have a feeling I might need all the sympathy I can get for myself if your killer's moved his base of operations over our border. If I can have those details?'

'Sure. You'll know from the newspaper reports that both our victims have been in their late twenties and blonde, and that our chappie likes to hang around back alleys waiting for his victims?'

Rafferty confirmed that he knew that much. Remembering the telephone call that Shore had mentioned, which had drawn Barbara Longman to her death, he asked, 'Any evidence that they might have known their killer? Such as a phone call before they left home, perhaps?'

'Funny you should mention that,' said the sergeant. 'Because we've reason to believe that they *did* both know their killer. Though the phone call aspect's out. The first victim didn't have a phone and the second was staying at her mother's for the weekend and the mother was adamant that it didn't ring the entire time her daughter was there. But both victims were married, and from what their neighbours said, we think they might both have been playing away. It looks as if they arranged to meet their killer close to where their bodies were found. We know they both set out on their own, and although we can't know if the second victim *arrived* there alone, as she drove her own car, the first one went by bus and the driver remembers her getting off the bus by the alley where she did. He told us no one else got off there, so it seems as if her killer might have been waiting for her.'

'How about the method of killing? I know they were suffocated, but have you any idea what he used?' Rafferty, aware that serial killers often had their own particular trade mark, knew that these details wouldn't have been released to the press. Stevens confirmed it before he went on. 'Stuffed the victims' panties in their mouths after he'd beaten them semiconscious and then held their nostrils closed with his hand. He's a vicious sod, this killer,' Stevens told him, 'and getting more so. I saw both victims, and although the first one had been pretty badly roughed up before he killed her, the second was far worse. You should see the autopsy report. Oh, and they were both raped, but *after* death, not before, as the papers assumed. Anything else you want to know?'

'Not just now, thanks. What you've told me has given me plenty to think about.'

'And do you think your killer and ours might be the same bloke?' With an apologetic laugh, Stevens added, 'Only it would be nice to have some news to give to DI Ellis when he gets back. We seem to be getting pretty bogged down with this one,' he confessed.

'I'm not sure, Sergeant. There are certain similarities, such as the age of the victim, and the hair colour. But the rest of your killer's MO doesn't match up.'

'Think you've got a copy-cat killer, then?'

'Could be. Thanks for all your help. Can you tell DI Ellis I rang and that I'd like to come over and see him as soon as possible?'

'Will do, sir.'

Thoughtfully, Rafferty replaced the receiver and told the hovering Llewellyn what he had just learned.

The Welshman frowned. 'It's not exactly conclusive either way, is it, sir?'

'No. Though, if it was the same killer, it's strange that he didn't beat her as he did the other victims. Especially as, since the other cases followed a predictable pattern of increasing violence, you would expect the third victim to be beaten far more brutally than the first two. Yet, this murder was gentle by comparison. Apart from a small bruise at her temple, he doesn't seem to have hit her at all. Dally doesn't think she was raped, but we'll know for sure after the post-mortem. Of course, that doesn't necessarily mean anything, he might have been disturbed before he could do so, though it seems unlikely as it was such a lonely spot.'

He picked up his mug of tea but it was cold and he put it down again in disgust. 'Anyway, I've left instructions for Ellis to contact me, as I'd like to compare notes more fully on this one. But as the information from Suffolk is inconclusive, we can't afford to rule anyone out of our suspicions. That means we'll have to speak to the dead woman's family again, get some statements from them. For one thing, I'd like more information about that phone message to the Shore house, and the farmer it mentioned. But we'll leave all that until after the PM. Dally tells me he's scheduled it for tomorrow morning.'

RAFFERTY WAS PLEASED Sam Dally had decided to exert himself on this one. Unusually, he combined two roles, and Rafferty surmised that his police surgeon half must have given his pathologist half a talking-to for not only did the post-mortem start on time but for once Dally didn't indulge his usual macabre line in jokes and it finished earlier than Rafferty had expected.

Henry had told them that his wife had been in the early stages of pregnancy, and now Sam confirmed it. He also confirmed that Barbara Longman had been suffocated. Or—as Sam had it—her death was 'consistent with suffocation', and, although he refused to commit himself as to the means, he thought it probable the killer had pressed something soft, like a cushion, over her face.

She hadn't been raped. Although an attempt had been made to make it look as though she was the latest victim of a sex killer, it was an amateurish effort. Her clothing had been disturbed, but that was all. There was no seminal fluid, no bruising to the soft flesh of the inner thighs, no *real* assault at all—apart from the undeniable fact that the victim was dead. To Rafferty, it was looking more and more like the work of a copy-cat killer.

Keeping a careful distance between himself and the body on the autopsy table, Rafferty asked, 'How much effort would it have taken to hold her down and suffocate her at the same time? Or do you think she was knocked out first? That bruise on her temple—'

'Might have stunned her, made her less able to fight back. But there are several indications that she was conscious before she died. And if you left that wall to hold itself up and came a bit closer, you'd not only be able to see the pinpoint haemorrhages in the eyes, consistent with suffocation, you'd also be able to see the grazes on the back of her legs. As if she'd scratched them on the rough grasses, as she tried to drag her legs up to remove a heavy weight.'

Rafferty took Sam's word for it and stayed where he was.

'And then, there's bruising to the skin around the wrists. I'd say her killer forced her bent arms up beside her head and held them there with one hand to stop her struggling—unnecessary if she had been unconscious.' He launched into further, more gruesome descriptions of the post-mortem details, to which, as a defensive mechanism, Rafferty found it necessary to shut his ears.

Rafferty nodded absently, and reminded Sam that the dry grass under her heels had been reduced to shreds, which suggested her shoes had beat a tattoo on the ground before she had died. All in all, it seemed pretty conclusive that she had not only been killed where she had been found but had been conscious at the time. Now, he tried another tack. 'I suppose we can take it for granted that she was killed by a man?'

'I wouldn't take *anything* for granted if I were you, Rafferty,' said Dally, as he threw his gloves in the bin and removed his blood-stained gown. 'Especially as

I doubt if it took much effort at all. She was only a slender little thing.'

It was funny, Rafferty mused, keeping his eyes averted from the cadaver on the table, although he knew the victim had a slight figure, he continued to think of her as a buxom woman, some sort of earth mother. The expression 'kind but firm' which Shore had used invariably produced such a picture in his mind. He toyed with the idea of asking Llewellyn, who had studied psychology, what the professionals would make of such a confession, but thought better of it. Psychologists usually managed to make the most innocent revelations sound perverted. Generally, as far as he understood it, they traced everything back to a fellow's mother and Rafferty didn't need an honours degree to figure out that they'd have a field-day with his.

'Thanks, Sam.' Rafferty headed gratefully for the door, and away from the assorted odours of the pathology department. 'I'll see you at the inquest, I suppose?'

'Wouldn't miss it, laddie, especially as it's being held in that hall next to the Green Man.' Sam beamed ebulliently at him. 'The publican there knows his trade. Keeps a very special malt for favoured customers, like yours truly. Want me to put a word in for you?'

After witnessing the post-mortem, Rafferty doubted he'd ever again have the stomach for *any* alcohol, and he managed only a sickly grin and a shake of the head before following Llewellyn out to the car. As all the shady places in the car park had, of course, been appropriated hours ago, they had had to park where they could find a place. And, after standing in the baking sun for so long, the inside of the vehicle was as hot as a furnace. Rafferty opened all the windows before he settled into his seat.

'Right, let's go and see the family again,' he said, as he started the engine. 'There are enough doubts now about the killer's identity to press them for statements. Hopefully, as—with the conspicuous exception of Mrs Shore—they're all supposed to have been so fond of the victim, they'll be only too happy to do their duty in that direction.'

His words reminded him of a duty of his own that he'd rather forget. But he knew if he didn't at least *ask* his ma would give him no peace, so he might as well get it over with before they were well and truly immersed in the eighteen-hour days of a murder inquiry.

'Speaking of happy families. How goes it between you and Maureen?'

Unfortunately, as Maureen was Rafferty's second cousin, and Llewellyn his partner, his ma took a proprietary interest in the romance and was continually badgering him as to its progress. He wasn't surprised when Llewellyn's reply amounted to no more than a brief, 'All right,' that more or less advised him to mind his own business. Llewellyn believed in keeping personal things personal, Rafferty reminded himself wearily. The trouble was, Kitty Rafferty didn't share the reserved Welshman's love of privacy. She either didn't, or wouldn't, understand that Rafferty had fostered the relationship from mixed motives of altruism and self-interest, he hadn't expected to oversee it personally. But convinced—with some reason, he had to admit—that the emotional hang-up lingering from a strict Methodist upbringing would render the otherwise perfectly capable Welshman inadequate in the rites of courtship, his ma felt that Llewellyn needed encouraging. Rafferty reflected that she was just the woman to do it.

She'd been driving him mad on the subject for weeks, and now that he'd finally broached it he blundered determinedly on, trying his best to ignore the closed-up expression on the Welshman's face as he recalled the latest leverage his ma had primed him with. 'It's Maureen's birthday tomorrow,' he commented, trying to sound unrehearsed, and hoping it would ease a revealing remark or two from Llewellyn. 'I suppose you'll be getting her a present?'

'Her birthday?' Llewellyn frowned. 'Are you sure? She didn't say.'

'Course I'm sure.' Although remembering birthdays wasn't something generally expected of a mere male in the Rafferty matriarchy, he was confident that his ma wouldn't get such a thing wrong. The women in the family did the remembering and the selecting, all that was required of him and the other males was that they coughed up the cash. And as present buying Rafferty-style had as many competitive elements as the Olympics, he reckoned he got off lightly.

Relieved to be able to abandon the agony aunt pose, and adopt instead that of the wise uncle, he went on, 'That's women for you. Expect you to know such things without being told and then get all sniffy when you fail.' He shook his head, pleased, for once, to be able to boast a superior knowledge. 'Women can be very unreasonable about such things, Llewellyn. Take it from me.'

'Not Maureen.' Llewellyn shook his head, and his lips parted in a rare smile. 'She's far too sensible.'

Rafferty looked pityingly at him. Although both
intelligent and intellectual, at twenty-nine, Llewellyn
was still something of an innocent where women were
concerned. With an air more of sorrow than superi-
ority, Rafferty put him straight. 'Listen, Taff, they're
all like that. Don't think just because Maureen's always got her head stuck in some old Greek geezer's
book that she's not the same.' If *she* wasn't, her
mother certainly was, he reminded himself, and if
they *did* end up getting hitched, it would be unwise
for Llewellyn to get on the wrong side of Maureen's
mother so early in the relationship. With a sly glance
at Llewellyn, he wondered if his sergeant had realized yet that that formidable snob Claire Tyler-
Jenkins was being primed by Kitty Rafferty as his future mother-in-law?

He had been surprised when his ma had taken a
shine to the Welshman. He had been even more surprised when Kitty Rafferty, a committed Roman
Catholic—who thought the Pope an infallible deity
instead of a poor old mortal like anyone else—hadn't
raised a murmur against the slowly burgeoning inter-
denominational romance between the Welshman and
Rafferty's Catholic cousin, Maureen. In fact, once
she had finally accepted that *he* and Maureen would
never become an item, she had been positively *encouraging*. No doubt, a change in the Welshman's
religion would be his ma's next campaign. It would be
just like her to even offer to give him Catechism in-
struction herself. Poor Llewellyn.

Rafferty said no more, but the thoughtful look on
Llewellyn's face was sufficient to satisfy him that his
point had gone home. Although Llewellyn had confided little, Rafferty felt that the little had been sig-

nificant. If Llewellyn was at the present-*considering* stage, it indicated a certain depth to the relationship. That suited him. He'd be happy if it deepened into something permanent—he favoured a *very* long engagement himself, because not only had the more irritating edges been smoothed off Llewellyn's personality since he and Maureen had got together, but, as a bonus, all his ma's considerable matchmaking talents had been concentrated away from *him*.

Pleased at his dextrous handling of the situation, he spared his reflection in the driving mirror a brief congratulatory glance. Two and a half years after being widowed, he was just beginning to savour his freedom, and he was very keen to keep it that way. Beside him in the passenger seat his sergeant was getting restless in spite of the welcome breeze brought by the car's movement.

'About this present, sir,' Llewellyn began, after another contemplative five minutes. Unlike Rafferty, he wasn't a man for impulsive reactions. 'What do you think I ought to get?'

'Call me Joe, for God's sake,' Rafferty commanded. Llewellyn's constant 'sirring' got on his nerves. He hadn't bothered to get on first name terms before because, although he had been happy to discover that the Welshman was very close-mouthed, he had still harboured doubts about their partnership. But, in many ways, he realized, they made a good team. Odd, perhaps, but better than he'd expected.

And it would almost be worth welcoming him into the clan to see the invariably neat and precise Welshman at one of the family's hooleys, jacket off, tie under his ear, as he leapt about with the rest, a half-pint of the water of life whooshing around inside him.

Rafferty smiled inwardly and permitted himself another piece of advice. 'I'd send her a bunch of flowers, Dafyd,' he counselled confidently, as he drove into the Shores' entrance. 'Can't go wrong with flowers.'

FIVE

Mrs Griffiths again showed them into the library, where Henry Longman was slumped in a large armchair. The curtains had been drawn, as if to shut out the world, and a soft lamp bathed the open pages of the wedding album—his own presumably—that rested in his lap. To Rafferty it seemed a morbid occupation for one so recently widowed. A bottle and a heavy tumbler half full of Scotch were conveniently within reach. From Henry's glazed expression, the freshly broken paper seals discarded on the table, and the level of the bottle, Rafferty guessed it wasn't the first of the day.

'I'm sorry to have to trouble you so soon after your wife's death, Mr Longman,' he began, 'but it's necessary to ask you a few questions.'

Henry didn't appear to have heard him. He was unshaven, and he gazed vacantly at the album with eyes red-rimmed from weeping, while his long, slender fingers stroked the glossy print of his dead wife's face. As Rafferty said his name again, Henry raised his head. Conscious of a feeling of intrusion caused by poking his officially sanctioned nose into heavy private emotions, Rafferty wanted to get the interview over as quickly as possible. But, before he could say anything further, Henry launched into a rambling reminiscence.

'Charles laughed at me when I told him I was going to marry Barbara, you know.' His voice was sluggish as though grief had slowed his mental processes. 'He hardly knew her then and he told me she was a gold-digger, and took pleasure in making sure she knew that *he* was the one with the money, not me. Thought that would be the last I'd see of her.' He gave a sad yet triumphant smile. 'But he was wrong. She still married me. She's been good for me, even if... Been good for me,' he repeated, before distress twisted his thin features. 'Was. Was good for me. Must remember. Got to remember. Hilary said... must face up to it.'

Rafferty and Llewellyn shuffled uncomfortably and avoided each other's eyes. God, this was awful, Rafferty thought. But at least he was bearing up better than Llewellyn, who looked as if he was praying for a visitation from the Archangel Gabriel to put an end to Henry's pitiful ramblings.

Though Llewellyn's prayers were only partly answered, neither of them complained to the Almighty when Charles Shore, presumably summoned by the housekeeper, strode into the room. As Shore took in Henry's slouched figure, irritation seemed to tighten his jaw. He twitched the album from Henry's trembling fingers and told him, 'Looking through that isn't going to bring her back, Harry.'

Rafferty winced at Shore's insensitivity, forgetting that he'd thought much the same only a few minutes earlier. But as he gazed at Henry, he decided Charles might have a point. Henry was the type who could turn mourning into a lifetime's occupation. It wasn't doing him a kindness to encourage him. Still, he remembered, it was early days.

'Have you told him yet?' Rafferty quietly asked Shore, after checking that Henry, his chin once slumped to his chest, was taking no further interest in them. 'That his wife was murdered, I mean?'

'I told him.' Shore shrugged and added, 'Though whether he's taken it in or not is another matter.'

Rafferty nodded. Approaching Henry, he pulled up a chair, and sat down beside him, giving his shoulder a gentle shake. 'Mr Longman, can you please listen to me.' Once he was sure he had Henry's attention, he went on. 'I understand that Mr Shore has broken the news to you that your wife was murdered?'

Henry nodded. He looked bemused. 'I don't understand it, though. Why would anyone want to murder Barbara?'

'That's what we have to find out, sir,' said Rafferty. 'That's why we needed to speak to you and the rest of the family. We hope you'll be able to help us. To tell us something about your wife's life, how she spent her time, what she did. If she had any enemies and...'

Henry looked shocked at the suggestion. 'She didn't have any enemies. It must have been a madman. She was a good woman. Everyone loved her, thought the world of her...especially the children. The children... Oh, God, who's going to tell Maxie? I can't do it. I really can't.' He turned a stricken face towards Charles. 'You know how much he loved her.' He clutched the arms of his chair tightly, as if he thought they were going to drag him out of it forcibly to break the news to his son.

Charles Shore took a quick impatient breath. 'Calm down, Henry. I've told him. I've told them all. Who else was there to do it?' he demanded, half to himself, with the first real show of irritation. 'He took it surprisingly well, considering.' He turned away, and

beckoning to Rafferty, led him out of earshot of
Henry. 'The post-mortem's been carried out now, I
take it?' Rafferty nodded. 'And? The results confirm she's the third victim of that serial killer?'

Rafferty shook his head. 'In fact, from our enquiries, I'm inclined to the view that her murderer was
someone else entirely.'

'Someone else?' Shore studied him for a moment,
before he asked quietly, 'What makes you think so?'

'I can't go into that, sir, but I can assure you there
are sufficient differences between the three cases for
there to be a reasonable doubt. That's why I shall
need your co-operation.'

Shore nodded once. 'Of course, anything I can do.
And Henry, naturally. You've only got to look at him
to see what all this is doing to him.'

Rafferty took a deep breath. 'Then he won't mind
providing us with a statement. In fact, we'll need
statements from everyone here. Perhaps we can start
with you, Mr Shore?'

'Statements?' Shore's cold grey eyes fixed un-
blinkingly on Rafferty's. Rafferty forced himself not
to drop his eyes. He didn't want Shore to think he
could intimidate him. 'You surely don't suspect that
one of us killed Barbara?'

'It's just routine, sir,' he quickly placated them.
'And you did promise your co-operation,' he reminded him. For a moment Shore looked as if he was
going to make an issue of it, but as Rafferty went on,
he subsided. 'As I said, I have my doubts that Mrs
Longman's murder and the ones in Suffolk are connected, though, of course, the possibility is still being investigated.

But in the mean time I have to carry on and eliminate as many people as possible. To do that, I need to ask questions that might seem insensitive.'

Shore drew in a deep breath. 'I see. Very well. You'd better get on with it, then.'

'Thank you, sir. If we could start with you? My sergeant'll take notes.'

Without further protest, Shore began. 'I was in my office in Elmhurst most of Thursday. It's near the bus station in King Street. I had to prepare for an important meeting the next day, as I told you, and needed to work on some figures—my staff will confirm it, if necessary. I reached home about 8.30 p.m. Thursday evening.'

'And you, sir?' Rafferty turned to Henry Longman. Henry seemed to have shrunk further into his chair. 'Mr Longman? I'm afraid we need to know where you were on Thursday.'

'Henry was in a meeting,' Charles answered for him. 'At the local Chamber of Commerce. It can't have broken up much before five as there was a lot to go through. Isn't that right, Henry? Henry?' he prompted, raising his voice slightly.

Henry's head jerked like a marionette's whose strings had been pulled. He ignored the question and asked one of his own. 'When will I be able to bury my wife?' It was simple and poignant and made Rafferty shuffle uncomfortably.

'It won't be just yet, I'm afraid, sir. We have to wait for the coroner to release your wife's body, and these things can take some time.'

Thankfully, Henry seemed satisfied with his answer and didn't press for more information. Rafferty had been careful to avoid mentioning the post-mortem to him. From past experience, he was aware that the phrase, and all it conjured up, sometimes brought on hysteria in a victim's family, so generally he did his best to avoid it. Not unnaturally, relatives could accept the death of a loved one more easily than they could the thought of them being cut about afterwards. Rafferty thought this could be because murder was at least a very human thing, brought about by hot emotions like lust and hatred that everyone had experienced. But the PM was a chilling clinical procedure, warmed only by irreverent black humour. Whenever he watched one, Rafferty imagined himself on the table, being discussed as if he was no more than a side of beef well past his prime, and he hoped to Heaven that when his time came he would die a nice simple death, so a post-mortem would be unnecessary.

Henry's head had sunk back to his chest. Reluctantly, Rafferty pressed him for an answer. 'Can you confirm that you were at a meeting at the Chamber of Commerce all day on Thursday, Mr Longman?'

Henry's eyes had a hunted look, and his words, as he answered, were slurred, as if reluctance, as well as the drink, had thickened his tongue. 'Er, yes. That's right. All day.'

'You're quite certain about that, Mr Longman?' Rafferty looked sharply at him.

Henry reached for his glass and swallowed what was left of the whisky. 'Course I'm sure. Chamber of Commerce... all day... witnesses.' He stumbled to his feet, almost falling over as he did so. ''Scuse me. Don't feel well.'

He wove a meandering path across the room. Charles followed, opened the door for him, and bellowed, 'Mrs Griffiths. Henry's not well. See to him, will you?'

He shut the door behind Henry without bothering to see if his order was obeyed. He was a man used to getting his own way. He walked back and came to a halt before the portrait of his father. After gazing thoughtfully at it for some moments, he turned and commented, 'They say history repeats itself, Inspector. It seems they're right. Did you know my father was murdered when I was fifteen?' Rafferty nodded and Shore added, as though the information was of much less consequence, 'Two months after my mother died from cancer.'

'Yes,' Rafferty murmured. 'A tragic loss.'

Shore's expression was as hard as a poker player's and he told them, without any trace of emotion, 'My father was blown to bits, Inspector. The force of the explosion sent parts of the vehicle a hundred yards away. As for my father—' He broke off and a muscle tightened in his jaw as he added, 'Let's just say there wasn't a lot to bury. It isn't difficult to believe someone could hate my father enough to kill him. He could be a hard man when crossed...hard, even when he wasn't. But why would anyone want to murder Barbara? I know you said you don't think it was the Suffolk killer, but...' He shook his head and muttered, as if trying to convince them as much as himself, 'It *must* have been a madman.'

'You didn't get on with your father, Mr Shore?' Llewellyn queried.

Shore stared hard at him, as if he considered the question impertinent, but then he shrugged. 'I fail to see what relevance that has to your investigation, Sergeant, but, since you ask, no, I didn't; my sister was always his favourite. He was the sort of father who expected a lot from a son. You feared him, respected him, obeyed him; he wasn't interested in such a mealy-mouthed emotion as *liking*. He believed that softness bred weakness. He always used to say to me, 'It's a hard world out there, Charles, and you have to be hard to survive.' He told me that by giving me—and Anne, to a lesser extent—proper English names, royal names, and by sending us to the right schools, he'd done his bit. The rest was up to us.'

He smiled bleakly and, for a moment, Rafferty glimpsed the vulnerable child beneath the powerful man; he imagined what it must have been like to be Charles, as a small boy, at the 'right' school, but with the pushy, un-English father and the *wrong* background. Pretty unpleasant, was his conclusion. He wouldn't have got much sympathy from Maximillian Shore, who had survived far worse.

Shore turned back to the portrait and Rafferty could no longer see his face. 'Of course, he had a terrible time in his youth, so it wasn't surprising that he should feel that way. He refused to accept that the more subtle forms of Jew-baiting and class hatred to be found in this country couldn't be overcome, if one were strong enough.'

'It seems he was right,' Rafferty murmured. 'Such obstacles didn't stop your father getting rich.'

'My father got rich in spite of his background,' Shore asserted, with a frown, as if Rafferty had just uttered a particularly vile blasphemy. Then he sighed. 'Perhaps, in a funny way, it was *because* of it. His parents died at the hands of the Nazis when he was a teenager. It caused him to be all the more determined to make his mark. With hard work and more hard work, he prospered. And wealth brought *him* acceptance—of a sort, even if, as children, it failed to do the same for Anne and me. Now, of course, I'm grateful for his training.'

And what of Shore's sister? Rafferty wondered. How had Maximillian's school of hard knocks affected her? He seemed to remember, from the reports of her father's death, that she'd married Henry when she was eighteen. To get away from her father? Rafferty wondered. Emboldened by curiosity, he asked, 'And your sister? Does she feel she has reason to be grateful, too?'

'Anne? Probably not. Especially as our father cut her out of his will when she insisted on marrying Henry. They were only reconciled a few months after Maxie was born. Unfortunately for her, Father was killed before he could reinstate her—if such was his intention.'

This time, Rafferty had a glimpse of another side to that lonely boy. For a second, Shore's expression was cruelly self-satisfied, as if, even so many years later, he got immense pleasure from the knowledge that the more favoured sibling had unwisely thrown away her pre-eminence, and with it had discarded money, status, success. All the things that Shore relished and possessed in large measure.

'But then she was always headstrong. Insisted on marrying Henry before she had any qualifications. Of course, a baby was soon on the way and it didn't take her long after that to realize she'd made a poor choice. Nothing would make her admit it, of course. I've had to support her all these years—her and Henry and the boy.'

He gave a short, malicious laugh. 'Give Anne her
due, she stuck it out. They only split a few years
ago—her choice, of course. She should have divorced years ago, because by the time she got around
to it she had—other problems to contend with.' He
smiled with a certain grim satisfaction, but didn't
elaborate.

There was a small, uncomfortable silence after that.
God, this family, thought Rafferty. What was the
matter with them all? In mitigation, Rafferty reminded himself that, if not as appalling as his father's youth, Charles Shore, too, had survived a hard
boyhood. The trouble was, of course, that not only
did such miserable early experiences often stunt the
gentler emotions of the sufferer, they had a knock-on
effect on his immediate family as well.

Feeling as if he had disturbed dusty family ghosts,
Rafferty cast round for an avenue of escape. Gestur-
ing at the quantity of books on the shelves, he enquired, 'Were they your father's?'

Shore nodded. 'Most of them. Of course, I and
some of the rest of the family have added to them, but
the bulk were his. He read voraciously, always about
other people's lives.' He paused, and when he continued, his voice had lightened, even held a touch of
mockery. 'Did you know he wrote his own autobiography? You should find it behind you. They're all in
alphabetical order.'

Rafferty turned, and his fingers traced along the
spines until he came to it. It had a curious title—*A
Phoenix Life*. Gently, he eased it from the packed
shelves and flipped through it.

Like Henry, Charles Shore seemed to be in the
mood for looking back. 'My father discovered a taste

for writing after that. Tried his hand at intellectual theorizing. Fancied himself something of an expert on a number of topics—you name it, and he had a theory about it; crime and the habitual criminal, marital breakdown, success, failure, poverty. He collected quite an impressive number of statistics, too. And when he'd been turned down by everyone else, he decided to publish his theories himself.'

'And did he?' Rafferty asked, peering again at the shelves from which he'd taken Shore's autobiography.

'No.' The younger Shore's face tightened. 'He was murdered before he got the chance.'

This brought another uncomfortable silence. To break it, Rafferty asked conversationally, 'And where are they now? All his papers?'

Shore shrugged. 'God knows. Probably thrown out with the rest of the rubbish. My father was a terrible hoarder, Inspector, and we had a grand clear-out after the funeral. If they're still about and you're that interested, Mrs Griffiths might know where they are.'

'Ah yes, your housekeeper. That reminds me. I'd like a word with her about that telephone message she took for Mrs Longman.'

'Certainly. If you think it'll be helpful.' He went to the door and shouted for her. 'She'll be along directly.'

Mrs Griffiths must have taken the shouted summons to indicate an order for coffee, for several minutes later, she struggled in carrying a loaded tray. The ever-gentlemanly Llewellyn relieved her of it and placed it on the table by the window, earning himself a rare smile.

Mrs Griffiths had begun to pour when Shore told her, 'Leave that. The inspector wants to hear about the telephone message you took for Mrs Longman.'

After inviting her to sit down, Rafferty asked her, 'Perhaps you could start by telling me exactly what the message said?'

Evidently irritated at being expected to face this three-man interrogation squad, her reply was short and abrupt. 'All he said was that Cyril Thomson was about to plough up the wild flowers in Tiffey Meadow and she should get there directly. He asked would I be sure and pass on the message to Mrs Longman and I promised I'd do so straight away.'

'Did you recognize the voice?' he asked, with little hope of receiving an affirmative.

'No.' She shot him a sharp-eyed look. 'Not at the time, but now that you mention it, there was something vaguely familiar about it. But the voice was muffled, as if the caller had a sore throat, or as if he was calling from a long way away.'

'You said you recognized the voice. Are you sure you don't have any idea who he was?' He wondered if she might be trying to protect someone.

'I said it sounded familiar.' The housekeeper's lips compressed, as though she had already had enough of his questioning, without having to correct his mis-interpretations of her answers. 'I didn't say I *recognized* it. I told you, I don't know who it was. Something about it struck a chord, that's all. He gave me a name, of course, but I really can't be expected to remember now if he called himself Jack or Jim or Joe. I know it was *something* like that,' she defended herself. 'But he must have been a friend of Mrs Longman's. How else would he have known the telephone number? It's unlisted. He said he was with the Conservation Society, so you shouldn't have any difficulty in finding him and asking him yourself.'

'He actually *said* he was with the Society?' Rafferty pressed her. 'Or did he merely imply it?'

Mrs Griffiths looked sharply at him, as if she had just realized the possible significance of all these questions. 'Are you saying you think whoever made the call *killed* her?'

'I don't think anything in particular at this stage, Mrs Griffiths,' Rafferty assured her. 'I just want to get things clear in my mind, that's all.'

If the housekeeper was upset by the possibility that she had spoken to Barbara Longman's murderer, she gave little sign of it. But then, as Rafferty had already concluded, she wasn't the type to have hysterics. Still, she appeared grateful for Llewellyn's solicitude, as he poured her a cup of her own coffee. She sipped it quietly while Rafferty resumed the questioning.

'Can you tell me what this man's *actual* words were, Mrs Griffiths? It could be very important. Cast your mind back to just before the call if it helps.'

She nodded. Rafferty was glad to see that the shock, and the strangeness of sipping coffee in her employer's library, seemed to have softened her manner. The resemblance to Mrs Danvers faded. 'I was busy making the season's last batch of raspberry jam, and I wanted to get back to it. Those two boys Maxie and Edward had been in and out of the kitchen a little earlier and I was nervous about leaving such a big pot on the stove in case they came back and caused an accident. Especially as the day before I'd caught Maxie messing about with my previous batch.

Anyway, I returned to the kitchen after taking the message, and I was too relieved to see my jam was safe to think any more about it. Fallgold variety it were. Admittedly, not as well flavoured a raspberry as the early Mallings, but still pleasant.'

Shore gave a *hrmph* of impatience at this meandering explanation, and Mrs Griffiths took the opportunity to get in an obviously much felt grievance. 'Of course, if I could have relied on that Carlotta, who was supposed to be helping me, I might have been able to spare more attention for what he said, but half my mind was on the jam, as I wouldn't trust her to watch grass grow.'

'Carlotta?' Rafferty queried.

'The Italian au pair,' Shore supplied tight-lipped. 'One of Barbara's less successful ideas, wasn't it, Mrs G.?'

Whatever effect he might have on the rest of his staff, it seemed Mrs Griffiths wasn't in awe of her employer. In fact, it now appeared they shared the familiarity and frankness of old sparring partners, as her agreement was vociferous. 'It certainly was. Au pair, she calls herself. All I know is, that she spends more time making eyes at young Maxie's holiday tutor than she does helping me. If she was any use I'd have had all the jam made the day before and no need to worry about it being ready. But I'd promised Mr Shore only that morning that I'd let the local Tory party have some for their bring and buy sale and I was anxious about getting it finished. It was unfortunate that I'd already given all the jam I'd made the day before to Mrs Shepherd, the mother of Maxie's friend Tom, especially as she wasn't a bit grateful.

Said it had given her lad the stomach ache. Cheek of her. As if my jam would—'

'Yes, yes,' Shore burst in. 'I really don't think we need to go into all that now, Mrs Griffiths. The inspector wanted to know what the man said,' he reminded her testily.

'Yes, well, I'm sure I'm doing my best.' She sniffed. 'All this upset—how am I supposed to remember?' She smoothed a few wispy bits of hair back into her greying bun. 'He said . . . now let me see. He said something like, "Can I speak to Barbara?" And I told him she wasn't available and asked if I could take a message. He said, "My name's Jack,"'—or Jim or Joe, Rafferty silently supplied. 'The line went a bit crackly then, but I'm almost certain he said he was from the Society. Anyway, he said *something* about the Society,' the housekeeper insisted, with a look that implied Rafferty had tried to make a liar out of her. 'And did Mrs Longman know that Cyril Thomson had a tractor with a plough hitched up to it and was about to plough up Tiffey Meadow—it's protected, you know, because of the rare flowers,' she added. 'Anyway, he was very insistent that I pass the message on to her straight away and I promised I would.'

Shore broke in. 'That farmer chap, Thomson, would stand looking into, in my opinion. Surly individual.'

'You went to see him when Mrs Longman hadn't come home that evening?' Shore nodded, his olive skin flushing, and Rafferty guessed that the farmer had been less than deferential. 'What did he have to say?'

'Said he hadn't seen her since their last run-in earlier this year. Denied he'd ever intended to plough up the meadow when I taxed him about it. Told me that was the last thing he'd be likely to do. Said he couldn't care less if Barbara had rounded up a dozen of her conservation friends and staged a sit-in for a month to stop him planting in it.' Shore's jaw tightened and Rafferty heard his teeth grinding together. 'The idea that she might do just that even seemed to amuse him. Told me to go and look round the meadow myself if I was that concerned, as he had better ways to spend his free time.'

Rafferty sat up straight and looked sharply at Shore. 'And did you?'

Shore shook his head. 'I looked over the fields from the road, and called her name, that's all, but there was no sign of her. I didn't see any point in blundering about. I assumed she would have answered if she'd been there.' Suddenly, his expression was grim. 'I was looking for a live woman, Inspector, not a dead one. Besides, I didn't really expect to find her.'

Slowly Rafferty nodded. It was a few seconds before he resumed the questioning. 'You didn't see her car? We found it parked up that lane at the side of the meadow.'

'No. The lane's the other side of the meadow and I didn't go that far. I parked on the main road, so her car might have been there, but, as I said, if it was, I wouldn't have seen it. That's when I returned home and rang you.'

Llewellyn asked, 'Is there any reason why Mrs Longman's husband didn't contact us himself? I would have thought . . .'

Shore's gaze narrowed and fixed steadily on Llewellyn. 'That's Henry for you. Always likes someone else to make his decisions for him. He was reluctant to contact the police even when I arrived home and established that she *was* missing.'

Rafferty and Llewellyn exchanged surreptitious glances as Shore went on. 'I insisted, of course. He left it to me to try to get hold of someone at the Conservation Society's offices, as well as the caretaker of the hall, and that farmer. They all said they hadn't seen her. I even asked the caretaker to search the hall and outbuildings, just in case she'd got shut up somewhere.'

Mrs Griffiths broke in. 'Can I go now? Only I do have work to do.' She sounded put out. Apparently, she liked being ignored even less than she liked being questioned.

Rafferty did his best to soothe her ruffled feathers. 'Of course. Thank you, Mrs Griffiths. You've been very helpful. There is just one other thing. I don't know whether you can explain it, but Mrs Longman was wearing a rather unusual dress. Do you ... ?'

'Oh, that.' She tutted disparagingly. 'They were having a dress rehearsal in the church hall. They're doing Shakespeare.'

Although hers wasn't a particularly expressive face, it was clear she considered the great Elizabethan playwright vastly overrated. Rafferty hadn't yet got around to adding Shakespeare to his book list, so he couldn't comment.

'It was Mrs Charles's idea,' she told them, with a glance at Shore. 'She used to be an actress, of course.'

Rafferty got the impression that she regarded anything to do with the entertainment world as no better than it ought to be, whether it was Shakespeare or the sleeze-pots of Soho. Perhaps, he mused, as he caught the faintest lilt of a Welsh accent, she had been brought up a strict Methodist, like Llewellyn? It would certainly explain her demeanour. 'You said it was Mrs Charles's idea,' he commented. 'Wasn't she in it as . . . ?'

Shore interposed again. 'My wife wasn't interested in taking part in a tin-pot village production, Inspector.' The idea seemed to amuse him. 'I imagine she only suggested it to get the children from under her feet during the school holidays. Not that she's ever here for long enough to have to worry about that, anyway.'

'I see.' Rafferty nodded at Mrs Griffiths. 'Please go on.'

'Mrs Longman was playing Titania, Queen of the Fairies or some such,' she continued. 'As Mr Shore says, all the children are in it, though the boys aren't too keen. Not to be wondered at really. What boys want to parade around a stage wearing tights, especially in this heat?' A ghostly smile lightened the housekeeper's sallow features. 'Little devils, they knew what time they were expected to be ready, and had made themselves scarce. Of course, when I told Mrs Longman, she couldn't waste time getting changed again to look for them. Told me to send the boys on to the church hall when I saw them.'

With a satisfied expression, she added, 'I don't know where Edward got to. Maxie showed up not much more than twenty minutes after she'd driven off, but I couldn't persuade him to wait for the

4.00 p.m. bus to Elmhurst and follow her. Claimed he didn't feel well and he did seem a little pale and tetchy, not his usual self at all. But what else can you expect with this unhealthy weather? I made him a drink and persuaded him to go to bed. Jane—Mr Charles's daughter—had already left for the hall with a little friend and her mother.'

Rafferty thanked her again and let her go. He found he was still clutching Maximillian Shore's autobiography. On an impulse, he asked if he could borrow it.

He thought Shore was going to refuse. Instead, he commented succinctly, 'I wouldn't have thought you'd have much time for reading with a murder to investigate.'

Rafferty gave him a winning smile and confided, 'I find it essential to be able to relax when I'm in the middle of a murder inquiry, even if it's only for a few hours. The old grey matter often works much better for the break.'

Shore shrugged with an air of indifference. 'Borrow it by all means. Though why that should interest you, particularly...'

Rafferty smiled. 'Let's just say I'm hoping he'll inspire me.' He heard the lining of his pocket tear as he stuffed it into his jacket. Llewellyn had several times advised him that he ruined the line of his suits through his schoolboy habit of cramming his treasures into every available pocket. But, at thirty-seven, he knew he was unlikely to change. He wasn't sure he wanted to. 'Before we go, sir. Could we speak to your wife again and get her full statement? And if you could let me have your sister's address, I'd be grateful.'

Shore's eyes narrowed. 'I'm afraid my wife's not at home, Inspector. As for my sister, you can have her address, by all means, but I don't understand what you think she can contribute to your investigation.'

Rafferty assured him once again it was just routine and, with just a trace of his former reluctance still lingering, Shore supplied his sister's address. Then, in what appeared to be a burst of brotherly concern, he added, 'You'll go easy with her, won't you? This is a shocking business and my sister never did stand up to shocks very well.'

'Don't worry, sir.' Rafferty was surprised at Shore's solicitude for his sister after the apparent animosity he had shown earlier. But his next words revealed that he wasn't concerned so much about his sister as about himself.

'I don't want her coming here upsetting Henry. He's bad enough without adding my sister and her hysterics to the brew. And I've got to live with him.' He looked thoughtful as he showed them out and added, almost to himself, 'For now, anyway.'

SIX

'FUNNY ABOUT that phone call,' said Rafferty as they parted from Shore and got into the car. 'I thought so when it was first mentioned, but then it looked as though our killing was definitely tied up with the other ones, and it just seemed like an unfortunate circumstance. Now, I'm not so sure.'

'Didn't it strike you as odd, too, that the dead woman's husband didn't contact us himself?' Llewellyn asked. 'I know Mr Shore didn't seem to think there was anything strange about it, but even so...'

Rafferty nodded. 'I know what you're thinking. If the case has no connection with Suffolk, it's possible one of the family could be implicated. Certainly, whoever made that phone call knew his victim very well. It's an unlisted number—no stranger would be likely to have access to it. And he knew of her interest in rare flowers and was able to use that as bait to tempt her to that meadow. And, as we both know, most domestic murders are carried out by the spouse, so if it does turn out to be a domestic killing, chances are the husband's implicated. Shore's no fool and must realize the direction our suspicions are likely to take. He's probably just trying to protect Longman.' He tapped the book he had borrowed from Shore. 'I thought this might help us to learn a little more about the family. I know this is old stuff, but it'll give the background. It might be useful.'

Although Barbara Longman *hadn't* been raped—in spite of other suspicions—a sexual motive for the killing couldn't be ruled out, so, while waiting to hear from DI Ellis in Suffolk, Rafferty had given orders that all known sex attackers should be brought in for questioning. However, as he discovered on his return to the station at lunchtime, the results were disappointing.

Rafferty shut the interview room door on the one skinny old man—all the team had brought in. Turning to Constable Hanks, he demanded, 'Is this it? Just old Albert? Surely you can do better than that?'

'He's the only one we've got, I'm afraid, sir,' Hanks defended himself. 'The rest are either banged up, dead or have solid alibis. Old Albert's the only local sex attacker who couldn't produce an alibi for Thursday afternoon.'

Rafferty sighed. Hanks had done his best. He always did, he was a bright lad, and now Rafferty felt he had been unfair to take his frustration out on him. It was just that, after his conversation with Suffolk CID, he was less than sanguine that the cases were connected and he had begun pinning his hopes on the possibility that one of their own local weirdos would prove to have been Mrs Longman's murderer. If not... But he didn't want to think of the 'if not' aspect just yet. Rafferty managed to dredge up a smile for the earnest young constable. 'Go and grab yourself some lunch while Sergeant Llewellyn and I have a word with Albert.'

But old Albert was beyond understanding any of Rafferty's questions. Years of drink had pickled his brain and he met Rafferty's gaze from faded blue eyes that looked as if they had been through one too many cycles on the washing machine of life. Rafferty couldn't believe that the old man was still up to attacking anybody. Besides, his favourite victims had been little girls, not grown women. 'We're wasting our time,' he told Llewellyn as they shut the door on the tramp. 'He's not our man, I'd stake my love life on it. But tell Hanks to check out all his usual haunts, anyway. Someone might have seen him drinking in the town when Mrs Longman was killed.' Just then, his stomach gave a mighty rumble. 'And get me some cheese and pickle sandwiches from the canteen on your way back,' he called before Llewellyn disappeared round the corner.

There were more reports waiting for Rafferty when he got back to his office, and while he waited for Llewellyn to return he made a start on them. But when the first few he picked up proved as short on information as the earlier ones he sat back and let his mind drift. Sometimes if he just emptied his brain of all the swirling images that made concentrated thinking so difficult it let one vital element filter back, the one that made all the difference. But, today, try as he might, he couldn't single out anything. He gave up when Llewellyn returned with his sandwiches. Taking a huge bite, he pulled the rest of the reports toward him and started to read again.

IT WAS past midnight when Rafferty closed Shore's autobiography and turned out his bedside light. *A Phoenix Life* might be a strange title, he reflected, but it was certainly apt. As a lad of fifteen, Maximillian Shore had been left for dead in a mass grave of his fellow Jews. Uninjured, he had fallen with the rest as

Nazi bullets had thudded into emaciated bodies. Shore had described the guards' chilling laughter as they finished off their victims and Rafferty could almost hear it ringing in his ears as he tried to settle. But the images of the deaths, with their attendant terror, blood and debasement, were still too vivid for sleep to come easily.

He could see the young Maximillian Shore crouching for hours in the stinking hole, his only company the corpses and the buzzing flies that tormented him all that long, sweltering afternoon as he waited for darkness. His dead friends had apparently given him a macabre comfort, a strength to endure and survive that stopped him from going mad. With the coming of night, he had crawled from the hole, bade those who had shared his vigil a silent goodbye and set off. The days that followed would have filled half a dozen adventure novels. Travelling only at night, he had narrowly missed capture several times but, finally, after many hazards, he managed to contact an influential non-Jewish friend of his father, who had got him out, first to Switzerland and from there to England. It was the beginning of a phenomenally successful life; a life of chances taken and risks overcome; until a hidden bomb had done what the Nazis had failed to do. It certainly gave him more insight into the family background, but as to helping him solve Barbara Longman's murder...

Rafferty was still pondering Shore's incredible success and his own anticipated early rising the next morning when sleep finally came.

RAFFERTY HAD JUST got into the office on Sunday morning when DI Ellis got back to him. 'Morning, Joe. Thought I'd find you working. My sergeant tells me you think our killer might have started spreading his favours around.'

'That's right,' said Rafferty. 'Though, from what he told me about your bloke's MO, it doesn't match ours. But could we get together and discuss it?'

'Might not be necessary. Did Stevens mention that I'd been to Ipswich to question a suspect?' Feeling an uneasy sense of *déjà vu* as he became aware of the euphoria in Ellis's voice, Rafferty confirmed it. 'When does the pathologist think your victim died?'

Rafferty told him, 'Some time Thursday afternoon.'

'Sorry, Joe, but it sounds as if you've got a copycat on your patch. Because the chap we've arrested had been held in custody at Ipswich since 11.00 a.m. that morning.'

Rafferty, who had been holding his breath, now slowly let it out. Dispiritedly, he forced himself to ask the obvious, though he didn't doubt that Ellis had got his facts right. 'You're sure about that, Frank?'

'Positive. Not only has he been singing like a poor man's Pavarotti, providing details that only the murderer could know, but the DNA tests prove he's our boy. It's a relief, I don't mind telling you. I haven't had a decent night's sleep since this case started, but I'll sleep tonight.'

Doubt if I will, thought Rafferty glumly. Ellis's news had confirmed his growing doubts that Barbara had been a victim of the serial killer. And with the local weirdos also out of the running, the possibilities were lessening, drawing closer to home, closer to Barbara Longman's family and friends. Swallowing his depression, Rafferty congratulated his opposite number and put the phone down.

SUPERINTENDENT BRADLEY had decided Rafferty should hold a press conference on Monday afternoon to tell the media of his progress so far in solving Barbara Longman's murder. Rafferty didn't know what Bradley thought he could tell them. He knew as well as Rafferty did that their progress had been zilch. The farmer, Thomson, denied he had been anywhere near the meadow, the Conservation Society, when telephoned, had been emphatic that not only did they have few male members none of the ones they did have had a forename beginning with 'J'. The alibis they had thus far been able to check held up. According to Shore's personal secretary, he hadn't left his office all Thursday afternoon. And although, because he was away on business, they hadn't been able to contact the chap at the Chamber of Commerce with whom Henry had had the meeting, it was unlikely that Henry would be so idiotic as to lie about something so easily checked.

Despite the fact that nobody had ever seriously suspected him, even old Albert had turned out to have an alibi; one supplied by an ex-policeman security guard at the Priory View Shopping Centre, way over at the north-west part of the town. He'd let the old man sit on one of the benches in the centre for most of the afternoon of the murder, until he began to abuse the shoppers. It had been late-night shopping on Thursday, and normally, if Albert behaved himself, he let him stay till the shops closed at 9.00 p.m. But, that day, he'd moved him on at 5.30 p.m. and though early it was still much too late for him to have murdered Barbara, even supposing him still physically capable of it.

And, in spite of the best efforts of their forensic, house-to-house and other enquiries, they had no other leads. No witnesses—not even the usual time-wasters—had yet come forward. For all the reports that had so far come in, Barbara Longman and her car might as well have become invisible as soon as they left the Shores' drive. No one had seen her for the entire ten minutes that it would have taken her to drive to the meadow, a fact which Rafferty found so incredible that he ordered the descriptions of the victim and her car circulated again. *Someone* must have seen her, he reassured himself. It was just a matter of time before a witness came forward. It *was* still the holiday season. It was possible someone had gone on a late break abroad after witnessing Barbara driving to the meadow and was unaware of the call for witnesses.

Superintendent Bradley took the news from Ellis well, considering. But Rafferty took his emphatic assurances that he would have his full support with a big pinch of cynicism. Bradley had a knack for claiming the laurels of someone else's victory for himself, whilst, if there was any blame to be allotted, it was certain Rafferty would receive it in full measure. He knew that the Yorkshireman's support was a delicate plant. Bradley was a career policeman determined on carving himself a path right to the top, and Rafferty didn't doubt that he would get there. He had all the essential attributes for high office: the morals of a politician, the machiavellian mind of a con man, and a wife who was related to half the top brass in the Force. He couldn't fail.

As he left his superior to his machinations, Rafferty reminded himself of his mother's frequent exhortation. Just do your best, lad, that's all you can do. No one can ask for more. Like hell, they can't, he snorted. Bradley can—and will.

After briefing Llewellyn and the rest of the team, Rafferty put aside his pessimism. To hell with Bradley. This was *his* case, and he'd tackle it his way. And now that the Suffolk killer was definitely out of the running, they could direct the full force of their enquiries on the information they *did* have. Among other things, that meant checking out the Conservation Society a little further. Privately, Rafferty doubted they would find their killer among their members—why would he deliberately set the police on his trail? But it was likely the killer had *connections* with the Society, through a member who was his wife, sister or friend. How, otherwise, would he have any knowledge of the victim, or the family's unlisted telephone number?

They had phoned Miss Colman, one of the committee members of the Society, but she had been unhelpful. Although obviously upset about her friend's murder, she seemed to feel the police were adding insult to injury by suspecting her precious members. Perhaps, Rafferty remarked to Llewellyn, a visit from the inspector in charge of the case would persuade her to be more co-operative?

IN SPITE OF its grand-sounding name, the Conservation Society was based in a mean little fifties terraced house, near the recreation ground on the poorer, eastern outskirts of Elmhurst. Its scuffed front door opened straight off the pavement into a similarly scuffed hallway.

The painfully plain middle-aged woman who opened the door bore all the hallmarks of the committed 'Green' campaigner: rope-soled canvas shoes, natural cotton skirt suit, even the 'Save the Whale' badge proclaimed her dedication. But Rafferty got the impression her dedication had only grown as other areas of her life had become increasingly barren. Miss Colman wore no wedding ring, and, as he sensed that the Society had come to replace the husband and children that fate had denied her, he knew he would have to tread warily. Beneath her unnecessarily antagonistic manner she seemed to nurse disappointment at life and bitterness at men in about equal measures.

She confirmed her identity and, after examining them with all the enthusiasm of a vegetarian for a plate of congealed beef stew, demanded what they wanted *now*. 'I told you on the phone that you're wasting your time questioning *my* members, as few of them are men and none have the initial "J". Even if they did, it's certain that none of the Society's members can have anything to do with Barbara's death.' She capitalized the pronunciation of her baby like any proud new mother and added self-righteously, 'Green campaigners are into life, Inspector, not death.'

'I'm sure they are,' he told her, placatingly. 'But whoever killed Mrs Longman certainly isn't, and from the information we have, it's apparent that, although he probably wasn't a member, the killer had *some* connection with the Society and knew of Mrs Longman's involvement with it. As her conservation work brought her into contact with a wide variety of people, it's essential we look into any connections, however tenuous. Checking the membership list seems the logical place to start.'

'I see.'

Her hostile stare wavered slightly and Rafferty was relieved to see that, of the two emotions that were evidently waging a war within her breast, the natural desire to have her friend's killer caught seemed to be overcoming her dislike of men and her antipathy to any criticism of her Society and its members. And, although it was obvious Miss Colman still found the thought of her Society being investigated by chauvinistic policemen a double intrusion, Rafferty's explanation had at least taken away some of the sting of suspicion.

'Well.' She relented. 'I suppose as long as you only want to *eliminate* my members from your enquiries...' She turned and led the way through to the office along the narrow damp-smelling hallway. 'It was the thought that you suspected one of them that I found abhorrent.' They might be *men*, her manner implied, but they *were* members of the Society, which, in her view, obviously saved them from the worst perversities of the male species.

'I was very fond of Barbara,' she told them. 'There was no nonsense about her. She did whatever was required without any of that dreadful girlish flirting which some of my members seem to find essential whenever there are men around. It would be too awful if someone *I* knew had—killed her. But that's ridiculous, of course. After all, according to the papers, you policemen think she was killed by that disgusting pervert in Suffolk. Any connection with the Society is obviously just an unfortunate coincidence.'

Rafferty decided it would be foolish to rouse her protective instincts for the Society all over again, so he didn't tell her the Suffolk killer was now out of the running. She would discover it soon enough when she watched the television news.

The office was situated in the front room and was obsessively neat and workmanlike. A functional and unlovely government-surplus grey filing cabinet was lined up as though awaiting inspection to the right of the window, and beside it, situated to get the best of the limited light, was an equally ancient metal desk. The smell of damp was less keen in here, Rafferty noticed. Presumably, in the winter, the two-bar electric fire kept the worst effects at bay.

Miss Colman, less strident now she had convinced herself the Conservation Society could be absolved of any possible guilt, became quite chatty. 'Barbara was a friendly woman, but a little too *trusting* in my opinion. I thought it was most unwise the way she gave *men* lifts in her car. Just because they were husbands or boyfriends of our members didn't make them above suspicion, as I told her. She used to laugh at me, but,' her chin rose as her feelings about the general male population had been amply vindicated, 'her death proves I was right. If she had listened to me, she . . .'

Before she managed to get into her stride about the wickedness of men, Rafferty quickly reminded her that they needed to see the membership list.

She drew herself up with a sniff. 'I'm aware of that, but there's a slight problem. Barbara put it on the computer. I've never had much affinity with the

wretched things, but, if you think *you* can work it...'
Her dismissive glance told Rafferty that, whatever
else he might delude himself about, she was sure his
accomplishments wouldn't include anything *useful*.

Unfortunately, as far as the current skill require-
ment was concerned, Rafferty had to admit she was
right. Computers were far from being his strong suit
and he sighed as he eyed the blank-screened box that
sat importantly in the centre of the desk. In spite of
the Force sending him on various computer courses,
he still felt intimidated by the wretched things and
insisted on tapping his reports out on a battered old
Remington manual.

'Barbara got it for us,' she went on in a milder tone,
evidently gratified that her earlier assumption about
his abilities had been correct. 'She said being able to
do a *mail-shot*'—the jargon tripped no more naturally off her tongue than it would have off his own,
Rafferty noted—'would make it easier to circulate
information to the members. She intended to teach
the other committee members how to use it, but...'
She sniffed and turned away, blowing her nose into
what looked like a handkerchief made of recycled
blotting paper. 'There's a manual in the drawer, I believe.'

'Don't worry, sir,' said Llewellyn. His voice,
though polite as ever, betrayed a hint of triumph.
Pulling out a chair, the Welshman observed evenly,
'It's an Amstrad, I've got one of these at home, so I
think I'll be able to extract the information without
too much trouble. With your permission, of course?'
He glanced at Rita Colman, as his hand hovered at
the side of the screen.

At her tight-lipped nod, Llewellyn switched on. Almost instantly the screen brightened and he opened a plastic box at the side of the keyboard, selected a disk and inserted it. 'Just loading the program,' he informed them. As they watched, the screen went black again and short lines of white text appeared.

In a little while, the printer hummed, columns of information emerged on to the screen and it seemed they were ready for action. Llewellyn removed the first disk, inserted another and settled happily, tapping at the keyboard with an air of expertise. After a few minutes spent bringing likely looking files on to the screen, Llewellyn exclaimed, 'Ah. This looks like it.'

Miss Colman confirmed it. The list of familiar names and addresses flickering on the screen seemed to bring back her antagonism, and she rushed to the defence of her members again. Rafferty shut his ears, and, as if realizing that she had lost her audience, she went out closing the door loudly behind her, as though to make it quite clear that she dissociated herself from their actions.

Llewellyn pressed several more keys in quick succession and, with a just discernible smugness, told Rafferty, 'I've instructed it to start printing, sir.'

Nothing happened for a few seconds and Rafferty, a bit put out that his sergeant had, once again, managed to make him feel like an uneducated knownothing, seized happily on the hold-up. With an acid smile, he remarked, 'It doesn't seem to be working, Sergeant,' just as the printer pounded into life.

Disgruntled, Rafferty retreated to the other end of the room, and for the next few minutes, he watched with a dismay that grew in proportion to the pile of

computer paper produced. In no time it had turned
out sufficient lists of names and addresses to gladden
the hearts of a dozen direct-mail junkies. It looked
like more than the hundred members Rita Colman
had claimed during their telephone conversation. Investigating them, *and* all their friends and relations,
would probably be the total waste of time she had
claimed. And it would take forever, tying up precious manpower in the process.

How likely was it that this 'J', if he was the murderer, would leave such an obvious trail for the police to track back? Rafferty asked himself. Unless he
was playing a clever game of double-bluff, he thought
it likely the man was simply taunting them, knowing
they'd have to spend valuable hours checking the Society out.

It would be common knowledge among her friends
and acquaintances that Barbara Longman was fierce
in defence of those wild flowers. 'Green' concerns was
the one area of her life where she *was* fierce, apparently, the one area where kindness never entered the
arena. Anyone who knew her even slightly could be
pretty certain that, after such a warning phone message, she would head straight for the meadow ready
to defend the flowers from all comers. For a murderer, keen on certainty and privacy, it had all the
charm of a sure thing to a compulsive gambler. And,
obligingly, Barbara Longman had gone to the
meadow, and died there in that desolate spot with
only her precious wild flowers and the Sniffy Tiffey
as witnesses.

He slapped at the pile of paper. 'Now that we've
got them, I suppose we'd better give this lot to Hanks
and the house-to-house team to copy and check out.

And one of us had better make time to go and see this farmer chap again.' With the unkind but fervent hope that a muddy farm and a surly farmer would humble his know-all sergeant, he told Llewellyn, 'You can do that. Speak to my neighbours while you're at it. Find out what's known about him. Check with the computer to see if he's got a record for violence.'

Llewellyn gave a stiff nod.

Rita Colman came back. 'You got what you wanted, then?' Her voice was sharp and she gazed with a proprietary air at the pile of paper in Llewellyn's arms.

''Yes. Thank you for your help. It will probably come to nothing,' Rafferty assured her. 'But we have to be thorough.'

Given the mysterious telephone call that had lured her to her death and the fact that the Suffolk killer and the local weirdos had been eradicated from their enquiries, Rafferty knew he had to consider other motives than rape for Mrs Longman's murder. After all, she hadn't been raped; it was possible her killer had decided that a copycat killing would effectively conceal an act of personal vengeance. It had been done before. And, as far as Rafferty had so far discovered, the only area of Barbara Longman's life that attracted controversy was her conservation work.

He eyed Miss Colman thoughtfully. Being a despised male, he was wary of rousing her ire again. 'Perhaps we could ask you one or two further questions?' he suggested tentatively. She nodded. 'Do you know if Mrs Longman had made any enemies over her conservation work? I know it's a subject on which many people have strong opinions, even those on the same side don't always agree about methods so—' He broke off as she looked suspiciously at him and became aware that his way of expressing himself had been less than tactful.

'It doesn't mean to say that any of us would go in for murder, Inspector,' she assured him frostily. 'All our members got on very well with Barbara. And as you believe she was the third victim of the Suffolk killer, I don't see why you should be so interested in any enemies she made in her conservation work.'

Rafferty had forgotten he had let Miss Colman go on thinking the Suffolk killer was the prime suspect and his head echoed to his ma's mocking voice. 'O what a tangled web we weave, when first we practise to deceive.' She was right, as usual. Rafferty wondered how best to conceal his deceit without antagonizing the woman. Especially as she now had the impression that he was going to start hounding her members...

'We *did* believe that, certainly,' he admitted cautiously. 'Didn't I say that was no longer a possibility?'

'No,' she told him abruptly. 'You didn't. You let me believe that my members weren't under suspicion and...'

'But they're not,' he told her disingenuously. 'That wasn't what I was thinking at all. If Mrs Longman had an enemy, an enemy who wished to harm her, then wouldn't you say he's more likely to come from among the *anti*-conservationists?'

He was gratified to see that he had adopted the right tone, for she nodded slowly and said, 'And you want to know if there was anyone in particular that Barbara had crossed swords with?'

'That's the idea,' he encouraged.

To his astonishment, she actually smiled. She leaned forward confidingly, her expression eager. 'Now that's *much* more likely. Especially as there *was* someone. Barbara was always in the forefront of our campaigns and took on some very powerful people: big business polluters, men who put profit before the environment.' She paused and gazed at him from brown eyes bright with malice. 'One of them was Charles Shore.'

AFTER RETURNING to the police station, Llewellyn went back out again to speak to the farmer and Rafferty took himself off to the public library. An hour later, he sat back and stared at the front-page story on the library's microfiche. What Rita Colman had said *hadn't* been just the malicious tittle-tattle of an embittered woman, as he had suspected. Two and a half years earlier, Barbara Longman had accused Charles Shore's chemical firm of deliberately discharging chemicals into the River Tiffey. Her accusation hadn't been substantiated and Shore had denied it. But, strangely, he hadn't sued her for slander, libel, defamation or anything else, which Rafferty felt was uncharacteristically forgiving of him.

Rafferty paged forward over issues covering the following months, but there were no further mention of her accusations. The story had just petered out. But it wasn't hard to understand why. Rita Colman had told them that Charles Shore had bought up the local newspaper chain and put his yes-men in charge, effectively ending the paper's support for the Society's campaign against polluters. She had told them that, at the time, she hadn't understood why he should go to so much expense. He had never pre-

tended to care about 'Green' opinion. And it wasn't
as if he couldn't afford the piddling amounts such
polluters were fined. But, she had gone on to explain, recent events had provided a probable reason
for his actions. Ill-health had persuaded the local
Tory MP to step down at the soon to be held by-
elections and Barbara had told her that Charles
Shore, who had long nurtured political ambitions,
had grabbed his opportunity to put himself forward
to the Tory party selection committee.

Rafferty had been surprised that Charles Shore
should consider running as an MP, with all his other
commitments, and had remarked on it.

Rita Colman had smiled condescendingly at his
naïvety and said, 'Think of all the powerful business
contacts he'd make at Westminster. But for that, he
needs to get selected, then elected. It's a fairly safe
Tory seat, even in the midst of a recession. Unfortunately for him, a free local newspaper has recently
started up in Elmhurst which he hasn't so far managed to gag with his money. And they commissioned
Barbara as a freelance to work on a series of investi-
gative environmental articles. Barbara was always
very strong on honesty and truth. If she found out he
was still polluting the river, she wouldn't hesitate to
make it public again. I doubt if the Tory selection
committee would be quite so keen to select him then,
do you?'

Rafferty nodded. Such bad publicity could end his
political ambitions before they had even got off the
ground. And Shore would know it. 'But her husband
works for Shore—they live in his house,' he had objected. 'Would she put their security on the line for a
principle?'

She gave him a look that demanded, what could a mere *man* know? 'Barbara had strong principles. I don't expect you to understand that. I doubt if Shore did, either. She wouldn't consider abandoning them even for such personal considerations. She was an admirable woman in many ways.'

'But do you have any proof that he's polluted the river lately?'

'No,' she admitted reluctantly. 'But maybe Barbara had. And perhaps, this time with the Environment Protection Act to help her, she thought she might get somewhere. She had certainly discovered *something* recently that upset her, but she didn't tell me what it was—she probably wanted to tackle him about it first. And if he had been up to his old tricks, do you really think it's likely he'd let her stand in the way of his ambitions? We already know he can be utterly ruthless, just like his father.' Her voice was suddenly harsh, condemning and filled with hatred. 'He wouldn't think twice about killing her. He'd snuff her out like a candle, if it suited him. Make no mistake about it.'

SEVEN

RAFFERTY SWITCHED OFF the microfiche with a flourish and looked round as if he expected a round of applause for his techno-wizardry. None being forthcoming, he strolled back to the desk, thanked the assistant for her many patient explanations as to the gadget's operation and returned to the station.

He found Llewellyn back in the office, busily typing away. 'Rita Colman's story checks out,' he told the Welshman. 'The local paper had a big front-page splash about Barbara Longman's accusations against Shore over two years ago. I printed it out for you,' he added casually, carefully forgetting that it had been the librarian's skill rather than his own which had produced the printout.

'So what do you think?' Rafferty asked, after Llewellyn had read the report.

Llewellyn looked steadily at him. 'You really want to know?'

'Of course.'

'Very well. For one thing, Shore's a very powerful and influential man. I don't think either of us should go at this in a bull-headed manner.'

Rafferty gave him a belligerent stare. 'Meaning me, I suppose?'

Loftily, Llewellyn told him, 'You did ask.'

Rafferty sighed. 'I did, didn't I?' He gave a rueful smile. 'Don't worry, Dafyd. I'll go easy. I don't have much choice. We've no proof that Barbara Longman had discovered anything damaging against Shore and, so far, his alibi checks out. Quite possibly there's nothing in it at all, and it was something else entirely that was worrying her. But, if he had been illegally dumping chemicals in the river and Barbara found out about it and threatened to put an end to his political ambitions, it would certainly provide him with a powerful motive.' Rafferty twirled himself gently in his chair for a few moments before turning back with a grin. 'And if there *is* anything in it, I know just the person to find out.'

Llewellyn, noting the grin, gazed steadily back and said, 'Meaning me, I suppose?'

'Meaning you. I—as you've implied on several occasions—have all the finesse and discretion of a bull elephant with wind. Whereas you...' Satisfied that Charles Shore, his reputation, habits and ambitions would get a thorough but discreet going-over by Llewellyn, Rafferty switched the conversation to another suspect. 'What did you manage to find out about that farmer?'

'He's got a record. I'm typing the report now, if you want to wait and read...'

Rafferty waved the offer away. 'Just tell me.'

'He has a couple of drunk driving and drunk and disorderly convictions, but nothing more—at least nothing on record, though none of his few neighbours had a good word to say for him. I can't say I'm surprised, as he's as surly an individual as Charles Shore claimed. He said he hasn't had a tractor in that meadow for years. Said he isn't allowed to, as the rare flowers there are protected, though I doubt if that would stop him. His neighbours told me he argued with everybody and went out of his way to be obstructive and unhelpful. Last year he had to be taken to court to stop him blocking access to a public footpath on his land. The year before that he just missed being prosecuted for threatening to set his dogs on one of his elderly neighbours. He also has something of an open feud going on with the Conservation Society. I'm surprised Rita Colman didn't mention him.'

'I imagine Recycled Rita prefers to drop the big boys, like Charles Shore, in it. Much more satisfying. Still, as you say, he's another possibility. Small farmers like Thomson are generally anti-conservationist to a man. If they thought there was a profit in it most of them would plough up their granny's grave and plant it with rape seed.'

'Speaking of profit,' Llewellyn remarked, 'I would imagine there were money problems there, too. The farmhouse looked as if it was about to fall down.'

'Don't see how that helps us. It's not likely Barbara Longman remembered him in her will. What sort of alibi has he got?'

'Told me the same story he told Hanks—that he was busy on another part of the farm during the relevant time. Said his mother would substantiate his story when she returned from town.'

Rafferty smiled. 'What? Dear old mum? Not exactly watertight, is it? In my experience, mothers can generally be relied upon to save their sons from nasty policemen and their questions. I reckon if you laid the lies of all the mothers in the world end to end...' Aware of Llewellyn's implacably intelligent gaze, his mind thrashed about trying to come up with an appropriate metaphor and failed. He concealed his lack of success by carrying on smoothly, 'You'd wish you hadn't started the job. Perhaps I should go and see old Ma Thomson myself?'

It was a pleasant afternoon; the dead heat of a few days before had mysteriously faded. And, he realized, a bit of fresh country air would help clear his lungs of some of the remaining sludge from his smoking. He swore, as he realized he couldn't go. His successes at the library had made him forget that Bradley had arranged a date for him. He would have to make it another day. Still, the weathermen forecast a similar outlook, he consoled himself. And before he saw Ma Thomson there were one or two other people of more pressing interest. Shore's sister—Henry's first wife—for instance. He was sure she'd have some interesting things to say about her brother, her ex-husband, and the rest of the Shore menagerie.

But first he had to get through the press conference.

ALTHOUGH RAFFERTY TRIED to keep calm, the ladies and gentlemen of the press were evidently in a bullish, police-baiting mood. As the conference wore on the tension in the room heightened, the questions became increasingly hostile and Rafferty cursed the absent Superintendent Bradley under his breath. 'Trust him to be "unavoidably detained" elsewhere,' he muttered. As Ian Haslam, senior crime reporter with the *National Bulletin,* leapt to his feet again, Rafferty gritted his teeth.

'Can we expect this case to end in the same way as your last one, Inspector?' the sharp-faced newsman taunted. 'With no arrest and no conviction?'

Rafferty forced a smile past his teeth. Although his last case had brought no conviction, it was considered closed and successfully concluded—a fact of which Haslam was well aware. The newsman's taunt forced a reply from Rafferty that lacked even the elementary diplomacy that he had so far managed. 'It's early days yet for *this* case, Mr Haslam. But,' he mocked, 'for future reference, might I suggest you ask one of your colleagues to explain the difference between a solved closed case and an open *unsolved* one?'

Rafferty was relieved when his sarcasm was greeted by a guffaw of laughter. Haslam sat down again, an ugly flush on his face. Rafferty guessed he had made an enemy, but for the moment he didn't care and he took advantage of the suddenly lightened atmosphere to bring the conference to a close.

BY THE TIME Rafferty had escaped the attentions of the media, it had been too late for them to go to London to see Anne Longman. They drove up the following morning. The first Mrs Longman lived in St John's Wood, an area of north-west London in which the straying husbands of the previous century had often housed their mistresses. Quite a few of the pretty Italianate villas still existed, but Rafferty was surprised to discover that Anne Longman didn't live in one. Instead, she had a flat in an anonymous sixties block. It had a run-down look which suggested the leaseholders were more interested in short-term profits than maintenance. It certainly wasn't the sort of home in which Rafferty expected one of the mega-rich Shores to live.

'I'm surprised Charles Shore didn't find somewhere a bit more salubrious for his only sister to live,' said Rafferty as he pressed the button for the lift. 'He was careful enough of his public image to spend a pile in buying up the local newspaper chain in order to conceal his dirtier habits, so you'd think he'd realize that the way an aspiring politician treated his nearest and dearest was also important. It's not as if he couldn't afford a decent place for her.'

Llewellyn treated him to one of his more sagacious glances and commented, 'But we don't know that he can, do we? Companies larger than Shore's have suffered from the fluctuations of the Stock Exchange.'

'What—do you think he might be more style than substance?' It was something Rafferty hadn't considered.

Llewellyn gave the tiniest of shrugs.

'It's possible, I suppose,' Rafferty conceded. 'But, somehow, in Shore's case, I don't think a shortage of the readies is the reason he houses his sister in a sixties concrete block. With him, I get the impression that the satisfaction he gets from keeping her down is amply worth the risk of a little bad publicity. Besides, if she's that dependent on him, he's safe enough. She's not likely to tell the press.'

The lift arrived and groaned its way up to the second floor. Rafferty knocked on the door of number fifteen and waited impatiently, curious to find out what Shore's sister, and Henry's ex-wife, would be like.

She wasn't what he had expected, but then, in his experience, people rarely were. He knew she was in her early thirties, three years Charles's senior, but she looked older. Her thick dark hair hung lifeless, and her face, although attractive in an ageing *ingénue* way, wasn't made-up with any great care. Her mascara had smudged and been left that way, as if correcting the small imperfection would entail too much trouble.

Rafferty showed his warrant card and, after raising not quite matching pencilled eyebrows, she remarked, with a callousness intended to shock, 'I suppose you've come about the sainted Barbara? My brother rang last Friday, and told me she'd been murdered. Thoughtful of him not to leave me to read it in the papers.' Her lips twisted in a parody of a smile. 'Poor Henry. He seems to have trouble keeping his wives.'

Rafferty got the impression that, under the juvenile desire to shock, her words were a form of camouflage for feelings that might otherwise overwhelm her. There was an air of suppressed excitement she couldn't quite conceal and he guessed that the whisky he smelt on her breath as she moved back to let them in had heightened it. It was only half-past eleven and such early, solitary drinking hinted at instability, the need of a crutch to get through the day. Charles had hinted that she had a 'problem'; presumably that was it, though he had implied that her problem hadn't existed before her youthful marriage to Henry. Rafferty could well believe that Henry wouldn't exactly be a Rock of Gibraltar in the husband stakes. Had his ineffectualness and general air of helplessness driven her, despairing, into alcoholism? Or would she have followed the same route without his steering? With its succession of broken lives and tragic deaths, insecurity seemed to run in the Shore family.

'Welcome to Chez Squalor.' She spread her arms wide as she led them into the living room. Her description wasn't far wrong. With its balding rugs and grimy, smoke-stained walls, the interior of the flat was a good match for the exterior. 'My darling little brother's the last of the big spenders, you can see.' Her next words confirmed Rafferty's earlier conclusions. 'I think it amused him to provide me with a cheap flat in this area.' She gave a bitter laugh. 'He likes to remind me I'm a kept woman. I was my father's favourite, you see, at least until I rebelled and married Henry. It always rankled with Charles. This is his revenge.'

Despite the drink, she was sharp, and was well aware of the reasons behind her brother's lack of generosity. There was something of the jealous child in all of us, he mused, and even international executives weren't immune. Hadn't he always known that he was his ma's favourite? Her inadequately concealed preference still brought pangs of guilt long after childhood. He remembered his younger brothers and sisters watching to make sure he didn't get the bigger helping, the better presents, the greater attention. Growing up didn't change the jealousy, it merely drove it underground. He wondered what Maximillian Shore's favourite child had seen in Henry?

'He was kind,' she told him, startling him with the ease with which she seemed able to tune into his train of thought. But then his ma had a similar knack. One of his sisters, in a moment of candour, had told him his face was too open. A handicap in a policeman. 'Don't look so surprised, I'm not witch, it's just that that's what everyone always wondered. At least I thought he was kind,' she went on. 'It was only later that I discovered his so-called kindness stemmed more from weakness, from taking the line of least resistance, than from compassion. That's when I began to despise him. When you've had a father like mine, you need kindness. Or perhaps I should say I thought I did.' She shrugged and pushed her hair behind her ear again, in a gesture that betrayed the surface bravado.

Turning her back on them both, she gazed out of the window, watching as storm clouds, buffeted by a chilly east wind, chased each other across the sky. Rafferty wasn't altogether surprised that the weatherman had got it wrong again and he was glad he'd had to postpone the visit to old Ma Thomson. He'd have been squelching in mud up to his armpits.

Anne Longman appeared lost in contemplation and seemed to have forgotten their existence. Rafferty got the impression it was something she did often, a vanishing trick to shut out life's problems, like Henry and her father.

But, as the rain started in earnest and began a tympanic clattering against the windows, she turned back to face them, indulging, once again, in the drinker's need to confide, to explain away their weakness. 'My father accused me of trying to take the easiest route through life by marrying Henry.' She gave Rafferty a thin smile. 'And he was right—I was. Ironic isn't it, that it often turns out to be the hardest route in the end?'

Given the chance, Rafferty was all for the easy life himself, and having, like Llewellyn, lost his father at a young age, he wondered how it must have felt to have a parent like old Maximillian? As he recalled the unyielding expression of the portrait, with its hint of ruthless fanaticism, so well captured by the artist, he decided he'd had a lucky escape. It was hardly surprising that she'd married young. Defiance, they called it. Rebellion against authority. Hardly surprising either that she'd chosen a man like Henry.

She'd been only eighteen when she'd married him. At that age it would be easy to mistake weakness for kindness. He pulled himself up short before he got to the stage of inviting Llewellyn's psychological opinion. You're not here as a father confessor, Rafferty, he reminded himself. Get on with it.

He cleared his throat. 'Barbara Longman was murdered, as your brother told you. Do you know anyone who might have wished to harm her?'

'Apart from me, you mean?' she asked flippantly, again displaying that juvenile need to defy both good sense and convention that seemed an integral part of her character. Perhaps that need had set in early? Had she attempted to shock her father in order to gain some freedom? Perhaps she had hoped that by going against his express wishes often enough he would give up on her? Or perhaps, he thought wryly, it was just the drink talking, and he should leave the analysis to Llewellyn? 'Who could possibly want to murder the sainted Barbara? Everyone loved her.' Her mouth turned down. 'She was the fairy on top of the Christmas tree.'

'You didn't like her though.' She'd made no attempt to hide her feelings on the point and he saw no need to ignore it.

'Would you?' she countered. 'In my position?' She played restlessly with assorted bangles on her thin wrists. Rafferty found her fiddling distracting. 'She was the reason Henry got custody of Maxie, my son. If it wasn't for her...' Two bright spots of color stained her cheeks and her hands tightened on the back of the chair. 'She had no right to him. He was *my* son, not hers.'

Predictably logical, Llewellyn remarked reasonably, 'But surely, your son would have been about twelve, thirteen when the custody hearing was held? Old enough, I would have thought, to be asked his preference. If he'd rather stay with you, he had only to say.'

Anne Longman's eyes were scornful, as she demanded, 'What do you know about it? Charles made sure he *didn't* want to stay with me. Poisoned his mind against me.' She gave a sardonic laugh. 'He thought I didn't understand why, but I know my brother. Charles can be charming when he wants something. And you can be sure he pulled out all the stops on the charm front for Maxie, promised him all sorts of things that I could no longer give him, just to make sure Henry got custody and I didn't. Even as a boy, Charles was obsessed with getting his own way. I remember once, when we were children, we had a puppy that preferred me. He killed it out of spite. He could never bear anyone to have something he wanted. If he couldn't have it, he'd prefer to destroy it. Just like he destroyed the puppy.'

She stopped her tirade for long enough to light a cigarette. The pungent smoke made Llewellyn cough, but she took no notice, so intent was she on pouring out her grievances. 'Of course, with Barbara in court, looking as sober and saintly as Mother Teresa, and promising to provide Maxie with a stable home life, I knew no judge would grant me custody. I could see that no matter how hard I tried . . .' Her voice broke with the easy emotionalism of the drinker and she took a couple of shuddering breaths, before drawing quickly on her cigarette. The smoke seemed to calm her, for as her gaze settled on the bottle of cheap whisky on the sideboard, her eyes gradually hardened, and she took on an astonishing resemblance to her father. 'As long as Henry was with *her,* I knew I'd lose.'

'Her death would seem to have removed that difficulty,' Llewellyn remarked quietly.

She gave a harsh laugh. 'You sound as if you think *I* killed her.' The possibility that they might suspect her didn't seem to trouble her. With a wide-eyed and deceptive serenity, she added tauntingly, 'I might have done, at that—if I'd thought of it.'

'We don't know who killed her yet, Mrs Longman,' Rafferty told her quietly. How deep was the grudge she harboured against her successor? he wondered. Deep enough, certainly, to convince herself that the loss of her son hadn't been her own fault. It was strange, because, in spite of her penchant for drama, at heart she struck him as a realist. As much of a realist as her brother in her own way. Was she really capable of convincing herself that if it hadn't been for Barbara and her brother, a judge would have awarded her custody? Even if she managed to fool herself, would she have been able to pretend sobriety for long enough to fool the court? he wondered.

There would have been social reports and the rest. Custody hearings could be nasty, with all the little human failings thrown into the ring. Hadn't he heard the way of it often enough from his divorced colleagues in the Force? Although he was a Catholic, he was of the lapsed variety and had no strong feelings against divorce. If Angie, his wife, had lived longer, they'd probably have had kids and he might have followed the same route himself. With or without Barbara's presence in the court, it was likely Anne

Longman's drinking habits would have got a good
airing. She must know it too.

Llewellyn took up the questioning again. 'As this
is a murder investigation, you'll understand that we
need to ask certain questions? Perhaps you can tell us
where you were during last Thursday afternoon?' She
didn't respond, but Llewellyn persisted. 'Were you at
home?'

Anne Longman took her time replying. Only after
she had slid another cigarette from the packet of
Gauloises and lit it, did she speak. 'I imagine so.
Where else would I be?' She frowned, as if the question made her realize that she *didn't know* where she
had been, and, for a moment, her drunken forgetful-
ness seemed to worry her, but then she smiled and
flung her arms wide in a gesture that invited them to
come up with a suggestion. When they didn't respond, she repeated, 'Where else would I be?' Bra-
zening it out, she added, 'I've no money to go
anywhere. Charles made sure of that.'

Llewellyn tried again to get a firm answer from her.
'I'm afraid we need a more definite answer than that,
Mrs Longman. Can you please try a little harder to
remember.'

Rafferty glanced at his sergeant with a wry admiration for his perseverance. Personally, he didn't
think they'd get much out of her today. If they
wanted to prise a straight answer from her, they'd
have to get here early, before she'd braced herself with
alcohol.

But the Welshman was a creature of duty and although it was plain that Anne Longman's emotionalism made him uncomfortable, Llewellyn did his best

to counteract that by adopting a firm no-nonsense policeman demeanour. On the surface, they were a walking cliché, Rafferty realized with amusement—the soft cop and the hard one. And even if it wasn't strictly a true evaluation of their roles or personalities, the customers didn't know that.

'I *am* trying,' she insisted. 'But I can't remember, and badgering me won't help.' Taking another deep draw on her cigarette, she blew the smoke out and gazed at him coolly through the grey haze. 'Put me down as "at home all day", Sergeant, if it makes you happy.'

Rafferty got the feeling she was playing with them. It seemed Llewellyn sensed it too, because his Welsh accent, which was normally barely discernible, became more pronounced; a sure sign of annoyance. 'I'm afraid guesses aren't good enough, madam,' he asserted, his expression grim. 'Is there no one else who could confirm you were here?'

'A boyfriend, you mean?' She shook her head with an arch smile. 'Strictly *verboten,* don't you know? My darling brother thinks I'm a naughty girl and he made it plain, on the day I moved into this grace and favour flat, that it was simply to provide a roof over my head and to keep him above reproach. No followers allowed. The only male I can have staying here is my son, but they've succeeded in brainwashing him to such an extent that even that's a rare occurrence.' Her lip curled. 'I'm sure Charles pays my next door neighbour to spy on me.'

She crushed her cigarette out in the ashtray and lit another, before enquiring in a tone of bright interest, as if she were enquiring about a friend's pet cat,

'How's she supposed to have died, anyway? I gather from your questions that I'm included in your list of suspects, so surely I'm entitled to know? Charles didn't say and I rarely get a newspaper.'

As the media had already reported the brief details he had supplied at the press conference, Rafferty saw no reason not to tell her. 'According to the post-mortem, she was suffocated.'

Anne let out a peal of laughter. 'How disappointing for her.' With a glance of Llewellyn's stiff expression, she gibed, 'I don't know why you should be so shocked that I find it amusing. Death by suffocation's hardly in the best tradition of saints, is it?'

Rafferty stood up. He felt they had provided her with enough fun for one day. He hoped she wouldn't find their next interview quite so amusing. 'If you *do* remember for certain where you were on Thursday afternoon, perhaps you'd get in touch?'

She nodded and said quickly, as if anxious to get rid of them, 'Of course. Is that it?'

'For the moment.' Llewellyn's voice was sharp. 'We'll need to speak to you again, of course.'

As they let themselves out, Rafferty caught the crash of bottles from inside the flat. It seemed she hadn't been quite so relaxed about their visit as she made out. The thought made him realize he could do with a drink himself. And it *was* lunchtime. 'Fancy a bevvie?' he asked Llewellyn. 'I think we can spare half an hour.'

'No thank you, sir.' After a pause, he added, 'I don't drink.'

Rafferty wasn't altogether surprised. 'Taken the pledge, have you?' he joked.

'That's right. Took a vow when I was young.'

Rafferty gaped at him as he realized his joking had been spot on. 'Really? I thought that sort of thing went out with the Ark. You mean you've *never* drunk alcohol?'

Llewellyn nodded, and as he took it in Rafferty slowly shut his gaping mouth. In all his years in the Force, he couldn't recall a colleague who had willingly forsworn God's great comforter in such a way. To be able to hold your drink was almost as much a badge of office to the average copper as his warrant card. To him, Llewellyn's youthful teetotal vow was akin to a novice nun swearing to give up sex before she'd even tried it. Surely, he reasoned, bemusedly, it was the sacrificing of *known* pleasures that counted on the heavenly scoreboard? His shoulders slumped as he remembered he'd taken a vow himself to go on the wagon till this case was solved.

'It's not unheard of, you know,' Llewellyn went on. 'Lots of youngsters took a similar vow in the area where I lived. It was a small community, traditional. It's not so common now, of course. I remember the girls used to be encouraged to take a vow of chastity, to save their virginity for their wedding night.'

'And I suppose some of them combined the two?' Rafferty joked heavy-handedly. 'Shades of—"lips that touch liquor shall never touch mine".' Of course, his joke fell flatter than a Shrove Tuesday pancake.

'I didn't expect you to understand.'

Llewellyn sounded put out and Rafferty couldn't really blame him. He'd undergone enough religious indoctrination himself in his time to know what it was like, and with Llewellyn's father having been a minister, he'd have received more than most. Hadn't the Catholic Church done its best to turn his own youth into a desert of denial? As he recalled, everything had been a sin. Even to *think* naughty thoughts was wicked, though how you were supposed to control thoughts when they sprang unbidden he'd never understood. Luckily for his libido, he'd never paid too much heed to the squinting Father O'Brien, Old Wink, Blink and Nod One Night, as they'd called him. Now, he cleared his throat and wisely changed the subject. 'What did you make of the first Mrs Longman?' he asked.

Llewellyn shrugged. 'Very prickly, very defensive. It's obvious she's bitter about losing custody of her son and blamed the dead woman.'

Rafferty nodded. 'Could be a possible motive there. And she was vague about her whereabouts at the time of the murder. But unless she had an accomplice, she would seem to be out of it, as she couldn't have made that telephone call. Besides, the woman's a lush and they're not noted for either the excellence of their memories or for being cool-headed enough to get away with murder.'

He opened the entrance door and they ran for the car to get out of the downpour. Aware of Llewellyn's opinion of his driving, and feeling guilty about his earlier insensitivity, Rafferty handed the car keys to his sergeant. 'You drive.'

'I don't know about her drinking habits,' Llewellyn remarked, as he started the engine and edged cautiously out into the traffic, 'but she seemed a neurotic woman. The sort who might behave impulsively.'

'Mm. That's my conclusion, too,' agreed Rafferty. 'But even if we ignore the fact that the telephone caller was male, if she was going to kill Barbara, I can't see her suffocating her. She felt that Barbara had robbed her, not only of her son, but also of his love. I get the impression that all that anger would demand a more bloody revenge, as, apart from the drink, the boy seems to be the only thing in her life that she values.'

'That's hardly surprising, as there doesn't appear to be anything else in her life *to* value. We always prize highest that which we cannot have,' pronounced Llewellyn. 'She married very young, too. She was still only eighteen when she had her son, and her brother said she never acquired any qualifications. What sort of job could she get now, do you think, with no qualifications, no experience and a drinking problem? She must feel she's got a lot to be bitter about and she has all the time in the world to brood on it. It's an unhealthy mixture.'

Yes, but had it become a dangerous mixture, too? Rafferty wondered. Unlike Henry, he thought she'd have sufficient daring to kill Barbara. But daring alone wouldn't have been enough, it would have required coolness, too. A couple of stiff whiskies could have provided that, he supposed. If she had the sense to restrict herself to the two. She'd also have had to find a man friend to entice Barbara to that meadow.

The car slowed and stopped as the lunchtime traffic built up. Rafferty fretted, as usual hating the trapped feeling a traffic jam invariably induced in him. Of course, he had become used to quieter roads. Unsurprisingly, Llewellyn, with his dislike of rushing anywhere, took the stop-start progress in his stride, which irritated Rafferty even more. He found himself drumming his fingers on his knee, as the windscreen wipers did their best to hypnotize him.

'I want you to go to Charles Shore's business premises again when we get back, Dafyd. Have a look at his office if you can, and speak to anyone there you didn't speak to last time. Find out if there's any way he could have gone out without anyone else being the wiser. We also need to have another chat with Hilary Shore, pin her down a bit tighter on her claimed appointment times.' They had visited Harvey Nichols and Mrs Armadi before seeing Anne Longman and discovered the gap between her appointments was sizeable, even though Hilary Shore had given the impression that one had more or less immediately followed the other. Before he returned to his brooding, he added, half to himself, 'They're a bit too loose for my liking.' Glancing at the calm profile of Llewellyn, he asked the question that had often intrigued him. 'Why did you join the police, Dafyd?'

Llewellyn was silent for a moment, as though reflecting on his own reasons before he replied. 'Philosophy starts up in the air and remains there,' was his cryptic observation. 'Which is mainly why I gave it up at university. With police work, particularly at this level, there's an answer at the end. A resolution. I like that.'

'Not always, there isn't,' Rafferty pointed out and immediately wished he hadn't. It didn't do to tempt the Fates, to put ideas into their too suggestible heads, especially as experience had warned him that, unlike the nun, the Fates had no divine pressure to resist temptation.

Rafferty needed to think, and it seemed a cup of hot sweet tea in the station canteen was the nearest he was going to get to liquid inspiration. Luckily, when they reached the M25, it was fairly clear. So he ordered Llewellyn to get into the fast lane and put his foot down.

EIGHT

LATER THAT AFTERNOON after Rafferty had downed several cups of tea, each of them singularly failing to provide any inspiration at all, Llewellyn cautiously nosed the car out of the back exit of the police station. Turning right into Bread Street he took a short cut towards the southern outskirts of Elmhurst, carefully avoiding East Hill and its roadworks. But for once Llewellyn's usual efficiency must have deserted him, for they were held up for five minutes at the level-crossing in Church Road as, surprisingly dead on time, the express from Liverpool Street Station roared past.

'Should have taken Station road and gone under the bridge,' Rafferty informed the Welshman. After pointedly sighing, frowning at the crossing barrier and looking at his watch, Rafferty finally glanced at Llewellyn and remarked casually, 'You know, as we seem to be rapidly eliminating everybody else in the case, I'm becoming more and more convinced that one of her family killed her, especially as, so far, only Charles Shore's alibi has held up. The question is—which one of them did it?'

Rafferty took no notice of the long-suffering sigh that escaped Llewellyn's thin lips at this pronouncement, and went on. 'Of course, we'll have to continue checking out these other suspects—the Conservation Society members, and the farmer, and you can call me suspicious if you like, but, the more members of that family I meet, the more it strikes me there's something not right, something downright unhealthy about them. You've only got to look at that bloody morbid house they live in to see that.'

Llewellyn's lips tightened, but, apart from commenting that impressions weren't evidence, he didn't betray his irritation further.

Rafferty was into his stride now and wouldn't allow Llewellyn's natural caution to deflect him. There were undercurrents in that house; undercurrents that had only confirmed his suspicions. 'For instance, take Hilary Shore. For all her tears, she didn't strike me as exactly grief-stricken at Mrs Longman's death. And her alibi's a bit shaky.'

The barrier rose just then, and broke his train of thought, but as Llewellyn put the car into gear and bumped over the crossing, he began again. 'At least we can eliminate everyone known to have been at the house before 3.30 p.m. I had Hanks test how long it would take to drive to the meadow from the Shores' house. Putting his foot down hard—not that he could do too much of that because the roads are so winding—it still took nearly ten minutes, and then he had to cross the field to where the body was found. So, if someone in the house killed her, they wouldn't have got back there much before 3.30 p.m. According to Mrs Griffiths, Barbara Longman left the house right on 3.00 p.m. She remembers the library clock chiming the hour. Did you check out if they all drive?'

Llewellyn nodded. 'According to the Licensing Authority at Swansea, they've all got licences.'

'So, if it took ten minutes to drive to Tiffey Meadow and the same time to get back, plus the time to cross the meadow, kill Barbara and then return to

the car, that lets out the housekeeper, the tutor and
the au pair. As I said, it lets out anyone known to
have been at the house *before* 3.30 p.m.' With a sideways glance at Llewellyn, he demanded, 'So, who
does that leave us with?'

'Henry Longman, Anne Longman, and Charles
and Hilary Shore,' the Welshman intoned. 'But, apart
from Anne Longman, they've all given alibis.'

'I *know*. But, if they're crackable, I intend to crack
them. Don't forget that telephone call must have been
made by someone who knew her, someone aware of
her interests, who also knew the ex-directory number. The housekeeper admitted the voice sounded familiar, so that means it's not likely to be a casual anti-
conservationist acquaintance. She also said the voice
sounded muffled, which indicates that they were deliberately trying to disguise it, indicating, in turn,
someone far closer, someone who knew their voice
would be recognized.'

'Do you really think it's possible to disguise one's
voice?'

'It's obvious you've led a sheltered life, Taff,' Rafferty scoffed. 'You'd be surprised how much a handkerchief over the mouthpiece can alter a voice. My
brothers and I used to think it was a great trick when
we were young. One of us would ring up the school
pretending to be my father and say we'd all suffered
food poisoning.' He grinned. 'We got away with it
several times, until my old man met us in the street.'

'Speaking of telephone calls,' Llewellyn interrupted his reminiscences, 'I went to see the Shores'
housekeeper while you were in the canteen. I thought
if she *did* have any ideas about the identity of the

caller, she might be more forthcoming to me with us both being Welsh.'

'And was she?'

'No,' Llewellyn admitted. 'But she did confirm that Shore had put his name forward to the Tory party for selection. She told me something else as well.'

Impressed that his sergeant had managed to get *any* information out of the tight-lipped housekeeper, Rafferty waited.

'She said that Anne Longman had planned to contest the custody ruling, but changed her mind only a few weeks before Barbara Longman's death. Apparently, her legal advisers finally convinced her she would lose. I gather she didn't take it very well. Rather blamed Barbara Longman. Unfortunately for her, of course, the dead woman was a...'

'An angel, a wonderful woman, beloved by all,' Rafferty intoned. 'In fact, the sort of woman who no judge would think of removing a child from.'

Llewellyn murmured, 'From whom no judge...' under his breath.

Rafferty couldn't decide which was getting to him more; Llewellyn's pedantry or the supposed saintliness of the victim. He wasn't sure if he was intended to hear the correction, wasn't even sure if Llewellyn realized he did it half the time. But if he could do nothing about the victim's aggravatingly upright character, he could certainly nip the other irritation in the bud.

'Who from—from whom—who cares?' he demanded. 'You're not at that bloody university now, so just stop trying to teach me the Queen's English, OK?' Llewellyn's mouth shut with the snap of a Venus fly-trap. Rafferty did his best to ignore the hurt silence that formed an aura around him. 'So,' he continued a few seconds later, before Llewellyn retreated into a total huff, 'you're saying that Mrs Griffiths hinted that recently there's been even less love than usual between number one wife and number two?'

'Oh, I don't think there was any animosity on the part of the *second* Mrs Longman,' Llewellyn replied with clipped politeness. He applied the brake with rather more force than necessary as they approached the crossroads near the Shores' home. 'No, all the bad feeling stemmed from the first wife. According to Mrs Griffiths, there's a trust fund for the boy. And whoever acts as his guardian controls it.'

'And the lad's mother would like to get her mitts on it, is that it?'

The Welshman nodded.

They were about to turn into the Shores' drive when a woman waved them to a halt. 'Wonder what she wants?' Rafferty mused, as he wound the window down and watched in the rear-view mirror, as she parked her shopping trolley neatly on the grass verge and waited for them to reverse towards her. 'Back up, Dafyd. Let's find out.'

The woman stuck her head through the open window and demanded of Rafferty, 'You the police?' He nodded. 'I thought you were. I've seen you in and out of the Shores' place since Barbara was taken. I've been waiting and waiting for you to come and see me, but no one has.'

Rafferty glanced at Llewellyn. How did she get missed in the house-to-house? his eyebrows asked.

I don't know, Llewellyn's expression signalled. But I'll find out.

With the smoothness of long practice, Rafferty concealed the cock-up. 'Sorry it's taken so long, but we're here now, Mrs . . . ?'

'Mrs Watson.' Glancing over her shoulder, she leaned forward conspiratorially, button-brown eyes round and sharp nose aquiver. 'I hear that Barbara's long stick of a husband claimed he was in a meeting all day last Thursday. Well, I can tell you for a fact he wasn't.'

She gazed at them with a kind of expectant triumph, and Rafferty said, 'Perhaps you'd like to pop yourself in the back and tell us all about it? Sergeant, get out and open the door for Mrs Watson, like a gentleman, there's a good chap.' Expressionlessly, Llewellyn did as he was told.

Settled comfortably in the back seat, Mrs Watson proceeded to admire the upholstery, the floor carpet, the winking lights on the dashboard, until Rafferty began to get a crick in his neck from craning round waiting for her stream of inanities to end. Thankfully, she finally said something that interested him.

'I live in the cottage at the back of the Shores' place,' she explained. 'And I saw him just after 2.30 p.m. on Thursday, parking at the rear entrance to the big house. Saw him with my own eyes, I did. Furtive he looked. That's the only word for it. Furtive. Gardening I was. Saw him through the hedge, but he couldn't see me.'

Rafferty and Llewellyn exchanged significant glances. So they'd discovered the first lie. Rafferty wondered how many more there'd be? 'You're sure it was Henry Longman?'

She gave him a scathing look. 'Course I'm sure. Think I wouldn't recognize that long streak of bacon anywhere? Besides, he was only across the lane from me—a matter of eight or nine feet. And short-sighted I'm not. You ask old Boyd, the optician in the High Street, if you don't believe me. I recognized his car an' all—that fancy car that Charles Shore bought for him. Think I wouldn't recognize that?'

After the scrutiny she'd given *their* car, Rafferty had to admit she had a point.

'It were Henry Longman, I'm telling you. He parks that car in front of my house often enough, while he skives off work with his weak belly or his irritable bowels or whatever. Man's a walking 'condriac. He was talking on that car phone of his when I saw him. S'pose he was on to his doctor again, though you'd think he could manage to wait till he got to the house to do it.' She smiled with a grim satisfaction. 'From the look on his face the doctor refused to come out.'

Rafferty glanced at Llewellyn to see if he had any criticisms to make of Mrs Watson's grammar. But if he had he kept them to himself and Rafferty returned his attention to the woman.

'Going to arrest him, are you?' she demanded.

'As for that, we'll have to wait and see what he has to say for himself,' Rafferty observed quietly. 'But thank you, Mrs Watson. What you've told us is very helpful.'

'Never liked that Henry,' she announced, settling back against the admired upholstery as if she intended taking up residence. 'Feckless and useless he is. Whatever a fine woman like Barbara saw in him I don't know. And him with a troublesome great lump of a lad for her to worry about as well. As if *he* wasn't enough, with his weak stomach and his *nerves*. What cause has he got to have nerves, I'd like to know? She had more right to nerves than him, I'm telling you. Woman was a saint, why she—'

'Yes, thank you, Mrs Watson,' Rafferty put in hurriedly. Surprised that he had managed to stop the flow, he cocked a mischievous eye at Llewellyn and added, 'Perhaps my sergeant here can drop you home and get a formal statement from you?'

She had started to preen at the prospect of being chauffeured home in the car for the neighbours to see, but it was apparent that she didn't find the making of an *official* statement quite so enticing.

'Nothing to worry about,' he assured her. 'Only we do like to have things nice and tidy. For the records.'

She nodded slowly. 'Not one for mess and disorder, me. Keep a clean house and a clean life. *I've* nothing to sweep under the carpet, I'm sure. Not like some.'

Rafferty looked pointedly at the Welshman. Find out who *had,* the signal passed between them. Rafferty slipped quickly out of the car. 'Drive carefully, Llewellyn,' he instructed. As if he ever drove any *other* way. 'You've got a valuable witness there.' To his amusement, the woman's preening resumed. 'You can leave visiting Shore's office again for now. It'll keep. Check out Mrs Watson's neighbours, while you're at it,' he added in a murmur. 'Find out if *they* saw Henry that afternoon. You can come back for me when Mrs Watson has finished with you.'

From the resigned look on Llewellyn's face, he suspected it might be some time before his sergeant managed to get away. Still, it might be better to listen alone first to whatever explanation Henry Longman came up with. Might get more out of him without

Llewellyn there, wearing his permanent air of slight disapproval of the human race and their goings on.

He manhandled Mrs Watson's shopping trolley into the car, said goodbye to her and shut the door. As Llewellyn drove off, Rafferty raised a hand in reply to the woman's self-consciously regal wave, before heading up the drive.

NINE

RAFFERTY'S PROGRESS towards the house was made at a caterpillar's crawl as he digested Mrs Watson's evidence. It was a development he hadn't expected— although he had told Llewellyn he suspected one of the family had killed Barbara Longman, he found it difficult to *seriously* cast Henry in the role of murderer. *Murderee*—yes, he snorted. He had no problem imagining that at all.

Even though he made allowances for the fact that Henry had just lost his wife, it was apparent that his personality had always been ineffectual. When he considered the frustration this would be likely to cause in a marriage, it was a wonder one of his two wives hadn't murdered *him* years ago.

Perhaps they'd succumbed to other temptations instead? he mused. Had one or both of them taken a lover? Although it seemed unlikely that the saintly Barbara would do such a thing, it wasn't impossible. After all, was Henry likely to be any more stimulating a personality in bed than he apparently was *out* of it? And it would certainly provide Henry with a motive.

But even with Mrs Watson's evidence, Rafferty found it difficult to get excited about the chances of an early arrest. Still, now that he'd been pushed into considering the possibility more seriously, he had to admit Henry had behaved oddly. For instance, why had he looked as if he had taken to sackcloth and

ashes even *before* he had learned of his wife's *death,*
never mind her murder? Surely, as an executive in the
Shore empire, it would hardly be his normal attire?
Charles Shore would be unlikely to tolerate such
sloppiness, and would expect the house and its permanent residents to keep a certain standard. It
wouldn't be the sort of place to lounge around in
scruffy comfort. It would be more an extension to the
office than a real home and Rafferty thought it unlikely there would be much opportunity for relaxa-
tion. There would be business lunches and dinners,
where deals would be thrashed out between the soup
course and the cheese and biscuits. Even in Shore's
absence, the show would be expected to go on. As the
saying went, 'time was money', and every hour, every
minute, would be exploited in order to count towards the profit.

He frowned speculatively at the capering figures
decorating the roof-line of the house, as his slow pace
drew him closer and he returned to pondering about
Longman. Had Henry already known his wife was
dead when they had first seen him? But how could he,
he reasoned, unless he had killed her? And if he had
murdered her, was he stupid enough to don his odd
mourning gear, from a combination of guilt and remorse, without considering the effect this would have
on the investigating policemen?

But, if he had murdered his wife, it would certainly explain why he had preferred to wait for
Charles Shore to come home and report her missing.
He would have needed time to get himself under control, scared he might betray his guilt if they questioned him sooner. Had he also hoped the delay

would make the calculation of the timing of his wife's death more difficult?

As far as Rafferty could see, the only thing likely to stir Henry out of his lethargy, to induce in him a murderous rage, would be if Barbara *had* been having an affair. The trouble was, they had found nothing, so far, to indicate that this was a possibility. But that didn't mean there wasn't anything to find, he reminded himself.

According to Mrs Watson, Henry had sneaked home the back way when he should have been working, on more than one occasion. On a previous truant exercise, could he have overheard something not meant for his ears? Something that made him suspect his perfect wife was cheating on him? Did the supposed lovers use a code for messages so simple that even Henry could crack it? Had he done so last Thursday, and heard and understood the message that Mrs Griffiths had taken and guessed it was another lovers' tryst? It gave a time—immediately—and a place—Tiffey Meadow.

Rafferty doubted that the passion of any affair could be great enough to transform the uncomfortable dry grass and weeds into a cushioned mattress. But then he realized that no such transformation would have been necessary, as there had already been a mattress there. Stained, it was true, but comfortable enough if covered with a car rug.

He reminded himself that it was unlikely Henry had ever had reason to hold his head up—till he had married Barbara. He didn't seem too bright; in business he was propped up by nepotism; and as a parent he had fathered one son, a son, moreover, who was by all accounts as lacking in intelligent application as himself. All in all, he had not had a lot going for him. Yet in Barbara he had hit the jackpot. Everyone they had spoken to had said what a fine woman she had been. That quality would have reflected back on to Henry and provided him with a reason for the pride that had eluded him most of his life.

What would his reaction have been if he had discovered this paragon had been cheating on him? Would he have erupted in a jealous rage, followed her and killed her? Was he even capable of such passion? He scowled as he realized he had neglected to check with Mrs Watson whether Henry's car had remained parked in front of her house all afternoon, or if it had vanished during the crucial time from 3.00 p.m. to 3.30 p.m. If it had remained where he had parked it, and he had been unable to borrow one of the other household vehicles, he might have the motive to kill his wife but he would lack the opportunity. For without a vehicle, Henry would have been unable to get to the meadow easily. The nearest bus service was a good fifteen-minute walk away, and then only ran once every hour. If, as the housekeeper had said, the call for Barbara had come just before 3.00 p.m., he'd have had to wait till the next bus at 4.00 p.m. to follow her. By the time he could have reached the rendezvous, his wife and her possible lover would both have been long gone.

In turn, Rafferty considered the likelihood of Henry using a taxi or a push-bike. He didn't think Henry was cool enough to hire a taxi to take him to kill his wife, and as for the push-bike, he tried, and failed, to imagine Henry on a bike, his long, gangly legs pumping furiously towards the lovers' trysting spot. The image was just too comic. But both possibilities would still need to be checked out.

He stopped dead in his tracks in the middle of the drive as another theory occurred to him. But if *Henry* had been the one to leave the message, disguising his voice, in order to deceive Mrs Griffiths, time wouldn't necessarily be a factor. Hadn't Charles Shore complained that his mobile phone had gone missing the day before the murder? Henry would have had as much opportunity to take it as anyone. He could have already been at the meadow when he'd phoned the house to lure his wife to his chosen killing field. Mrs Watson had said she had seen Henry at 2.30 p.m. and that gave him time to get to the meadow. As long as he left his *car* parked at the house, he'd have a good chance of sneaking out and back undetected.

And if that was what he had done, the murder had been premeditated rather than committed during a jealous rage. But again, Rafferty doubted that Henry was capable of such calm planning. He'd have made a botch of it.

Rafferty glanced again at the grinning faces of the scampering satyrs on the roof and wished he didn't get the feeling they were laughing at *him,* silently mocking his groping deductions. Quickening his step, he reached the front door, glad to get out of their line of vision.

The front door was slightly ajar and he stuck his head round the jamb, but there was no one in sight. Tentatively, he pushed the door wide and walked into the hall; this time no delicate roses wafted their perfume toward him. The gloom of the hall, unrelieved by what could only have been Barbara Longman's floral displays, unnerved him and he considered retracing his steps and knocking. But then he heard a voice coming from the direction of the library, and as he walked towards the open door he told himself that he could always say he'd knocked if he was challenged.

He was surprised to see the teenage boy he had encountered on his first visit to the house. He was standing in front of the portrait of Maximillian Shore. He hadn't noticed Rafferty and appeared to be in earnest conversation with the portrait.

'I miss her so much, Grandfather. It's awful here without her. Edward's even more hateful now than he ever was.' He sniffed, sounding thoroughly wretched. 'I wish I understood it.'

Poor kid, thought Rafferty. He was obviously desperate for understanding from someone. It was sad, that in a house that contained father, uncle and cousins, the person he should seek comfort from should be his long dead and rather terrifying grandfather. Especially as he could have been no more than a baby when the old man had been murdered. As he glanced over the boy's shoulder at the formidable face in the portrait, Rafferty reflected that it was probably just as well that the lad's grandfather *was* dead, as from what he'd so far discovered about old Maximillian he would have had scant patience with the tears of a sensitive teenager. But then, self-delusion was a privilege of youth. Rafferty sighed as he reflected that age brought other problems.

The boy spun round as he heard the soft expulsion of breath behind him. He wiped his eyes quickly on his sleeve before staring accusingly at Rafferty. 'Who are you?' he demanded. 'What are you doing in here, spying on me?'

Caught eavesdropping for the second time in just a few days, Rafferty felt his colour rising, and his embarrassment increased when he saw the boy's grief-stricken face. Rafferty didn't blame him for reacting angrily. He'd have probably done the same himself in similar circumstances. Apologetically, he explained, 'I'm a policeman. I came to see Mr Longman, if he's around.' He gave the boy what he hoped was a compassionate smile. 'You're Maxie Longman, I think?'

The boy drew himself up. 'My name's Maximillian, not Maxie. And I'm a Shore.'

Rafferty didn't bother to argue with him. Instead, he said simply, 'Your grandfather's name?'

Maxie nodded. He half turned away and surreptitiously wiped the rest of the tears from his face, before remarking, 'My uncle told me you're in-investigating Barbara's d-death.'

'That's right.' Rafferty took a pace towards the boy and held out a cautious hand. 'I'm sorry to have to come plodding in here in my size twelves, when I'm sure you'd much rather be alone. Your uncle told me you were very fond of your stepmother.'

Maxie nodded, blinking rapidly as though to ward off more incipient tears. The earlier ones had been bitter enough, to judge by the boy's swollen eyes, and Rafferty guessed Maxie's aggression was a protective measure, a reaction to having his emotional outburst witnessed by a stranger. It seemed to Rafferty a great pity that, having lost one mother to divorce, a murderer should cost him a second, especially as, as far as Rafferty had seen, she had been the only member of the family who seemed to have had any time for the children.

'There's nothing to be ashamed of in a few tears, you know, lad,' Rafferty gruffly remarked. 'I've been told your stepmother was a kind lady. I hope someone thinks enough of me to shed a few tears when I go.'

Maxie said nothing, but turned abruptly away and stared out of the window. He looked miserable, and his profile suggested that Rafferty could keep his words of comfort, but as he gazed out at the dark yew hedging, he became unexpectedly confiding.

'I wish she wasn't dead. Everyone else makes me feel I'm stupid, because I'm not as quick as my cousins, but she always made me think I could be a success like Grandfather. She used to tell me there were more roads to success than my uncle imagined and it was just a matter of finding the one that was right for me. And I believed her. I worked so hard, reading and studying book after book. I thought I *had* found the road.' He sniffed and, in a voice that was little more than a whisper, he added, 'But I was wrong. I know now I'll never amount to anything. It was all for nothing.'

Before Rafferty could reply, Maxie seemed to remember who he was and why he was there, for he turned suddenly and demanded with another show of aggression, 'Why do you want to see my father, again? Mrs Griffiths told me you've already seen him twice.'

Sorry his attempt at befriending the boy had failed miserably, Rafferty tried to remember himself at the same age and failed again. It wasn't surprising, of course. He had surely been nothing like this intense boy, whom everyone but his stepmother seemed to neglect. Selecting his words carefully, Rafferty said,

'Usually, it helps to learn something about the victim. How she lived, her friends, her family, her loves and hates. That's why I wanted to speak to your father again,' he lied. With unconscious irony, he added, 'There might be something he's forgotten to tell us.'

Maxie spun round wildly, his hands bunched into fists at his sides, and an anxious expression on his face. Biting his lip, he asked, in a stilted voice, 'You don't... you don't suspect my father, do you?'

Rafferty tried to reassure him, but it wasn't easy. How could he tell him, that after what Mrs Watson had divulged, they had to suspect him, question him again? Guardedly, he said, 'There are one or two points I need to clear up, that's all.' With a heartiness that didn't quite come off, he added, 'Nothing for you to worry about.' From Maxie's face, with its shocked pallor and wary, red-rimmed eyes, he could see the boy didn't believe him and his next words confirmed it.

'My cousin said you'd think my father did it.' His voice rose in the beginnings of hysteria. 'He didn't do it. I know he didn't. You can't...'

'All right, lad, calm down.' Stupidly, Rafferty found himself wishing that Llewellyn was there to add a bit of moral support. But, of course, he'd be no use at all, he assured himself. Dafyd Llewellyn was an only child and far less accustomed to dealing with overwrought teenagers than Rafferty himself, with his ever-increasing brood of nephews and nieces.

Maxie ignored him. He seemed to be working himself into a terrible state. 'I'm not a child,' he screamed at Rafferty. 'I won't have you treating me like one.' He wiped his eyes on his sleeve as the tears slid through the bravado. 'If you try to arrest my father, you'll regret it. My uncle's a rich man. He'll get the best lawyers. You'll see.'

Rafferty wasn't quite sure how best to respond to this, but he decided to try the stern policeman role. 'The law doesn't weaken before rich men, Maximillian. Don't you know that?'

Between bouts of hysterical laughter, the boy told him something that sounded suspiciously like a parrot-fashion repetition of his uncle's beliefs. 'I know they say British justice is blind, but it still has good ears to hear a first-class defence lawyer and that's what my father will get. If he needs it.'

As Maxie stared at Rafferty, his eyes dark pits of misery in a face even whiter than before, Rafferty reflected that Charles Shore was the sort of wealthy man who would hold such sentiments. And with good reason. Hadn't his expensive lawyers successfully defended him in several cases that had set the financial world reeling over the last few years? Scandals that less wealthy men would never have survived.

Rafferty was at a loss and found himself praying that the housekeeper would come and take the lad off his hands. Instead, to Rafferty's relief, Henry Longman stuck his head round the door. He looked as if he'd made a bit more of an effort today, Rafferty noticed. The shirt and trousers he wore appeared to have recently encountered an iron, and the faraway expression, though still evident, had lessened.

'I didn't know you were here, Inspector.' Worriedly, he glanced from Rafferty to his son. 'What's going on? I heard you shouting from upstairs, Maxie. I know your mother never used to think there was anything wrong in screaming at people, but I won't have you behaving that way. You're growing up now. It's about time you learned some self-control.'

Maxie glared at him and Henry ignored this and tried to jolly his son along. 'I thought you'd be out on the river with your cousins,' he told him. 'It's a shame to waste the nice weather.'

Maxie muttered, 'How can I when the paddle broke two weeks ago? You said you'd replace it, but you never did.'

'I *did* ask you to remind me, if you remember. Why didn't you?'

Maxie shrugged. 'It doesn't matter now, anyway. Even if it wasn't broken, I wouldn't want to do it any more. Not with them, and Barbara said . . . Barbara said I didn't have to. They spend all their time ganging up on me, laughing at me, calling me names.'

Henry looked at a loss. 'They're only children, Maxie,' he protested weakly. 'You should make allowances.'

From the boy's sulky expression, Rafferty guessed that was the last thing he was willing to do. Presumably, they were talking about Charles's two children, and judging from the spiteful way they had been teasing him on Rafferty's first visit, he couldn't blame the lad. Still, he thought, what example did they have? Henry was weak and ineffectual; Charles Shore, with his business empire to run, would be unlikely to have much time for them. And from the one occasion he had met the mistress of the house, she had struck him as having far more interest in herself than in the children.

Barbara Longman appeared to have been the only person who had been fond enough of any of them to attempt to turn the efficiently run and ugly old Shore house into a home. No wonder the boy looked so wretched at her loss. Rafferty wondered what would become of them all now that her influence had been removed? He supposed they'd acquire a nanny—a succession of nannies. But they weren't *his* problem, he reminded himself. His problem was solving Barbara Longman's murder. He didn't seem to be getting very far with it.

Henry had obviously been searching desperately for some way to occupy his son that didn't involve *him* personally. Now, he suggested: 'If you can't get on with your cousins, why don't you go over to Tom Shepherd's house? I thought you two were friends.'

'That was before he pushed me out of the tree in the Easter holidays,'' Maxie retorted. 'Anyway, I can't. He's convalescing.'

This seemed to be news to his father. But then, Rafferty imagined most things would be. 'Convalescing?' Henry frowned. 'Why? What was the matter with him?'

Maxie shrugged with typical teenage unconcern. 'Had to have his stomach pumped out, according to Mrs Griffiths.' He pulled a face. 'You know what a terrible cook his mother is.'

'Well, I don't know,' said Henry with a sigh. 'Surely you can find something to do. A great lad like you?' He certainly didn't want to be bothered, his manner implied. Maxie took the hint and slouched disconsolately out of the library.

There was more than a suggestion of a whine in Henry's voice as he told Rafferty, 'I don't know what to do with the boy. I think even Barbara must have been beginning to find the usual teenage tantrums a little trying, as she suggested, only last Thursday morning, that it might be a good idea to send him to boarding school.' He dropped heavily into one of the armchairs and ran his hand through his hair. 'Maybe she was right and I ought to send him away to school, like Charles's two.' Henry looked hopefully at Rafferty, as if he expected him to make his decision for him. 'What do you think, Inspector?'

Rafferty wasn't about to get sidetracked into a discussion on the subject. He had work to do. And he intended to begin by asking Henry a few penetrating questions. 'I've really no idea,' he said, his manner dismissive. It was about time Henry started to sort out his own problems, he decided. He could begin by explaining why he had lied to them.

TEN

BEFORE RAFFERTY could ask Henry any questions—
penetrating or otherwise—someone rang a piercing
demand for entry on the front doorbell. Almost trip-
ping over his own spiderlike legs, Henry scurried out
to answer it. He returned with Llewellyn in tow; a
Llewellyn who, to Rafferty's secret satisfaction,
looked to have had the puff removed from his pedantry by the garrulous and ungrammatical Mrs Watson.

Damn good job, too, thought Rafferty. It might
make the Welshman think twice before pulling *him* up
again. He turned his attention to the whey-faced
Henry and was about to begin questioning him when
the man made for the door.

'Please excuse... Don't feel well.' He clasped his
hand over his mouth, dived for the door and disappeared—again.

Irritated at the latest delay, Rafferty began a resigned browse amongst the bookshelves. He was surprised to find a biography of Hitler amongst the
Shore collection and commented on it. 'I wouldn't
have thought they'd have given houseroom to a book
on old Adolf.'

Llewellyn came and gazed over his shoulder. 'A
case of "know your enemy", perhaps?' Perking up,
he went on. 'A wealthy Jewish family like the Shores
will always attract people who want what is theirs.
And who can be sure where the next megalomaniac

obsessed with "ethnic cleansing" will spring up? Just because Britain's the oldest democracy in the world doesn't mean it can't happen here. This country's as capable of racial violence as the rest. Ask an Asian shopkeeper.'

Rafferty sighed. Mrs Watson might have temporarily subdued Llewellyn's educating zeal, but, like a weed, it had strong roots and had obviously staged a full recovery. Sensing the flowering of an imminent lecture, Rafferty tried to steer Llewellyn to the shelves containing psychological tomes, but the Welshman wasn't to be deflected.

'Yes, we can all learn a lot from the study of history and its personalities,' Llewellyn expanded. 'It can widen one's horizons, and make up for an inadequate education.'

He's implying *you* ought to try it, the inadequately educated Rafferty concluded. The cheeky Welsh git.

'For instance, the study of wealth and power—how to get it and keep it—tells one a great deal about human nature, which is, of course, essential in police work. And if you look at the Shores' bookshelves, you'll see they agree with me.' He tapped the spines of several books, one after the other. 'Abraham Lincoln, David Lloyd George, Kemal Ataturk, Henry Ford. Even'—he took the book Rafferty was holding and replaced it on the shelf—'Adolf Hitler, all show that early difficulties can be overcome. For instance, did you know that as many as sixty-five per cent of British Prime Ministers, up to the Second World War, suffered the loss of one or both parents in their youth? I was reading an article about it the other day and—'

'I'm sure that's all fascinating,' Rafferty broke in desperately. 'But never mind those old politicos, Dafyd. If it's human nature you're after, I'd have thought this lot would be far more instructive.' He persuaded Llewellyn over to the philosophy and psychology shelves. 'They've got the lot here.' He read a few of the easier names at random. 'Freud, Pavlov, even that German bloke whose name I can never pronounce.'

'Nietzsche. As I was say—'

'That's the one.' Determined not to allow Llewellyn to settle back in the lecturing saddle, Rafferty proceeded to loosen the girth. 'For myself, I reckon the best study of human nature is the study of human beings themselves. But I suppose for an intellectual like yourself, with neither nose nor instinct for the common and not so common man, books are the only answer.' He took another book from the shelves and thrust it at Llewellyn with a half-pitying smile. 'I'm sure Charles Shore would let you borrow some if you asked him nicely.'

Llewellyn took the hint and the book, and replaced the latter on the shelf. 'I wouldn't dream of doing so,' he said, adding pointedly, as he turned away. 'And I might lack a nose, as you say, but there's nothing wrong with my memory. *I* don't forget that this is the home of a murder victim, not a lending library.'

Oh, hoity-toity, Rafferty muttered, as the gibe went home. Since returning Shore's autobiography, he'd asked and been given permission to borrow more books. And in spite of Llewellyn's tart comment, Charles Shore had seemed more amused than offended by his request. It certainly had an advantage over the public library, in that he was unlikely to demand fines for their late return.

As Henry came back, Rafferty turned to him with relief. At least *he* was unlikely to harp on about his shaky scruples or his low-level intellect. Of course, as he enquired if Henry was feeling better, Rafferty reminded himself that the man was hardly in a position to find fault with him on either matter.

Henry, his face now an interesting pea-green, nodded uncertainly and Rafferty decided he'd better be quick in case Henry performed a third vanishing act. Especially as Llewellyn, in this mood, was quite capable of using the time to put the metaphorical boot in from some other totally unexpected side of the stirrup.

'Then perhaps we can get started? Sergeant?' He watched with a wicked gleam in his blue eyes till Llewellyn had flipped past the neat notes recording Mrs Watson's volubility, nearly to the end of his notebook, before he continued. 'You told us you were at a business meeting at the time of your wife's murder, Mr Longman.' Fixing him with what he hoped was a steely gaze, he went on. 'That wasn't true, was it, sir?'

Henry looked owlishly at him. 'How…how did you find out? I thought Jeremy Ingatestone was away for another week.'

'He is. It's not the Chamber of Commerce buddy you stood up who told us. But that's not important. What matters is that we *did* find out. Perhaps you'd like to tell us about it?'

Henry's face took on a trapped look. He floundered, opening and closing his mouth like a landed fish, before he finally blurted out, 'I knew I should have told you. It looks so bad for me. I told her it would.'

'Told who?'

'Hilary.'

'And what has this to do with Mrs Shore?'

Henry glanced quickly at him and away again. 'N-nothing. That is to say—' He broke off.

'Are you saying that Mrs Shore advised you to lie to us?'

'Yes—no . . . all I mean is that she said I'd be a fool to tell you I'd come home early that day, she said it would create—unnecessary complications. I felt unwell.' His eyes took on a feverish light. 'Yes, that's right, that's why I came home.' He blinked owlishly, as the implications of Rafferty's question penetrated. 'You surely don't think . . . ?' He swallowed hard and tried again. 'It—it was nothing to do with my wife . . . at least, not in the way you obviously mean. I loved Barbara. I would never have hurt her.'

That's what they all say, thought Rafferty cynically. Henry defended himself with a vigour that surprised him. But then, even a cornered fox often surprised his attackers; not that Henry struck him as particularly crafty. An air of unworldliness shone from the man, and Rafferty was almost convinced he was telling the truth—almost. But he was an experienced policeman, and he had learned the hard way that swallowing statements whole generally caused investigatory indigestion. He chewed over what Henry had said, while the man rambled on and wondered why it was he should have the increasing impression that Henry had been rehearsed in his story.

'I've been painting a portrait of my wife—I was an artist once. It was to have been a gift for our second wedding anniversary. I was painting it in secret—I didn't want any of the family knowing about it. It was for my wife's pleasure, nobody else's. I particularly didn't want Charles to know what I was doing till it was finished, especially as I painted during daylight hours whenever I managed to escape from the office. I thought once it was done, Barbara's delight would stop him saying much. He was—fond of Barbara.'

His face twisted with grief, misery, and something else that Rafferty couldn't quite fathom. 'I set up a basic studio in the loft of one of the outbuildings. Sometimes, when I don't feel well, I find painting a help, it relaxes me, so I thought I'd try it that afternoon. But it was no good, the turps made me feel sick, so I gave it up almost immediately, and went to bed. I tried to get into it again the next morning to take my mind off my anxiety about Barbara and what might have happened to her, but I was in such an anxious state that I couldn't control my brush strokes, so I gave up again and went to my room. I wanted it perfect, you see.' With a touching simplicity, he told them, 'A portrait was the one gift I could give her that all Charles's money couldn't buy. A portrait, painted with love. It's still in the loft where I left it.' His lip trembled visibly, as he added, 'Perhaps one day I'll have the heart to finish it.'

Henry's story was believable in so far as it explained the disreputable clothes he had worn on their first encounter. He had sought to bury his anxiety about his missing wife in his painting, perhaps as a way of feeling close to her. When Mrs Griffiths had roused him from his sickbed, he had simply put on the clothes he had discarded earlier.

'So, you see why I didn't want to tell you with Charles there that I wasn't where I was supposed to be. Shock made me forget that, with Barbara dead, it didn't really matter any more. Nothing mattered. Not Charles and his obsession with the great god profit, not my ex-wife and her put-downs.'

His next words showed him to have a practical streak amongst all the other-wordliness. 'Only, of course, they do matter, don't they? Somehow, I still have to live, and who's likely to employ me if Charles doesn't? We both know I'm not really cut out for earning a good living, but I've got a son to think of and I've acquired some expensive tastes.'

Suddenly, every pore seemed to ooze resentment, as though infuriated by his dependence on the Shores. 'You know what matters in this family, Inspector? Success—that's all. In the Shore philosophy, words like happiness and contentment are only for fools. God knows how often Maximillian Shore drummed it into my head that I was a failure. When my ex-wife and her father were reconciled shortly after Maxie's birth, I was scared the old man would make my son's life a misery, too, if he failed to live up to the Shore standards. Admittedly, the old man doted on him— first grandchild, and all that, but the old man had always expected most where he loved most. I was relieved he died just a few months later, before he could twist my son's mind the way he had those of his own children.'

Rafferty got the impression that Henry had repressed such feelings for years. It had taken his wife's death to release the simmering angers, the belated realization that, as he seemed to find his executive suit as restricting as a strait-jacket, he might have been happier sticking with art and poverty.

Somewhere in the house, a door banged. The sudden noise made Henry jump and his habitually anxious expression returned. He ran his hand over his face and blinked, as though startled by his own outburst. 'I—I'm sorry. What must you think? I don't usually...' He looked uneasily from Rafferty to Llewellyn and back again. 'I hope you won't feel it necessary to mention what I said to Charles. Hilary convinced me it's best he doesn't know—anything. He'd be furious, I see that. It's too late for me to start again now and I need this job.'

Henry had a point, thought Rafferty. From what he'd seen of Charles Shore, he was his formidable father all over again. He wouldn't be likely to countenance slackness, especially not from Henry, who was probably only tolerated for the boy's sake. And especially not when the slacker had made a fool of him into the bargain. And when all was said and done, Shore was paying his salary—quite a generous one, by all accounts.

Rafferty didn't attempt to make any promises. He got the impression Henry hadn't really expected him to. There were just one or two things he wanted to get clear. 'When you came back from the studio the day your wife went missing, you said you went straight to bed?'

'That's right.'

'What time would that have been?'

'I don't know. I suppose it was about a quarter to three.'

'Did you see your wife?'

'No. I didn't see anyone.'

'Your wife would have had to come up to get changed for her rehearsal. Surely you saw her then?'

'No. We have separate bedrooms,' Henry explained. 'She'd have had no reason to come into my room.'

Rafferty wondered who had decided on the separate bedrooms, and got the impression it hadn't been Henry. It made his unlikely theory that the sainted Barbara had had a lover a bit more plausible.

'You didn't call out to her? Ask her to make you a hot drink, perhaps?'

'No. I—I didn't want to bother her. Besides, I knew she was going out to the rehearsal of the play and wouldn't have time.'

'Very considerate of you.' Rafferty was sure he was concealing something. Henry, more than most men, looked as if he would be a demanding patient, expecting his wife to trot up and down stairs like a ministering angel whenever he got a sniffle. Rafferty decided not to pursue it for the moment. Perhaps he'd had a row with the sainted Barbara before he left the house that morning, and didn't want her knowing that he'd come home with his sickly tail between his legs?

'Mr Shore said that your wife wasn't the sort of person to just vanish without a word to anyone,' Llewellyn commented softly. 'In view of that, I'm surprised you weren't sufficiently concerned to contact us yourself when she failed to return home, rather than wait for Mr Shore to do it. Perhaps you can explain why you waited?'

Henry's eyes had the hurt expression of a wrongly chastised spaniel. 'I thought she might have—met someone, as Hilary suggested, and gone for a drink.'

Twin spots of colour appeared in his cheeks as he suggested the possibility, causing Rafferty to consider his lover theory even more closely. *Had* Henry suspected such a thing and, out of injured pique, refused to become concerned about the fact she was missing?

Henry continued to defend himself. 'I suppose, as well, I just hoped for the best, as one does, and kept thinking she'd turn up. Anyway, I still wasn't feeling well.' He sniffed and his eyes filled with tears. He pulled out a paint-splattered handkerchief and blew his nose noisily. 'Anyway, what does it matter what I thought, or didn't think, did or didn't do? She's dead. Whatever happens, nothing can bring her back to me, now.' Henry's face screwed up and he broke down and wept.

Awkwardly, Rafferty tried to comfort him. 'Your wife was almost certainly dead by three-thirty that afternoon,' he told Henry, in between the sobs. She must have been, Rafferty reasoned. Even though Dally hadn't been able to place the time of death quite so accurately, it seemed probable—unless she *had* been meeting a lover, and they had had a later falling out—that she'd died soon after reaching the meadow; she'd certainly never left it.

'So even if you *had* been up to going to look for her...' Rafferty continued, stopping as he realized, just in time, that—if Henry was innocent—telling him that all he would have found would have been his wife's dead body was hardly calculated to console him. Always supposing he *hadn't* killed her himself, of course, which was still a possibility.

His attempt at consoling Henry was no more successful than his attempt at consoling the boy had been, and he could only look on helplessly while Henry wept gut-wrenching sobs that seemed torn from his very soul. All that Rafferty could think of doing was to pat him ineffectually on the shoulder. Surprisingly, it was Llewellyn who had the presence of mind to pour the distraught Henry a stiff drink. Luckily, it seemed to calm him.

Rafferty had hoped to have a word with Hilary Shore. He wanted to get further details of her statement, as well as advise her that encouraging Henry to tell lies to the police wasn't a good idea, but, she was a difficult woman to catch and, on asking Henry where she was, they learned she was still in London. Rafferty wondered why she felt it necessary to keep out of their way.

'He's hiding something,' Rafferty commented, as they headed for the car.

Llewellyn nodded. 'But what he told us is believable enough—as far as it goes. Except for the saintly consideration for his wife. That doesn't ring true.'

Rafferty started the car engine and, glancing across at the passenger seat, asked deadpan, 'Did your friend Mrs Watson have anything more interesting to say, by the way? Any juicy gossip, for instance?'

Llewellyn nodded. 'But few facts. She had already told us all she knew. The rest was character assassination on the grand scale.'

'On the lines that Charles's wife was an empty-headed spiteful social butterfly, I suppose, and that Charles liked to console himself elsewhere.' Llewellyn nodded. 'Nothing about friend Henry?'

'Plenty. Most of it actionable.' Llewellyn's thin lips curled faintly upwards, as if, now that Mrs Watson's testimony was over and done with, he could manage a wry humour. 'I don't know why, but I got the impression she doesn't like him. She implied Barbara could have done a lot better for herself. Whether that's true or not is anyone's guess, as Mrs Watson's something of a romantic—you should see *her* bookshelves—full of kings and peasant girls and tycoons and typists. I think she had hoped to enjoy some vicarious grand romance, and Henry rather ruined the picture. She admitted she was disappointed when Barbara laughed and insisted that, whatever anyone else thought, she was a woman of simple tastes and was more than happy with Henry.'

'He's certainly simple enough,' was Rafferty's comment. 'I know they say that virtue is its own reward, but there are limits.'

'A virtuous woman,' Llewellyn quoted softly. 'Her price is far above rubies.'

'If you say so. Anyway, if she was as virtuous as Mrs Watson claims, that would seem to let Henry out. Shame really, as I was quite warming to the idea of the saintly Barbara being a bit of a floozie on the quiet. If she wasn't carrying on on the side, I can't imagine what other motive Henry could have for killing her. She didn't have any money for him to inherit. If anything, her death leaves him worse off, as she brought a small income from that part-time job at the Conservation Society.'

It also increases his ex-wife's chances of getting custody of the boy if she reapplies to the court,' Llewellyn observed. 'From what Anne Longman said, the fact that the court was aware that Henry intended to re-marry almost immediately after the divorce and to such an upright character as Barbara swayed them strongly in his favour. Without her...'

'I wouldn't imagine that the custody of his son would count for much with Henry,' said Rafferty, as he recalled his earlier conversation with him. 'From what Anne Longman said, it was Shore's spite that pushed him. It's obvious that Henry's at a loss what to do with the boy, though I suppose he's happy enough to take the money he must get as the boy's legal guardian.'

'There's another aspect to his wife's death that lets him out, you know,' Llewellyn remarked.

'Oh?'

'If Henry lost custody of the boy, who, after all, is Charles Shore's nephew, would Shore continue to provide a comfortable home and job for him?'

Slowly, Rafferty shook his head. 'I don't think he would. Don't you remember? He said he had to provide a home for Henry, but he added under his breath, "for now, anyway", which indicates that he was planning on his removal. So, it looks like her death had made him a loser all round. Her price really has been far above rubies for Henry.'

'And the children. Did you know that Henry's son fell out of a tree earlier this year and fractured his skull?' Rafferty nodded. 'According to Mrs Griffiths, the hospital only let him out early because his stepmother was an ex-nurse. He knocked himself senseless, apparently.'

Rafferty grunted. 'Didn't do much for his brain-power, either. Not, from what we've learned so far, that he exactly had a towering intellect *before* the accident.' He allowed himself a sour grin as another theory bit the dust. 'Must take after his father.'

ELEVEN

WHILE LLEWELLYN paid the delayed visit to Charles Shore's offices, Rafferty remained at the station and concentrated his mind on the other suspects and what they claimed they had been doing on the afternoon of Barbara Longman's murder.

Hilary Shore had said she had been in London, spending her husband's money. According to the staff of Harvey Nichols, Hilary had certainly been there and at the aromatherapist's, though as the fashion show had ended at 1.30 p.m. and she'd been half an hour late for her 5.30 appointment with Mrs Armadi there was an unexplained discrepancy. Rafferty was curious to know what she had been doing during the rest of the afternoon. Damn the woman, he thought. Why can't she return home, or at least telephone to let someone know where exactly in London she might be found?

The housekeeper, with or without the help of the Italian au pair, claimed to have been stirring her raspberry jam and the gardener had been in the nearest pub, it being his half day. His alibi, at least, had checked out.

The little girl had been at the church hall for the play rehearsal; the two boys, presumably, as Mrs Griffiths had suggested, not relishing the prospect of dressing up in ridiculous costumes, had disappeared before the telephone call, returning home once they could be sure Barbara was safely out of the house.

According to the housekeeper, however, they were both back before the 3.30 p.m. deadline he had set.

Then, of course, there was Henry, who after first lying to them had claimed to have taken his sick stomach to bed, and Anne Longman who *thought* she'd been at home, but who'd been careful enough not to swear to it.

As for the motive that Recycled Rita had imputed to Charles Shore, whether Llewellyn's enquiries had been applied with so much discretion that the people he had questioned had missed his point entirely, Rafferty didn't know, but the Welshman hadn't uncovered the tiniest rumour that Shore's chemical firm had polluted the river since the first accusation several years earlier. Of course, it was possible that Rita Colman's dislike of Shore and people like him, had encouraged the accusation. But Rafferty had told Llewellyn to keep digging anyway. 'But, for God's sake,' he added, 'don't let anything get back to Shore. If it does and he complains about harassment, Bradley'll have my balls for breakfast.'

'I'll carry on being discreet, don't worry,' Llewellyn had assured him. He had given Rafferty an elliptical glance before leaving for Shore's offices. 'I'm not brave enough to risk Mrs Rafferty's revenge if I deprive her of her longed-for grandson.'

Neither am I, thought Rafferty.

LLEWELLYN HAD SOME interesting information when he returned later that day. 'You were right. Mr Shore's alibi didn't stand up to deeper investigation. When I spoke to his personal secretary before, she told me he was working on some urgent figures that afternoon and had told her not to disturb him. She was adamant that he didn't go past her. But what she didn't say was that his private washroom has another door that leads down to a neighbouring street. Fortunately, neither Shore nor his secretary were there today, and I was able to speak to a more junior member of staff who wasn't quite so discreet.'

'Interesting. If Recycled Rita's accusations are true, he could easily have reached the meadow, killed Mrs Longman, and returned, in under forty minutes.'

Llewellyn nodded. 'But could he be sure his secretary *wouldn't* disturb him?'

Rafferty raised a sardonic eyebrow. 'Would *you* disturb him, if he'd ordered you not to? I wouldn't. Our Mr Shore is used to having his orders obeyed. I imagine he'd give his secretary hell if she dared to interrupt him.' He recalled some of Shore's exploits in the business world and added, 'Anyway, he's cool enough to take a chance. You checked if anyone in the neighbouring street saw him?'

Llewellyn nodded again. 'Nothing, I'm afraid. And he wasn't driving his BMW that day as it was in the garage and he'd hired a much less showy model.' He paused. 'No one saw that, either.'

'Typical.' Disgruntled, Rafferty shrugged into his jacket. 'I'm off to talk to old Ma Thomson. See if she *does* substantiate her son's story.'

FORTY-FIVE MINUTES later, conscious of the three sets of baleful dark brown eyes stabbing like a devil's pitchfork between his shoulder-blades, Rafferty walked with as measured a tread as he could muster from the tumbledown, weatherboard farmhouse across the glutinous black mud of the yard to his car.

The two lean mongrels dancing hungrily beside
Thomson flashed teeth far superior to their master's,
so it was with a sigh of relief that Rafferty reached the
car and opened the door. Annoyed that he'd allowed
the trio to intimidate him, he turned and scowled at
them. The dogs bared their magnificent teeth in angry growls, but Thomson took no notice. He was too
busy staring, with an expression of malevolent satisfaction, at Rafferty's ill-shod feet. Rafferty glanced
down and sighed. He *supposed* there were shoes in
there . . . somewhere, but he was damned if he could
see them under the mud. Normally, he kept a pair of
wellington boots in the car. Wasn't it just his luck that
the last time he'd taken them home to wash off the
accumulated muck he'd forgotten to put them back?

No doubt the wretched farmer was congratulating
himself on the urge that had inspired him to hose
down his battered old van ten minutes before Rafferty's arrival. Rafferty was almost tempted to do him
for using his hose-pipe during a ban, but he resisted
the impulse. Anyway, he wasn't sure of his facts. For
all he knew, a farmer like Thomson was entitled to
make free with large quantities of water during a
drought. In the CID, you tended to get out of touch
with such regulations.

Thomson's neighbours had been right about him.
The farmer had been as obstructive as possible and
Rafferty had got no more out of the uncommunica-
tive Thomson than had Shore or Llewellyn. The man
was adamant that he knew nothing about any phone
call and that he hadn't attempt to plough up the
meadow. 'It was still there, wasn't it?' he'd demanded belligerently—undisturbed, as the government and the Conservation Society decreed. As this

was irrefutable, Rafferty had had no choice but to agree.

But Thomson certainly had a short fuse, he reflected. He also had several scratches on his face. The man had an elemental quality, of basic instincts and primitive angers that wouldn't require much to set them off. Those large, calloused hands would subdue his victim easily enough, but in the process, Rafferty felt sure, they would leave more bruises on the body than Mrs Longman had sustained.

Unfortunately for Rafferty's latest theory, Thomson's mother had eventually confirmed his alibi. Her slowness in doing so might have seemed suspicious in another woman, but Rafferty didn't think her reluctance was due to an attempt to conceal the truth. The old woman had a warped sense of humour, and seemed to find her dour son's predicament amusing. For some malicious reason of her own, she had simply decided to cause him as much trouble as possible before confirming his alibi and saving him from being hauled off to the police station—she wasn't quite the picture of doting motherhood that Rafferty had imagined.

Still, those scratches were interesting, Rafferty reflected. And the old woman might easily have dozed off, sitting in the warm sun as she had been, even if she had vehemently denied such a possibility. Although it would probably be a waste of time, Rafferty decided to allow himself the satisfaction of checking the matter out further. He wasn't sure if Dally's report had made any mention of skin being trapped under the dead woman's nails, but it was worth checking.

LLEWELLYN WAS IN the office going through the statements when Rafferty got back. 'Anything new come in?' he queried, as he slammed the door noisily behind him.

The Welshman winced and shook his head. 'Nothing positive. None of the local taxi firms report picking up a fare at the Shores' or dropping anyone near the meadow. And, as far as Barbara Longman's car's concerned, one or two drivers on the road near the meadow mentioned noticing a red hatchback parked in that side lane where we found hers. The times point to it being the same one. Another man reported seeing *two* cars there as he passed on the main road, but he's vague on details. Though he did sound positive on the time. Said it was about 3.20 p.m.'

Rafferty looked thoughtful. 'I don't suppose he remembers any details about the second car? Things like make, colour, registration number, for instance?'

Llewellyn shook his head again.

It was too much to hope for, of course. 'Keep them at it, Dafyd. It might yet turn something up. Did you manage to get hold of Hilary Shore yet?'

Llewellyn shook his head. 'But Mrs Griffiths promised to ring me as soon as she returns.'

'What it is to have friends at court.' Llewellyn and the housekeeper had been getting very pally, Rafferty knew. Although she had made it clear she had no time for his boss, for some reason she had taken a fancy to Llewellyn. Of course, they were both Welsh, which probably explained it. Rafferty could imagine them sharing mutual grievances about him over hot tea and Welsh griddle cakes in the Shores' kitchen.

Rafferty smiled as he remembered a little chore he had saved for Llewellyn. 'I want you to go and see Mrs Watson again,' he told the housekeeper's confidant. Gratified to see that Llewellyn's long face grew appreciably longer at this news, he went on, 'She's not on the phone, unfortunately, and, although it seems Henry had no reason to kill his wife, we still ought to check if his car was parked in front of her house all afternoon on the day of the murder.' His eyes held a sardonic gleam as he added, 'Better get yourself a new notebook before you go. How are WPC Green and Hanks coming along with checking out the members of the Conservation Society?' He supplied his own answer before Llewellyn could utter any reproach. 'Slowly, I suppose?'

Llewellyn's nod indicated he supposed correctly. But did the Welshman have to look quite so pleased about it? Rafferty asked himself. 'You'd better get off now. I've got one or two things to do here.' Not wanting the Welshman to know he found Sam's reports pretty well incomprehensible, he waited till Llewellyn had gone before he picked up the phone to ring Dally. He started to dial, but then put the phone down again, as he remembered how much Dally always hated having to repeat himself. Why give the old duffer another chance to take a pop at him? Dammit, he'd have another go at it himself, he decided. It couldn't be *that* difficult. If he concentrated . . .

He looked vaguely around. Where was the blasted thing? If Llewellyn had put it away somewhere tidy... He began to drag out the neatly pigeonholed reports and statements, piling them haphazardly on the desk, till he came to Dally's. Stifling a groan of dismay at the length of it, he settled down to try to untangle the ponderous medical terminology. He was still at it when Llewellyn returned.

'I've checked with Mrs Watson, sir.' Llewellyn glanced resignedly at the untidy desk. 'And although none of the neighbours were at home that afternoon to confirm the times, she admitted that Henry Longman's car remained outside her house all afternoon. So, if he did it, he'd have needed the use of another vehicle, and the only other cars there were the housekeeper's and the van belonging to Higginbottom, the gardener. He'd left it there, with the key in the ignition, when he finished work. The boy's tutor was only there in the mornings and he left at twelve.'

'Does the gardener park his van in the same place as Mrs Griffiths?' Rafferty asked.

'Yes. They all use the largest of the old sheds behind the house.'

'And they're concealed by hedging, and aren't visible from the downstairs rooms. Very convenient.'

'They'd be seen clearly enough from upstairs,' Llewellyn reminded him.

'Only if anyone happened to be looking out of one of the back windows and we've already concluded that was unlikely. Apart from the boys—who might have been anywhere—and the au pair, who was at the front of the house, there was no one about to see. If Henry borrowed one of those cars, he could have gone out by the back lane. Where are the keys usually kept?'

'The gardener keeps his in his pocket, but that morning he had been unloading bags of peat and had forgotten to take the key from the ignition. He left it there the entire afternoon while he was in the pub, so anyone could have noticed the key and taken the car.

Mrs Griffiths leaves her keys in her handbag, which is hung in full view on the back door.'

'Hmm.' Rafferty tapped his nose thoughtfully. 'If he went out the front way, the au pair might have seen him, I suppose.'

'She didn't, sir.' For some reason, the usually sallow skin on Llewellyn's cheekbones were stained with two bright spots of colour, and Rafferty wondered if the bold-eyed Italian girl had made a pass at him. Llewellyn went doggedly on. 'She said Mrs Griffiths had told her to change the children's beds—apparently keeping the children's rooms tidy is one of her duties. She insisted on taking me upstairs to show me how far away from the window they are.'

'Now, I wonder why she did that?' With a speculative grin, Rafferty stared at Llewellyn, but the Welshman, although he looked discomfited, made no comment. 'I suppose Mrs Watson would have heard a car coming from that back entrance if he'd left that way?'

'Not necessarily, sir,' Llewellyn replied, as his cheeks gradually lost their glow. 'I noticed while I was there that I could hear cars passing quite clearly from the front room, but when she called me into the kitchen for a cup of tea, I couldn't hear any traffic. The kitchen is down a little passage at the back of the house and Mrs Watson admitted that, after she had seen Henry, she left the garden and went to make a pot of tea. So, if Henry had left that way, it's possible she wouldn't have known.' He glanced morosely at the clock on the wall. 'She seems to set as much store by the restorative powers of tea as Mrs Rafferty, sir, as she forced three cups on me. I thought I'd never get away.'

'You do seem to have a bit of trouble with the ladies one way or another, don't you, Taff? First Mrs Griffiths, now Mrs Watson and the little Italian girl. Isn't my cousin Maureen enough for you?' Llewellyn's lips compressed. 'I'm damned if I know what they see in you. Anyway,' Rafferty continued when his teasing brought forth no further response. 'It's all a bit inconclusive, isn't it? It's possible that no cars passed while you were there. It's a shame all Mrs Watson's neighbours were at work. If they hadn't been we might have discovered if Henry's or the housekeeper's cars *were* used.'

He sighed. 'I wish we had something more definite than all these coulds and mights and maybes. As the husband, Longman's still got to be in the running, however unlikely it seems that his wife was having an affair. He lied to us about his whereabouts, remember, and he may appear as innocent as a choirgirl, but then'—Rafferty directed a mischievous glance at his sergeant—'being Welsh, you'd know all about choirgirls. And this particular chorister was smart enough to wangle himself a nice cushy billet.' Which was more than he'd ever managed to do, Rafferty thought ruefully. 'His first wife's also in the running,' he went on. 'Especially as, as far as we've been able to discover, she had as strong a motive for killing the woman as anyone.'

Llewellyn reminded him that the telephone message had been from a man, not a woman.

'*If* there ever was a message,' he taunted him. 'Which brings us back to your friend, Mrs Griffiths...' He continued before Llewellyn was able to protest: 'Anyway, I'm no longer sure that the caller's gender is particularly significant.'

He swung round on his swivel chair. 'I've been thinking about it, and Anne Longman, for one, had only to persuade some man friend to leave the message for her. It's more than likely she would ignore her brother's veto on her bringing "followers" back to the flat. And even if Shore pays her neighbours to spy on her, they're likely to be out some of the time. I'm sure if she picked her moment, she could invite half the Argyll and Sutherland Highlanders up to that flat—as long as they didn't insist on playing their bagpipes—with no one any the wiser.'

Llewellyn nodded. 'She's attractive enough to persuade...'

'You noticed that, huh?' Rafferty grinned. 'But you're right. She'd be as well able as her brother to use charm to get what she wanted. And it wasn't as if she would need to ask a possible boyfriend to make any kind of threatening phone call. The message would sound perfectly innocuous to a third party. All she would have to do was tell him she was playing a joke on her *sister-in-law*. After all, their surnames were the same so it would sound believable enough.'

He tapped his teeth thoughtfully. 'It's possible that once news of the murder broke—if there was such a man—he'd have been too frightened to come forward. He'd have been scared we might suspect *him* of killing her. Of course, the problem with her is that unless she persuaded some man or other to drive her down to Essex and back, she'd still have to stay sober long enough to get here from London. If she had murder on her mind, she would surely not be reckless enough to risk being breathalysed so close to the scene of the crime.'

He swung his chair decisively round to the front. 'We're returning to London, Llewellyn. I want to see if Anne Longman's memory has returned. But, before we see her, we'll have a word with her neighbours and question them about any possible boyfriends and what cars they drive. It's a long shot, but worth checking. Mrs Griffiths may be able to help there, too. Pump her a little more next time you see her. We know Anne Longman hated the victim and, with her out of the running she might think she had a good chance of getting custody of her son.

'But before we go.' Rafferty silently admitted defeat and thrust Dally's pathology report at him. 'Have another read of that. I don't suppose it's significant, but you probably noticed when you saw him earlier that Thomson's face was scratched. If it's irrelevant, I want to get it cleared out of the way. You know how I hate a muddle.' At this, Llewellyn's gaze rested sardonically on the untidy desk. Impervious to such subtle criticism, Rafferty added, 'All I want to know is if the victim had skin trapped under her nails and I'm expected to wade through all that bloody mumbo-jumbo.'

'But Dally already told us there was nothing,' said Llewellyn. 'Don't you remember?'

Rafferty had been too occupied with keeping his lunch down at the post-mortem to have much attention to spare for Dally's colourful blow-by-blow account of his findings, but he wasn't going to admit that to Llewellyn and brusquely, he ordered him, 'Just read it, there's a good lad.'

Five minutes later, Llewellyn confirmed what he'd already said. 'No. No skin trapped.'

'Are you sure?' Rafferty frowned suspiciously at the speed of Llewellyn's perusal. It had taken him that long just to read the first page. And then he'd had to go back and read it again because he'd hardly taken in a word of it.

'It says so here, sir,' said Llewellyn, pointing to a particularly lengthy paragraph.

Rafferty skimmed the first few lines and decided to take his sergeant's word for it. 'Not that that lets Thomson out. Even if his mother does confirm his story, she's old and could have let her eyes droop for five minutes. The victim was only a little slip of a thing. He could have overpowered her quickly enough, and returned to the other side of the farm without his mother even noticing he'd gone.'

'You think he might have lost his temper and killed her accidentally?'

'Maybe.' Rafferty sighed and then admitted: 'But it doesn't seem likely. He's had a running battle with that Society for several years now, without killing any of them.'

His hunt for Dally's report had turned his desk upside-down and, as his gaze came to rest on the old photographs of Maximillian Shore that he'd had Llewellyn dig out of the files, he frowned, and re-marked, with a somewhat bashful smile, 'You know, Dafyd, this old man's face seems to haunt me. It's as if some sixth sense is telling me he had something to do with the murder.' He shrugged ruefully, as Llewellyn opened his mouth. 'Don't ask me how or why. I know it's illogical, but after reading his autobiography I feel even more convinced that there's something there, something that connects with this case. He was a despot, with family and business rivals both. His overpowering destructive personality still hangs over the family fifteen years later. For all his success, Charles strikes me as a deeply unhappy man,

Anne is a bitter drunk, he ruined whatever chances Henry might have had as an artist by pushing him to become a businessman. His evil influence has lingered even unto the second generation, as the children seem as incapable of happiness as the adults. They were a family waiting for further tragedy and now it's happened. Look at that face, man. Just look at it, then tell me you don't feel it, too.'

Obediently, Llewellyn came to stand beside him and studied the now faded photographs.

'Even though these photographs are old and grainy, you have to admit the man's personality still comes out of the picture and grabs you by the throat. He's the key that will unlock the door to this case, I know it.'

'I can see that, in his day, he must have wielded great influence,' Llewellyn admitted. 'But he's been dead for years. All right, I agree, they're not a happy family, but I'd have thought any tragedy waiting to happen would have occurred at the time he died—when that divisive will was read—not years later. Charles is the patriarch now. I just can't see what possible connection a man dead for fifteen years can have with this murder.'

Neither could Rafferty. All he knew for certain was that, far more even than these photographs, Maximillian's portrait seemed to act as a magnet for him. Each time he went to the Shores' house he found himself drawn to it, more and more convinced that the old man's formidable gaze held a message. However, if it did, he had yet to discover what it was. But, he realized, it might help his understanding if he found out more about what had made the dead patriarch tick. 'Didn't Charles mention something about his father's papers?' he asked, a few seconds later. 'Those theoretical papers he was working on. It might be worth digging into them.'

'He said they'd been thrown out, as I remember,' Llewellyn replied, his expression implying he had no interest in being led down this particular blind alley.

'He said they'd *probably* been thrown out,' Rafferty quickly corrected. Llewellyn's lack of enthusiasm for his idea made him all the more eager to pursue it, especially as, even though they had managed to turn up a few interesting items, they didn't seem to be getting very far with any of them. 'Ring Mrs Griffiths and ask her about those papers. I bet if anyone knows where they are it'll be the housekeeper. Lucky for us that with your Welsh charm you've got her wound round your finger already. I'll see you out by the car.'

However, according to the housekeeper, she was as sure as she could be that the papers would have gone on the gardener's bonfire years ago, which information somewhat hindered Rafferty's desire to learn more of the old man. Disgruntled, he slammed the driver's door and putting his foot down headed for London.

TWELVE

ANNE LONGMAN opened the door after their third ring. She seemed ill at ease today; the previous strained vivacity was missing, as was the bright hit or miss make-up. Something else was missing, as well, Rafferty realized. The smell of whisky. He assumed she was out of booze, and wondered if that alone explained her nervous state.

They followed her down the short hallway to the untidy living room, but when Rafferty attempted to question her, she flared up at him.

'For God's sake, can't you wait till I find a cigarette? Or is this country turning into another police state?'

Rafferty and Llewellyn exchanged glances. Ignoring them, she prowled from one end of the room to the other, like a caged tiger, her expression increasingly desperate as, one by one, jacket pockets and discarded cigarette packets were investigated and found to be empty.

'Damn.' The lid slammed on a cheap redwood box—presumably the last hope.

Rafferty, until recently a thirty a day man, tried to help. 'If you want to dash out to the tobacconist on the corner, we can wait five minutes.'

'Don't you think I would if I had any money?' she snapped. 'I'm broke. My allowance isn't due till tomorrow and knowing that bastard brother of mine, it'll be late.'

Suddenly, as though recognizing she might be alienating possible rescuers, her demeanour changed. She laid a hand on Rafferty's arm and gave him a devastating smile. 'With all that red hair, you must have your share of bad habits,' she murmured. 'For pity's sake, tell me smoking's one of them.'

Rafferty smiled ruefully. 'Sorry. I gave them up.'

Instantly dismissing him, she directed her smile at Llewellyn, but one look at the Welshman evidently sufficed to convince her that he was a paragon of clean-living virtues. She scowled, slumped in one of the worn armchairs and eyed them with dislike. 'Pity you didn't send the Vice Squad. Isn't it just my luck to get two policemen with not a decent human weakness between them?'

Rafferty, unwilling to be lumped together with Llewellyn as a Percy Prim, felt the urge to defend himself. But, as he watched her nicotine-stained fingers beat an erratic tattoo on the arm of the chair, he realized he might as well save his breath. Anne Longman was more concerned with her own deprivation than his manly pride. He realized something else as well. Deprived of her twin crutches of whisky and cigarettes, she might just let something useful slip.

'What do you want, anyway?' she snapped. 'If it's about my whereabouts when Henry's little bride was murdered, I still can't be any more definite than I was before. How many more times must I tell . . . ?'

'Until you remember, Mrs Longman,' Llewellyn asserted.

Their chats to the neighbours had elicited the information that Anne Longman had broken up with her last boyfriend some three weeks earlier. Apparently the split had been so acrimonious—with rau-

cous arguments and smashed crockery—that she had
declared herself off men. There certainly hadn't been
any male friends visiting recently, according to the old
lady next door. She had told them that all Anne's re-
lationships tended to break up in a similar manner.

The neighbour hadn't been able to tell them
whether Anne had been at home on the day of Barbara's murder. But the rest of what she had said certainly lessened the possibility that one of her past
boyfriends would have been willing to either make
phone calls for her or offer to chauffeur her all the
way to Essex. As, in Rafferty's estimation, this information dropped her a little further down the list of
suspects, he broke in before Llewellyn's officious
manner put her back up. 'We'll leave that for the
moment, though there is something else you might be
able to help us with,' he told her.

She gave him a sulky look. 'Oh?'

'It's nothing to worry about. It's just that Charles
told me your father had written a large number of
theoretical papers which he'd hoped to publish.' He
sensed, rather than heard Llewellyn's sigh, but went
doggedly on, anyway. 'The manuscript was kept in
the library, but it seems to have disappeared.' He
didn't mention Mrs Griffiths's conviction that the
manuscript had been destroyed, but went on, 'I wondered if you might know what happened to it?'

'Me? Why should I know what happened to it?'
Her eyes narrowed. 'Who told you I did?' Rafferty's
hopes rose as it became obvious that she was lying,
and, as though she realized that her denial had been
less than convincing, she immediately tried frankness. 'All right, so I did take it. What of it?'

She flopped back on the armchair and gazed at him with defiant eyes. 'I've as much right to it as my dear little brother. I thought I might be able to get Daddy's opus published. But there was no hope of that. From the parts of it I was able to read, most of it was case history stuff, the sort any practising psychiatrist would have reams of.' She laughed suddenly. 'A lot of it was in some kind of code—Father liked his little secrets. I couldn't figure the code out, but it must have been used for the more juicy bits or else why would Father put himself to so much trouble? Anyway, I knew that no publisher would be interested in publishing an amateur's little theories, juicy or not, especially as the coded sections were probably libellous.' She pulled a face. 'Pity, as I could have done with the money.'

Excited to discover that old Max Shore had felt the need to encode his work, and certain he was on to something definite at last, Rafferty asked eagerly, 'Do you still have the manuscript?'

She looked at him assessingly as if weighing all the angles, then she shook her head. 'No. I put it back in the library. But it had vanished last time I looked for it. God knows where it's gone.' With a half-teasing smile at Rafferty, she commented, 'You know, you've intrigued me, Inspector. Do tell me what possible use you think my father's old theories might be to you.'

After Llewellyn's criticism, Rafferty was defensive of his reasons. 'It was just an idea I had. Nothing of great importance. Anything that might help me solve this crime interests me, that's all.'

'What possible connection could my father have with Barbara's death?'

Feeling foolish, in face of so reasonable a question, he was forced to confess that he didn't know.

She gave a malicious smile. 'Sounds to me as if you're clutching at straws, Inspector. Barbara and my father never even met. Surely you know he died all of fifteen years ago?'

Rafferty nodded. He'd told her why he was interested in her father's papers, but he was damned if he was going to let her interrogate him, and he got up to go. He paused half-way to the door. 'Talking of your father, have you any idea who might have murdered him? I gather there were several theories at the time.'

'Obviously, you've read the police reports, Inspector. I don't imagine I can tell you any more than they can. There was certainly no shortage of suspects. My father's portrait might give the impression that he was more upright than Moses, but you shouldn't let it fool you. He made enemies with the greatest of ease. You don't get to be as wealthy and successful as quickly as he did without taking the trouble to discover where someone was most vulnerable. Of course, that Old Testament face of his made it easier to get under people's guard and cheat them. My father had no scruples, Inspector. He would stop at nothing to increase his empire. I called it his Attila complex.'

She returned to her armchair and with a lazy grace, swung her legs over one of the arms, displaying plenty of shapely thigh. She had a certain wanton charm about her, a reckless youthful bravado that was beguiling, and Rafferty couldn't help but stare as she stretched her body languorously, just like the cat he had likened her to earlier. Surprisingly, considering her drinking habits, she had kept her figure and it seemed to be giving Llewellyn the fidgets. But the

Welshman wasn't the only one affected by her, Rafferty admitted to himself. He got the impression she was fully aware of the effect she had on them and was amusing herself. No wonder she'd managed to persuade Henry up the aisle so easily, he thought. Henry, poor fool, wouldn't have stood a chance, wouldn't have realized that she was more suited to being a mistress than a wife.

Anne Longman still wore the look of the cat who had been at the cream as she showed them out. She stood at the door and watched them walk away and, as Rafferty glanced back, he got the impression that, like a teenager, from her early marriage to her conveniently poor memory, she got a kick out of cocking a snook at authority. Unfortunately, it was an attitude he felt a sneaking empathy with. Wasn't he a bit that way inclined himself?

Llewellyn didn't waste any time in reminding him that she still hadn't given them a satisfactory explanation of her whereabouts on the day of Barbara's murder. And as her neighbours had been unable to tell them anything incriminating, as a defence it was pretty effective. As with the other suspects in the case, it put the onus to prove otherwise squarely on them.

DWARFED BY THE red double-decker London buses and hemmed in by black taxis, tourist coaches, and the gathering gloom of a threatening thunderstorm, Rafferty blocked out the trapped feeling by forcing his mind to pick over what Anne Longman had said. If nothing else, the visit had given him more of an insight into Maximillian Shore, but he still wished he understood why the man preoccupied him so much.

What *could* he have to do with this case? What possible connection could there be with current events?

There was his autobiography, of course, but he'd read that and couldn't see that there was anything in it likely to bring on a murder now, fifteen years after publication, especially as it had been *Barbara Longman,* rather than one of the Shores, who had died. He was more interested in Shore's theoretical papers, as their disappearance inclined him to the conviction that they must hold some significance. At least if he'd read them, he might be able to discount and forget them. And it was certainly intriguing that he had felt it necessary to write part of them in code.

Broodingly, Rafferty cast his mind back, and as he reviewed Anne Longman's comments and Charles Shore's half-forgotten and somewhat disparaging remarks about them, a possible connection came to him, a connection so obvious, so exciting and potentially explosive, that he wondered he hadn't thought of it before. Rafferty glanced at Llewellyn and decided against confiding in him yet. He was discovering that it saved an ego bruising if he tried to think his ideas through before having them threshed by the Welshman's combine-harvester intellect.

Was it possible, that in his younger days, Maximillian Shore had been a *blackmailer?* His daughter had said he always seemed to know where a man was most vulnerable. She had also said that he had no scruples and had become wealthy surprisingly quickly. How else could he have done it? He'd been a poor immigrant, just escaped from the Nazi bloodbath in Europe, young and alone in a strange land, not speaking the language too well, if at all. How had he not only survived, but thrived?

After reading his autobiography, Rafferty felt he had learned something of what influences had contributed to Shore's success. He had seen and experienced all manner of evils; probably his own life had hardened him to the suffering of others. After all, had there been anyone to care a jot about what *he'd* been through? Experiences such as his often put a canker in a man's soul. Would he be likely to worry about the morality of it if blackmail could help transform him from a storm-tossed orphan, at the mercy of every jagged rock, to a king in an impregnable castle of wealth? Rafferty thought that, after such experiences, a man would be prepared to do whatever was necessary to safeguard himself from similar persecution in the future.

Shore's autobiography revealed that as a youth he had worked in a newspaper office. What better place for a lad with ambitions? In those distant days, with their obligingly discreet newspaper barons, there would be secrets in plenty, secrets that the general public never learned, secrets that could ruin a person. An observant young man, clever enough to keep his ears and eyes open and his mouth shut, could learn a lot. Had Shore achieved his ambition by stumbling fortuitously on the shameful secret of some wealthy man? Had he mined such a secret with the ruthlessness he would have observed daily in the camps? Mined it till it was played out and then gone on to the next, more wily now, more adept at winkling out the dark vices and secret susceptibilities that made powerful men vulnerable to little men like himself?

Maximillian Shore had been a man who enjoyed power. What could provide more power than a knowledge of others' weaknesses? Accumulating money had been like a religion to the man, Rafferty realized, and that made the possibility even more likely that, in his younger days, at least, he'd been a blackmailer.

Was that how his interest in theorizing had begun? he wondered. Had he developed a fancy to launder his own dirty little habit once he was established and successful? He wouldn't have been able to bring himself to destroy the material that had given him wealth and power. Where safer then to keep such explosive stuff than with the later theoretical papers that most of his family had no interest in reading? Charles had been amused by his little hobby, despised it even, perhaps, deep down, pleased to have a reason to feel superior to the father he had probably feared; his father, the dabbler in theories that no one wanted.

Charles Shore had apparently thought so little of his father's theories that he hadn't made any effort to keep them safe, had assumed they had gone on the gardener's bonfire and hadn't seemed particularly concerned about the possibility that they had been destroyed. Would Maximillian have confided to his son the probable truth about the source of the family wealth? As Rafferty pictured the old man's proud face, he thought it unlikely.

It was even more unlikely that Maximillian had confided in the wayward Anne. She had said she had taken the papers hoping to have them published. But on reading them, had she unravelled the coded secrets and had an even better idea? Had she tried to make use of the secrets her father had accumulated? Her anger when he had mentioned the manuscript made Rafferty believe that she *had* tried—and failed.

Any man Maximillian could have blackmailed would probably already have been middle-aged at the beginning of his blackmailing career. Presumably, most of them would be long dead by now—just like Shore.

But, as the papers seemed to have disappeared, he couldn't *prove* anything, either way. Not that he thought there was any mystery about how *that* had happened. Rafferty could imagine Anne Longman throwing them out in a drunken rage when they failed to earn her the fortune she sought, rather than replacing them as she had claimed to have done.

As another thought occurred to him, he sat rigidly in the passenger seat, frightened to move in case it vanished as rapidly as it had come before he got a handle on it. But what if she *hadn't* been lying when she said she had replaced them? What if, on failing to crack the code, she had lost interest? She wasn't the type to persevere. What if *Barbara* had discovered Shore's incriminating papers after Anne had replaced them? The indefatigable Barbara, who made everything her business, might well have come across them, in her enthusiasm for improving on the Shore housekeeping. She would have found deciphering the code easier than would Anne. From what they had learned of her, she would have had the patience, perseverance and intelligence to accomplish the task.

Of course, if he was right, he would have to abandon his favourite theory that one of the *family* had killed her. What possible secrets could *they* have had a decade and a half ago? Shore would have only been fifteen, Anne eighteen and Henry not much older when Maximillian had died. Any blackmail material that Barbara might have discovered would have been on outsiders, mostly long-dead outsiders at that.

Rafferty persisted. But what if one or two were still alive? What if Barbara had, in all innocence, let one of Maximillian's few still living victims know she was aware of their awful secret? What if she had attempted to reassure whoever it was that their long-buried secret wasn't about to be dredged up by her, and had failed to convince? Could a simple *misunderstanding* have been the reason for her murder? It could have been that way, Rafferty reckoned. With her moralistic ways, she would be likely to attempt to right a wrong, but, equally, would probably handle the guilty secrets of others badly.

Sure now that he was on to something, Rafferty determined to make another attempt to locate the papers. He would tackle Mrs Griffiths himself, when they got back. From what Anne had said it was evident that—whatever had happened to them since—they *hadn't* been destroyed at the time of Shore's death, as Charles had implied.

'THINK, Mrs Griffiths,' Rafferty implored. 'If Barbara removed the papers during a spring clean in the library, but decided they were worth keeping and didn't throw them away, where would she be likely to put them?'

She pursed her lips, though whether from annoyance at his persistence or from deep thought, Rafferty couldn't tell. 'Well,' she eventually admitted. 'They're certainly not in her bedroom, as I've given it a thorough going over and sorted through her clothes and things for Mr Henry and there was no sign of any such papers. They might be in one of the outhouses. Mr Charles hasn't bothered with them and she used to keep a lot of her own stuff stored in them;

furniture and so on from the flat she lived in before she married Mr Longman.' Her thin lips parted in the semblance of a smile. 'There's a lifetime's rubbish there for you to hunt through.'

Rafferty groaned silently. Still, he'd started now and he wasn't going to give Llewellyn the satisfaction of thinking he wasn't up to the challenge. Besides, although he had checked and eliminated the possibility of one of the local taxi firms being used by the murderer, he had yet to eliminate the other possibility. He could kill two birds with one stone and look for a push-bike or similar vehicle while he checked for Shore's manuscript.

SEVERAL HOURS LATER, tired, filthy, and in a thoroughly bad temper, Rafferty conceded defeat. They'd been through all the outhouses. They'd found rats and garden tools and old car tyres. They'd even found Henry's portrait of his wife. It was surprisingly good, and though it was unfinished, Rafferty gained a clear idea of Barbara's personality. She gazed calmly out of the portrait, exuding an air of wholesomeness, determination and devotion to duty that a nun might envy.

They found plenty of papers too, enough to convince Rafferty that the sole responsibility for the depletion of the Amazonian rain-forests rested with the Shore family. But of Maximillian Shore's theoretical manuscript, there was no sign.

He surveyed the last of the outhouses with distaste. It was the same hotchpotch as the others had been: ancient flowerpots with great cracks down their sides, apparently too valuable to throw away, a wheelbarrow with a wheel missing, a canoe with a broken paddle, fishing tackle, great sacks of fertilizer, seemingly brought here and then abandoned, a bike with no handlebars—the only one they'd come upon, and, regretfully, Rafferty put away his mental picture of a furiously pedalling Henry. The shed's only saving grace was that it was the smallest of the three outhouses.

'That's it, then,' he admitted, unwillingly confirming Llewellyn's opinion that they'd been on a wild-goose chase. 'Obviously this is where they stash their more *useful* rubbish.'

There were no great stacks of papers to be gone through anyway; he wasn't sure whether to be pleased or sorry about that. The blasted manuscript was obviously long gone.

The shed had a funny smell, composed of an esoteric mixture of damp earth, rotting wood, and long-dead tiddlers jettisoned in the bottom of the torn fishing nets. Another, more elusive odour was mixed with the rest, but Rafferty couldn't pinpoint it, until he spotted the damaged Airfix Spitfire resting in the wheelbarrow. With a nostalgic sigh, he picked it up. It still gave off a faint scent of glue and immediately plunged him back years. How many happy hours had he spent as a lad, putting these old kites together? he mused. Now youngsters preferred to sniff the glue.

The discovery of the Spitfire made him feel suddenly, inexplicably happy. He forgot the frustrations of the case, as he experimentally hefted the plane, and with a boyish grin, he guided it through an intricate flying manoeuvre, unable to resist providing the sound effects. 'Bandits at twelve o'clock. Bandits at twelve o'clock. OK, Algy, let 'em have it. *Rat-a-tat-a-tat.*'

Llewellyn heaved a long-suffering sigh as he watched Rafferty's antics. 'Hadn't we better get on?' he suggested, making purposefully for the door. 'The smell in here is affecting my sinuses.'

Rafferty snorted. It was the first he'd heard about any sinus trouble. But it sounded like just the sort of ailment Llewellyn would be affected with. He had to accept, however, that the Welshman had a point. The stink from the nearby Tiffey added to the other aromas to make a pretty powerful stench. Reluctantly he abandoned the Spitfire and followed Llewellyn outside.

It came as no surprise to him to discover that the Welshman had managed to remain relatively clean through all their rag-and-bone scavenging, though— if the disgruntled expression on his face was anything to go by—anyone would think that Rafferty had personally dipped him head first in the cesspit.

'You should have listened to Mrs Griffiths,' Llewellyn accused, unerringly voicing Rafferty's own conclusion. 'As I suspected before we started, we've been wasting our time. I can't understand, why, if you're so interested in this manuscript, you didn't arrange for properly equipped officers to tackle the job.'

'I *told* you. It was just an idea of mine,' Rafferty defended himself. Honestly, he muttered, with Llewellyn's carping, it was sometimes difficult to remember which of them was supposed to be the superior officer. 'It wasn't something I could expect Bradley to sanction. You know what a tight-fisted old—'

'Well, what next?' Llewellyn broke in, with a touch of asperity. 'Those papers are obviously long gone. Though what you hoped to...'

Irritated, Rafferty forgot his previous advice to himself and blurted out his suspicions about Maximillian Shore. 'If he *was* into blackmail and Barbara Longman found the evidence and contacted the victim, it would certainly be a motive for the blackmail victim to get rid of her.'

'That's true,' remarked Llewellyn.

Rafferty glanced suspiciously at him. Something in the Welshman's demeanour gave him an uneasy feeling that Llewellyn's combine-harvester brain was about to make clear of whatever chaff his latest idea was made. He wasn't wrong, he discovered, a few seconds later. Because, as Llewellyn told him, if she had been killed by a virtual stranger, it was extremely unlikely the murderer would have known her well enough to use the wild flowers in the meadow as a lure. Which logic not only put paid to Rafferty's latest idea completely but, as an unwanted bonus, ensured that Llewellyn well and truly had the hump.

After looking down at his dusty suit with an expression of distaste, the Welshman complained cuttingly, 'If you had thought to share your theory with me in the first place, we could have been saved all this menial labouring.' He sniffed the air and briefly closed his eyes, as though he offended his own sense of smell. 'I smell like a... like a...'

His imagination obviously wasn't up to describing what he *did* smell like, but Rafferty's wasn't so limited. With a gratification bordering on the sadistic, he proceeded to rub the usually meticulously groomed Welshman's nose in it. 'You stink like a particularly smelly old goat, Dafyd, my son,' he observed with relish. He sniffed. 'So do I. A couple of old goats perfumed by rotting fish.'

In spite of his attempted humour, the day's failure and Llewellyn's sour mood deflated him and his shoulders slumped. 'If it makes you feel any happier, I'll admit I was wrong, OK? Come on, let's go home. Today's been a dead loss all ways round. Perhaps tomorrow will bring a change of luck.'

THIRTEEN

IT HAD BEEN a long and particularly frustrating day. When Llewellyn dropped him off at 10.30 p.m., Rafferty knew just how he intended to spend what remained of it. He was going to climb off the wagon and into a hot bath with a comfortingly large whiskey. The last person he wanted to see was his mother.

Yet when he pushed open the living-room door of his flat, there she was, duster in hand, face glowing from exertion, as she gave the place a belated spring clean. Ever since his wife Angie had died two and a half years ago, his ma had insisted on doing it. He'd more than once told her not to bother, suspecting that the cleaning provided his mother with the perfect excuse to investigate his love-life.

'A bit late for housework, isn't it, Ma?' he asked caustically, as he sank wearily into a chair and let his eyes close.

'Better late than *never,* which seems to be your philosophy,' she retorted, as she pummelled a cushion into submission. 'Besides, I was on my way from the Bingo. Won fifty pounds, too.' As she clinked two bottles together he briefly opened his eyes. 'And I thought I'd come and celebrate with you. As you weren't here, I decided I might as well give the place a bit of a going-over while I waited.' She sniffed. 'Not before time either, judging by the odd smell.'

The lingering odour of old goat, Rafferty concluded.

'Was it that Dafyd who dropped you off?' He nodded and let his eyelids droop again. 'It's a pity he didn't stop, as I'd like a word with him about the present he got our Maureen for her birthday.' She sniffed. 'I can't say I was impressed.'

Remembering that the selected gift had been *his* idea, Rafferty opened his eyes again. 'Oh? What was the matter with it? Flowers, wasn't it?' he queried, all innocence.

'Yes. Yellow roses. I ask you! He's certainly got a funny way of courting a girl.'

Tired and irritable, he enquired, with a touch of belligerence, 'What's the matter with yellow roses?'

'Don't they teach you anything in that police force? For your information, when a man gives a girl yellow roses, it's a message that his love is waning.' Straightening a lopsided and romanticized view of Southend at night, she went on tartly, 'They also symbolize infidelity, and one or two other things, I shouldn't wonder. *Red* roses are for love. Everyone knows that. And if that sergeant of yours is playing fast and loose with our Maureen . . . I know he's your partner,' her voice wore on remorselessly, 'but you can tell him from me that if he's toying with our Maureen's affections he'll be sorry.'

The idea of the lugubrious Dafyd Llewellyn toying with *anyone's* affections, much less his bluestocking cousin Maureen's, rendered Rafferty temporarily speechless. How his mother imagined that Llewellyn had it in him to emulate even Casanova's shadow, much less the man, he couldn't fathom.

'So, if that sergeant of yours wants to stay in my good books, you make sure you tell him to send *red* roses next time.'

Rafferty nodded absently, gratified to discover that the know-all Llewellyn had made a botch of his gift-giving. He would enjoy passing on his ma's message.

RAFFERTY RETURNED to the office the next morning to find that, during their absence in London, more reports had accumulated. There were so many of them that Rafferty, who was beginning to feel swamped by a paper tide, forgot all about passing on his ma's warning.

As he had expected, no witnesses to the murder had come forward and although several people had reported seeing a red hatchback heading along the main road near the meadow Rafferty didn't feel he could place any reliance on their statements. The reported times varied wildly, and it was just as likely to have been another lone woman rather than Barbara Longman. She *had* driven one of the most popular colours of a very common car.

It was unfortunate that despite her good works in the town and her prominent links with several local organizations, none of the several people who had reported passing such a vehicle actually *knew* her by sight.

According to Recycled Rita, Barbara Longman had been in the habit of giving lifts to all and sundry, so it was possible that she might actually have picked up her murderer. The forensic boys were still going over her car, but Rafferty, increasingly desperate for a conclusive lead, as, one by one, his many theories had withered and died, knew he couldn't depend on one coming from that quarter.

The team searching the meadow had turned up nothing either, apart from a small amount of expected wind-blown litter. Of course, saliva-coated cigarette stubs, carelessly discarded by a tensely waiting murderer, were too much to hope for, but Rafferty felt it wasn't unreasonable to expect a *little* bit of help from the murderer's chosen killing field.

Frustrated on so many fronts, Rafferty was surprised when one area of frustration came to an end. They had tried on several occasions, without success, to talk to Hilary Shore again, but she was rarely at the house. Her visits seemed to be so fleeting that Rafferty was becoming convinced she was avoiding him. But they finally struck lucky that afternoon. She was on her way out in her car as Rafferty turned into the Shores' driveway and he had to brake sharply to avoid a collision. Llewellyn, who was becoming renowned at the station for the cautiousness of his driving, drew in a sharp breath at the near miss.

'All right. Keep your hair on,' Rafferty advised him. 'We missed her.' He ignored Llewellyn's muttered 'only just', got out of the car and approached the other vehicle.

'Mrs Shore. Glad I've managed to catch you. I wanted another word.'

Hilary Shore didn't look too happy about it, he noticed. Her voice lacked its previous flirtatious tone as she told him, 'I'm in rather a hurry, Inspector. Can't this wait?'

'I'm afraid not.' Their second interview had already waited long enough, as far as Rafferty was concerned. He didn't like being given the runaround. 'It's unfortunate that we seem to keep missing you.' Drily, he added, 'And I know, you being so fond of Mrs Longman and all, that you'll want to do whatever you can to help us catch her killer.'

She could hardly disagree with this. But her lips formed a sulky line as she nodded. 'Very well.' Engaging reverse, she executed a racy return to the house in her stylish if slightly dented sports model.

Llewellyn tutted his disapproval at this manoeuvre and commented on the dents. 'Looks like some poor devils haven't been so lucky.'

'Probably lacked my lightning reactions,' was Rafferty's quick-fire reply.

Llewellyn made a noise which sounded suspiciously like a snort and walked back to their own vehicle. Hilary Shore was waiting for them at the front door and led them into the drawing-room. As expected, it was opulent, and although like much of the rest of the house its walls were covered in dark panelling, this was offset by the three large and well-upholstered white sofas grouped around the fireplace. Cushions in jewel-bright primary colours were scattered the length of the sofas. Rafferty sensed the hand of the dead woman in here, as the room had a cheerful ambience that the rest of the house lacked. Perhaps, as the mistress of the house didn't seem interested, she had recently been given a free rein to make the sombre house more of a home, and had started in the obvious place.

Hilary Shore arranged herself on the sofa facing the fireplace and, with a moue of distaste, before bothering to invite them to sit down, flung the gaudy cushions from behind her back to the end of the sofa. The two policemen took a sofa apiece and Rafferty reflected that they looked like three ill-assorted party guests, each desperately hoping that some more congenial company would soon turn up. He hoped none did so before he had got the answers to his questions.

Hilary made a great show of consulting her watch, as though to remind them that her time was strictly limited. Rafferty took the hint.

'Now, Mrs Shore, on the day Mrs Longman was murdered, you said you were in London, first at a fashion show at Harvey Nichols, in Knightsbridge, and later in the day at your, em, aromatherapist.' She nodded, her expression suddenly watchful. 'You know, it's funny, but I got the impression that the two appointments were closer together than they in fact were,' he told her. 'But I've since discovered there was a gap of well over four hours between the two. Would you mind telling me what you were doing during that time?'

'Really, Inspector, what do you imagine I was doing?' Although she gave a deep, throaty chuckle as if amused at the absurdity of his question, Rafferty noticed her eyes had become increasingly wary. 'I lunched, of course, as one normally does at lunchtime.'

For four hours? Rafferty asked himself. 'Perhaps you could give me the name of the restaurant?'

She shrugged and told him, 'I forget. It wasn't one of my usual places. I know that it was dreadfully crowded and the service was appalling. They took simply ages to bring the quiche and salad I'd ordered.'

Rafferty persisted. 'If you could just give us a rough idea where it was, Mrs Shore. I imagine it was somewhere in Knightsbridge?'

She waved a hand airily. 'Yes, I'm sure it must have been. But after I left Harvey Nichols I did a little window shopping, and I'm sure you know what that's like, Inspector. You plunge about all over the place as items catch your eye.'

Very convenient, thought Rafferty, angered by what he sensed was a deliberate vagueness. That meant that half his officers would have to be tied up questioning the staff of the many restaurants in the area. Probably with no result to speak of. He gestured to Llewellyn to take over until he felt able to resume the questioning without revealing his anger. He sensed that, if he did so, she would consider his reaction a triumph of sorts and he didn't want to give her the satisfaction.

'How did you pay for lunch, Mrs Shore?' Llewellyn asked. 'Was it by cheque or cash?'

'Cash. Just as well I had the money, otherwise I'm sure I'd have been in there even longer.'

'And just how long *were* you in there?'

'Goodness, I don't know. Does it matter?' She gave another throaty laugh and crossed her legs, before adding, 'If I'd known two policemen were going to be so fascinated by my shopping trip I'd have taken notes.' In spite of her light remark, Rafferty felt sure she was trying to conceal something.

Her careless manner had put Llewellyn's back up, as Rafferty had known it would. Fortunately, anger took him in a different way to Rafferty, and the Welshman's voice was icily polite as he told her, 'We are investigating a murder, Mrs Shore. I'm sure I don't have to remind you that . . .'

She jumped up. 'Oh, for goodness' sake. It's not as if *I* killed her.' She ran her hands down her body and demanded, 'Do I look like a potential rapist?'

'Mrs Longman wasn't raped,' Llewellyn quietly reminded her.

Her hand waved this away as irrelevant. 'Obviously he was disturbed. Mentally *and* physically, I mean. You'll find it was some poor inadequate creature who attacked her, I'm sure. Probably one of those psychiatric patients that the government have thrown out of hospitals into the community.' She gave them a brittle smile. 'I don't want you to think I'm speaking ill of the dead, but no *adequate* man would choose to attack poor Barbara.' She smoothed her chic, and undoubtedly expensive, sleeveless silk dress with a satisfied expression. 'She was really terribly dowdy and had no interest at all in fashion. I tried to advise her, but'—she shrugged—'she preferred to spend her time in jeans and T-shirts. Said they were more practical. Practical!' The last word had a weight of contempt in its three syllables. 'Of course, even though she made no attempt to dress attractively, it was still foolhardy of her to traipse about the countryside on her own. I warned her that it was dangerous several times, but Barbara ignored me. She could be very headstrong.' She turned to Rafferty. 'If I were you, Inspector, I'd concentrate on the down-and-outs in the district. That's where you'll find your murderer, I'm sure.'

Rafferty didn't share her interest in fashion, or particularly want her advice. What he wanted were answers as to how she had spent the rest of that day, but he suspected that unless he got tough her remaining memories of last Thursday afternoon would be as vague as her sister-in-law's. Having got his temper back under control, he resumed the questioning. 'And after lunch, what did you do?'

She gave him a bright smile. 'More window shopping, I'm afraid.'

Rafferty sighed and wondered if spending money was the only thing that put an expression approaching animation on her face. If so, it was hardly surprising that with the heady first months of marriage long since past Charles Shore should treat her with something not far short of contempt.

'I saw this divine little suit in Harrods,' she enlarged. 'Black of course, and so simple, I thought it would—'

Rafferty cut her short. 'You used a charge card?'

She pulled a face. 'You must think me dreadfully extravagant, Inspector. I didn't buy it. Charles has been such a bore lately about the amount I spend on clothes and as I'd already purchased heavily at Harvey Nichols, I knew I'd risk a lecture if I bought anything else.' She sighed and, apparently oblivious of how callous she sounded, told them, 'It's such a shame, as it would have been perfect for poor Barbara's funeral.'

The pity Rafferty had previously felt for her had long since evaporated. Not only was he beginning to dislike her intensely, but he was also becoming increasingly annoyed at her evasive answers. He doubted that husbandly lectures would have bothered her, nor did he think it likely that she would have passed the greater part of an afternoon amongst the temptations of Knightsbridge without buying more clothes. If there was a woman alive capable of such self-restraint, and Rafferty doubted it, that woman certainly wasn't Hilary Shore. So, if she hadn't been pillaging the garment rails of the London stores, where *had* she been?

He decided to approach from another direction. Imbuing his voice with a compassion that was probably totally wasted on her, he remarked, 'It's been a dreadful business, hasn't it, this murder?' After one startled glance, she hastened to agree with him. 'Mrs Longman seems to have been a woman of many admirable qualities.' He watched her closely as he added, 'Your husband certainly seems to have thought highly of her.'

Her whole face seemed to tighten, as if she was struggling against the desire to blurt out some spiteful remark. Slowly, her expression relaxed again, and she allowed herself to comment, 'Charles can be a bit of a chauvinist, Inspector. He expected his needs to be put first and Barbara...well, she was one of those willing creatures who put her own needs way down the list; nothing was too much trouble. I think most men would have found such self-sacrifice admirable. She was an old-fashioned woman in many ways.'

'What about Mr Longman? Didn't he object to his wife turning herself into a servant for Mr Shore's benefit? Most husbands would expect to come first with their wives.'

She gave him a pitying look. 'You've met Henry, Inspector. Do you really expect him to have had the nerve to interfere? He's in awe of Charles, as most people are. Poor Harry, I used to tease him that he and I both had to play second fiddle. Him to Barbara's self-sacrifice and good works and me to Charles's business empire and his—' She stopped abruptly, an annoyed expression on her face, as if she had been about to say something she would regret.

'You were saying,' he prompted. '"And his..."?' Although Rafferty guessed what she was going to say, he wanted to hear her say it. However, this desire was to be denied him, as Henry Longman chose that moment to blunder into the room. As expected, when he saw them grouped around the fireplace, he immediately began to back out, uttering awkward apologies as he went.

Whether Henry's abject manner irritated her, or whether she wanted to use his presence as an excuse to escape further questioning, Hilary, after giving Rafferty an arch look, called out to him, 'For God's sake, Henry, come in. You do live here after all.' She consulted her watch again. 'And I *did* tell the inspector I had an appointment...' She again glanced at Rafferty, as if daring him to refuse her. 'So if you've finished with me...?'

Rafferty objected to being manipulated. He particularly objected to being manipulated by this woman and it made him stubborn. If she could make use of Henry, so could he, and, he reflected, a double whammy was always more satisfying that the singular variety. Perhaps it was time he frightened the pair of them? They had already colluded once to lie to him. It was possible there was something else they had agreed to keep quiet.

'You wanted to know why I'm asking so many questions, Mrs Shore,' he remarked slowly. 'I've decided to satisfy your curiosity. We believe that whoever murdered Mrs Longman knew her well—very well. They knew her habits, her interests, even the family's unlisted telephone number. I believe that whoever that person was deliberately tried to move the suspicion on to that serial killer in Suffolk. I asked myself why they should do that?' Unblushingly he added a patent untruth. 'And do you know, it didn't take me long to come up with an answer. It convinced me that the killer was closer to home. Much closer. Maybe even *in* her home.'

He paused to let that sink in, before he continued. 'So perhaps now you can see why I'm interested in the members of this family who have been particularly evasive about where they were last Thursday afternoon.' A swift glance passed between Hilary and Henry. Rafferty, having planted the seed of fear, got up and made for the door. 'I'll say good-day to you both.'

'Wait.' She stood up, fiddling anxiously with her belt buckle as she came towards him. 'If I tell you where I was that afternoon, will you promise not to tell my husband? He—wouldn't understand.'

Rafferty wondered what else he and Charles Shore were being kept in the dark about? First Henry had lied to him, now Hilary. How many other members of the family, before confiding their secrets, would demand that he didn't reveal them to Charles?

'I'm afraid I can't make any promises, Mrs Shore,' he told her, as he came back and sat down. 'But of course if I feel what you say to me is irrelevant to my inquiry, I shouldn't think there would be any need to mention it.'

She nodded. Resuming her seat, she said, 'I admit, I was doing a little more than window shopping that day.' Rafferty waited. 'I...' She stopped fiddling with her belt and now started on one of her earrings. 'I went to see a private detective.' She intercepted his surprised glance towards Henry and told him, 'Oh, Henry knows. Naturally, I told him all about it.'

Why *naturally?* Rafferty wondered and again he waited for the rest to come out. It was turning into something of an around the houses business.

'I've believed for some time that my husband has been having an affair. You don't know what a strain I've been under, suspecting, but not knowing for certain. I decided to do something about it. I had to. I couldn't go on as I was. I needed to know, one way or the other, even if I decided to do nothing.' She leaned towards him in a mute appeal for sympathy. With any other woman, Rafferty would have taken it as a natural gesture and done his best to accommodate her, but with Hilary Shore, he sensed the move was calculated. It made him more questioning of her motives, both in going to the detective agency in the first place and then in confiding the agency's discoveries to Henry. The indecisive Henry was the last person to sort out another's troubles; he couldn't sort out his own. Presumably, Rafferty mused, Barbara Longman had something to do with this mysterious business. Given her character, he would be interested to discover what it was. He gestured for Hilary to continue.

She squeezed a few tears out before she went on. Rafferty managed not to be too affected by them. 'As I said, I've suspected for some time that my husband was seeing another woman.' She raised damp eyes to his face. 'You can't imagine how upsetting such a suspicion is, Inspector. I had no one to turn to, only Henry. He's been such a comfort.' She spared Henry a grateful smile and laid a fleeting hand on his leg. Rafferty didn't miss the way Henry flinched from her touch, though Hilary seemed unaware of it. 'And then, of course, as Henry was already aware of my suspicions, when I found out the worst, I couldn't keep it from him. I felt awful having to tell him, after he'd been so kind.'

'Are you saying that this agency discovered the name of the woman your husband had been seeing?'

She nodded. 'That's where I went on the afternoon that I was up in town.' She paused and gave him a brave smile from her limited repertoire. 'It was *Barbara* he was seeing. And, although I already had my suspicions, you can imagine what a shock it was to have them confirmed. I knew Henry planned to skip work that afternoon, and I didn't want to call him at the house in case someone else listened on one of the extensions, so I called his car phone. After ringing the car number several times, I finally reached him about 2.30 p.m.' That must have been the telephone conversation that Mrs Watson had mentioned, thought Rafferty. With the news Hilary Shore had to impart, it was no wonder he'd looked so unwell.

'Thinking about it now, I know I should never have broken the news to him like that. But it was the shock, you see. I hardly knew what I was doing, but I had to confide in someone and Henry was as concerned as I was. When I got him, it all just came pouring out. Poor Henry.' She touched his leg again. 'It must have hit him like a sledgehammer.'

Rafferty found it difficult to hide his dislike. 'I'd like the name and address of this detective agency, please, Mrs Shore.'

'Of course. I feel it's engraved on my heart.' Radiating heartache and malice in about equal measure, she gave them the details. Now that her confession was out of the way, she looked rather pleased with herself. It wasn't difficult to understand why. If her story checked out, she was in the clear, but her revelations gave Henry a very strong motive for wanting to murder his wife.

Rafferty turned to Henry and breathed in sharply. Henry's hands gripped one of the gaily coloured cushions so hard that his knuckles had whitened and although Rafferty spoke his name, Henry didn't seem to hear. He just sat, gripping the cushion tighter and tighter, his gaze fixed on the wedding photograph of himself and Barbara that sat on the mantelpiece. It was as if he was in some other world, some other time, and it was only by standing in front of the photograph and breaking Henry's concentration that Rafferty could gain his attention. 'Mr Longman? Can you confirm what Mrs Shore has just told us? That she broke the news to you about your wife's affair about two thirty on the day she died?'

Henry nodded. He seemed to feel a need to justify himself, as he added, 'I didn't want to lie to you, but once we discovered the next day that Barbara had been murdered Hilary convinced me it would be foolish to do otherwise. At least I told you the truth when I said I felt unwell. You can imagine how much worse I felt when Hilary broke the news about my wife. I was in such a state, I didn't want to face anyone, so I went to my studio, where I knew I could be alone.' He put his head in his hands, and his voice, muffled now, continued. 'I practically collapsed when I got there. I couldn't think straight. I didn't know what to do.'

'You didn't consider tackling your wife? Asking her if it was true?'

Henry raised his head, his face was flushed and he glanced at Hilary as if for moral support.

She told them, 'I persuaded him it wouldn't be a good idea. I was scared Barbara would run straight to Charles. You don't know how vindictive he can be; he hates to be caught in the wrong.' She gave a brittle laugh. 'He's used to getting away with things, you see. He prides himself on it. He's capable of being completely ruthless, and I was worried Henry might lose his home and his job as well as his wife.'

Rafferty found her concern for Henry less than convincing. What she had been worried about was her own position. If Henry had challenged either his wife or Charles, it would have come out that Hilary had employed a private detective to spy on her husband. It wasn't difficult to imagine Charles Shore's likely reaction to that.

'I was fairly sure I would be able to get Henry fixed up with a job with my brother, so he would be in a position to take Barbara away from here, but it needed time to arrange. He's got his own business and is doing very well, so I've got one thing to thank Charles for. He set my brother up when we were first married.' Her voice was hate-filled as she added, 'Before he began to find other men's wives more to his taste.'

The sleek make-up on her face seemed to dissolve, the lines on her skin became more prominent, and Rafferty had a glimpse of what she would look like when she was old, and spite, discontent and self-obsession were permanently marked on her face. As though aware that Rafferty had witnessed what only her morning mirror was allowed to see, she turned away.

Henry broke in. 'Perhaps if I'd been more like Charles, Barbara would never had strayed.' With a sigh, he turned to Rafferty and the words began to spill out, slowly at first, and then more quickly, as if he had been bottling them up for too long. 'But I'm not anything like Charles. What Hilary told you is true. I didn't tackle Barbara. I didn't have the guts. I couldn't face her, not when I was such a wreck. I'd never understood what she saw in me, you see, and it was like a miracle when she agreed to marry me, especially when my first marriage had been so unhappy. I was scared if I pleaded with her not to leave me, she might begin to despise me. Everyone else seems to. I was terrified I might lose her altogether if I challenged her. And, of course, I'd promised Hilary I wouldn't do anything rash. The whole business affected her future every bit as much as it did mine.'

Rafferty said nothing, but, given Henry's character, it sounded plausible. His do-nothing mentality would be scared to do anything at all in case it made everything far worse. As Hilary had said, he might easily lose everything. There again, after finding out that his wife was having an affair, he might not care. The latest revelations certainly provided Henry with the motive that he had previously lacked.

'I thought I knew Barbara. I trusted her.' Henry looked bemused, hurt, angry, as he turned to Rafferty. 'Even now, if it wasn't for what Hilary told me the detective agency had discovered, I'd have been willing to swear she was totally faithful to me.'

Hilary turned on him, as though his loyalty to his dead wife infuriated her. 'Don't you think it's time you faced facts? Barbara played up to Charles for all she was worth once she sensed he wanted her, I don't know how you never noticed.'

Her words seemed to make Henry more bemused than ever. He simply sat, shaking his head as he had when Rafferty had told him his wife was dead, as if the physical denial of his wife's faithlessness would somehow make it true.

With an exasperated expression, Hilary turned away from him. 'You're a fool. There's not a woman alive—or dead,' she added spitefully, 'who wouldn't have got their claws into Charles given the chance. Barbara and Charles were having an affair, right under your nose, take my word for it. And your wife might be dead, but my husband is very much alive and I intend to hang on to him. All I ask is that you keep your mouth shut about their affair.' Thoroughly browbeaten, Henry just nodded.

'What's going on here?'

They all turned, shocked to see Charles Shore framed in the doorway. 'What mischief are you up to now?' he demanded of his wife.

FOURTEEN

RAFFERTY WONDERED how long Shore had been listening outside the door. Not that it really mattered, because, judging from the furious look he directed at his wife, he'd certainly heard enough. Hilary's shocked face told him that she realized it, too. Her face had drained of colour. She stared at her husband as if mesmerized, like a rabbit caught in a car's headlights, incapable of doing anything except shake her head in useless denial.

'I don't know what game you think you're playing,' he told her, 'but I'm going to put a stop to it. I knew you were jealous of Barbara, but I didn't think even you would make up such lies about her now she's dead.' He turned to Henry. 'Barbara and I were not having an affair. God knows how much I wanted her, but she turned me down flat. So you can hate me if you want, but you've no reason to hate Barbara, whatever this bitch says.' Surprisingly, this information failed to remove the look of utter misery from Henry's face.

Charles Shore was reputed to be a man of swift decision, and as he fixed his wife with a basilisk stare his next words confirmed it. 'Now that I've dealt with your lies, I'll deal with you. I want a divorce,' he told her. 'And if you know what's good for you, you'll agree and not make me wait for my freedom.'

Hilary gasped, but she recovered swiftly. 'Damn you, Charles, you can't divorce me. I won't let you. I know too much about you and . . .'

He didn't bother arguing with her. Quietly, he warned her that if she tried to threaten him, he had the power to make her wish she had never been born. She seemed to believe him, for her face became suddenly haggard and although her eyes glittered with frustrated fury she kept her mouth shut.

'God, how did I ever manage to persuade myself I loved you?' Charles seemed to marvel at his own folly. He slumped down on the white sofa beside Llewellyn, as if, now that the decision to split had been made, it had drained all his usual vitality. 'You're nothing but a vindictive, amoral, and over-priced slut. From the first time I set eyes on Barbara I realized I'd short-changed myself by marrying you. She intrigued me, enchanted me. She had qualities that I'd never encountered in a woman before, kindness, honesty, goodness, with a natural beauty that didn't need cosmetics, because it came from within. She seemed chaste, untouchable as a nun, and I wanted her.'

He glanced round at their stunned expressions and laughed. 'I know, it's ridiculous, isn't it? The thought of the wheeling-dealing Charles Shore falling so desperately in love takes some believing. All my life, I've chased profit, success, the next megadeal, and I never realized there could be something even more exhilarating—love. Of course, as soon as I met her, I wanted her for myself, and I tried to convince Henry that she was nothing but a gold-digger, but he wouldn't listen, unfortunately. When that failed, I

even offered them a home here after their marriage so
that she would be near me. I loved her so much.' He
closed his eyes, as if he didn't want to witness their
expressions as with difficulty the admission, 'And she
preferred Henry,' was torn out of him. 'Can you even
begin to imagine what that did to me?'

Softly, Rafferty questioned him. 'But if you loved
her, why did you—?' He broke off and glanced
guiltily at Llewellyn. Me and my big mouth, he
thought.

Shore frowned. 'Go on—why did I what?'

'Well, we've discovered that Mrs Longman suspected your chemical firm of discharging into the
river several years ago. I gather it happened shortly
after she met you and it's been suggested that—'

'That I might have been doing it again?' With a
weary expression, Shore brushed his hair back from
his brow. 'Tell me, Inspector—have you found a
shred of evidence to suggest that might be true?'

Rafferty glanced at Llewellyn before he told him.
'No, not so far.'

'Nor will you. Because there isn't any.'

'Then why did you buy up the local newspaper
group?'

'I'm a businessman, Inspector. I buy businesses.
And, in case you hadn't noticed, amongst other interests, I own several newspaper groups; that one was
just a natural expansion and its purchase had been
planned for some time. It had nothing to do with any
cover-ups, whatever you might think. I loved Barbara, I tell you, and when I promised her my firm
wouldn't pollute the river, I meant it. How was I to
know when I first met her that she was so involved

with Green politics? Once I knew how strongly she felt about such things, I made sure she would have no reason to regard me as an enemy. Anyway, even if I had polluted the river recently and Barbara found out about it, do you really think that would be a reason for me to kill her?'

Rafferty took a deep breath, ignored Llewellyn's restraining glance, and plunged on. 'It might. If she got in the way of your political ambitions. Especially once you knew you had no chance with her.'

Shore took his accusation surprisingly well. 'I don't think you've ever been deeply in love, have you, Inspector?'

Rafferty was about to deny it. But then, as he thought back over his life, over his early and mostly unhappy marriage to Angie, he realized Shore was right. 'No,' he admitted. 'I never have.'

Shore nodded. 'I thought not. Because, if you had, you would know I could never have hurt Barbara. Never. Besides, I'd already decided not to stand for selection a day or two before her death. Not that I expect you to believe that—I've no proof. And for the record, I wanted Barbara so much, I was prepared to wait as long as it took to get her.' With an unconscious arrogance, he told them, 'I always get what I want in the end.'

He made no further attempt to defend himself. Instead, he leaned back and closed his eyes. His skin had a grey tinge and he looked much older than his thirty years, as if the strain of concealing his true feelings for Barbara from her husband, his wife, and the police, the pain of her rejection and then the trauma of her violent death had suddenly become too much for him. He seemed much more human, much more vulnerable and suddenly Rafferty felt dreadfully sorry for him. Catching Llewellyn's eye, he made for the door.

Once safely out of earshot, Llewellyn asked, 'Did you believe Shore when he said he wasn't having an affair with Mrs Longman?'

'I don't know. I get the impression he had always thought love was for wimps like Henry, but whether he bedded her or not, his first grand passion obviously hit him hard. I should think Shore would be used to having any woman he wanted—probably despised them for it. He would have plenty of opportunity on his business trips. I doubt he was the man to disregard opportunity when it presented itself and, whatever his wife says, I'm sure she was well aware of the other women, and was prepared to put up with them. Obviously she sensed some stronger emotion than mere lust this time, and it frightened her. That's probably why she was in such a rush to tell Henry the news.'

Llewellyn nodded. 'Shore insists she was lying when she told Henry that Shore and Barbara were having an affair. But why would she lie?'

'Use your common sense, Taff. She knew her husband and his skill in getting his own way; and he wanted Barbara. Whatever Barbara felt about it was irrelevant. By convincing Henry the two *were* having an affair, she probably hoped to encourage him to take Barbara away, out of Shore's orbit. Maybe she even hoped Henry would have a brainstorm and kill her. But whether she suspected there was a chance of getting rid of her rival quite so finally, she's managed to turn Longman into suspect number one.

'Anyway, we'll hopefully find out if anything was going on between Shore and Henry's wife from that agency. You can drive up there this afternoon. And apart from finding out if Mrs Shore was telling the truth about her visit there, check when she arrived and left and exactly what the agency found out. I want all the juicy details—if there are any.'

WHEN LLEWELLYN still hadn't returned from the London agency by 7.00 p.m., Rafferty decided to have an early night; the first for nearly a week. As soon as he reached home, he ran a hot bath and a cold whiskey. Shedding his clothes, he eased himself into the hot water with relief. Bliss.

He sipped the Jameson's whiskey and sank lower, letting his eyes close and his mind drift, hoping that, this time, the conditions would be more conducive to intuitive deductive leaps. But something his mother had said broke his purposeful repose, and he sat up slowly, as it occurred to him that her words had inadvertently prodded him into coming up with the most unlikely theory yet on the murder. As if he didn't have enough of *those* to keep him busy for a month of Sundays, he groaned. He wondered how many more he would have to go through before he nailed the killer?

What was it she had said? Something about red roses symbolizing love and yellow roses symbolizing the waning of love. Was it possible, he wondered, that *other* flowers also had meanings? According to the botanists at the lab, the flower in the dead woman's hands had been a marigold, a cultivated marigold which would not therefore have grown wild in the meadow. Before, he had dismissed its presence there as one of those inexplicable things that every case seemed to throw up, but was it possible it could have more significance than that? he wondered. And if so, for whom in this case did flowers hold the most significance? Who else but Thomson? He and Barbara had fought over flowers—had she died over them, too?

Rafferty opened his eyes, and as he gazed admiringly at the DIY tiling surrounding the bath he asked himself sardonically, if there *was* anything in the theory, how likely was it Thomson would use a *flower* to express his feelings? Not very, he decided. And if that was the case, could the flower really be a clue of any sort? Anyway, what sort of message would the farmer be likely to have for Barbara? 'Up yours' seemed the most likely, and Rafferty doubted that any flower held such a meaning.

There was something else against the theory, he realized. Why would Thomson decide to kill her now? Presumably the protection on the wild flowers had been in place for years. Why would Thomson *suddenly* become enraged by Barbara's insistence that he abide by it? Besides, Rafferty had a vague idea that the EC actively encouraged farmers to leave fields uncultivated. Didn't they have some policy called 'set apart' or 'set aside', that compensated them for the trouble entailed in doing nothing to stop a particular piece of land reverting to nature? He wasn't exactly sure what it covered as the Common Market and its endless regulations had never greatly interested him.

He realized the whole thing sounded about as likely as the Inland Revenue giving refunds to good payers and he dismissed the idea. He had been right the first time—the marigold was just one of those inexplicable things the fates liked to throw in the path of the investigating policemen. Why did his ma have to put these ideas in his head? he demanded. As if he didn't have enough to think about. He drank some more of his whiskey, turned on the hot tap with his toes, and sank lower in the water. With a sigh, he decided he at least ought to check out the compensation angle.

'WHAT DID YOU find out at that detective agency?' Rafferty asked as soon as Llewellyn came through the door the next morning. 'Did they confirm what Mrs Shore said?'

'The chap I spoke to—when he eventually returned to the office—confirmed she was *there*, and why—after a little persuasion. But the receptionist thought she arrived well before her appointment time. She said it was more like 1.30 p.m. than 2.00 p.m. She remembers, as Mrs Shore said she was in a hurry and insisted on seeing Mr Skeets, one of the partners, straight away. She was out again after only ten minutes.'

Rafferty raised his eyebrows. 'In a hurry to resume her leisurely window shopping, no doubt. And her with no money to spend.'

'There's something else odd about her visit. According to this Skeets chap, although Charles Shore *had* apparently met a blonde several times in town, it wasn't Barbara Longman. He said there was no suggestion of any illicit liaison between her and Shore, which certainly supports Charles Shore's version. Skeets was insistent that he told Mrs Shore there was no foundation for her suspicions about that, at least.'

Rafferty nodded. 'What sort of an outfit are they?'

'They're quite a small concern, only a two-man business, but they struck me as being efficient.'

Rafferty gazed thoughtfully into space. 'It's my guess that she believed her position as Shore's wife was threatened. Of course she was aware of the depth of her husband's feelings for Barbara, and whether Barbara gave him any encouragement or not, Shore is an attractive man. I'm sure if he set out to charm, few women would be able to resist him. Certainly I doubt if his wife thought so. She judges other women's motives by her own, and I'm sure she felt that no woman in her right mind would stay with a man like Henry when they had the chance to land Charles Shore.

'She simply couldn't believe that Barbara wouldn't prove as grasping and manipulative as she is herself. So she came up with a plan to remove Barbara from Charles's orbit. All she had to do was to convince Henry that Charles and Barbara were having an affair. I imagine she worked on him for weeks before she "broke the bad news". And once that was done, she knew just how to make him keep quiet about it. She terrified him into believing that if he found the guts to challenge Barbara, she would leave him. In such a situation, Hilary would have been confident that the indecisive Henry would not only be incapable of any firm action, but that he would be only too happy for Hilary to make his decisions for him. She was even in the process of organizing him another job.'

'And then Barbara was murdered.'

'As you say, and then Barbara was murdered. I wonder which one of our little ménage killed her?'

'You think it was definitely one of those three?'

Rafferty shrugged. 'What do you think? Hilary Shore was certainly in an all-fired hurry to leave that agency. Can she really have been in such a rush to telephone Henry? Or had she decided that killing Barbara was a great improvement on her original plan? If she left the agency at 1.40 p.m., she had time to return to Elmhurst, leave that telephone message, and kill Barbara before driving back to London for her appointment with Mrs Armadi, especially at the speed she drives. Her voice is deep enough to be taken for a man's over the phone. As for Henry and Charles, they were on the spot, with no alibi worthy of the name. Maybe, for once, Henry managed to make a decision all on his own and act on it?'

'What about Shore?'

'A man like that doesn't fall in love with such a bang more than once in a lifetime. He had never wanted anything in his life as much as he wanted Barbara and she rejected him. Do you remember what his sister said about him?'

Slowly, Llewellyn nodded. 'That if he couldn't have something, he was quite capable of destroying it.'

Rafferty nodded. 'It's possible Charles Shore, like his father before him, decided that "the fact that I wish it is reason enough for doing it". Or, in his case, "If I can't have her, nobody else will".'

Llewellyn sighed and sat down rather heavily. 'And all we have to do is find out which possibility is the right one and then prove it.'

Rafferty gave him a suspiciously bright smile. 'That's all. Got it in one.'

Had Charles, spurned by Barbara as he had been by the puppy in his youth, chosen to destroy her? Rafferty wondered again. He was certainly ruthless enough and—if he had lied about deciding to remove his name from the Tory selection list, he would have a double motive for getting rid of her.

Then there was Henry; weak, ineffectual, indecisive Henry. No wonder he hadn't seemed overjoyed at the prospect of Barbara having a baby; after what Hilary had told him, he couldn't have been sure it was his. Although he had claimed to have felt too sickened by Hilary's disclosures, too bound by his promise to think about tackling Barbara, the pregnancy made it more likely that he had done so—with devastating results. Henry had a great capacity for hiding from reality. If he had killed her, he would hide from the truth, might even manage to convince himself that he hadn't done it.

As Rafferty had concluded earlier in the case, the discovery of his wife's supposed infidelity would be the one thing likely to stir him out of his lethargy. The one thing likely to kindle in him sufficient rage to overcome his natural indecision. He would, presumably, know where Mrs Griffiths kept her car keys. He could have disguised his voice as easily as anyone else. And he would know that the au pair had a habit of borrowing Shore's mobile phone, and that she would be blamed when it went missing. It was possible they had taken Henry's weak character a little too much at face value. Because, although such people were often afraid of expressing their own anger, fearful of the consequences to themselves if they should dare to give way to it, when something enraged them beyond bearing, they were likely to go completely out of control.

The trouble with that scenario was that Rafferty still found it hard to imagine Henry in the role of murderer. His picture of an out of control Henry didn't jell with him calmly leaving that telephone message. The two simply didn't go together. If such a rage had taken hold of Henry, it would spill out of him in an unpremeditated fashion. He would come out of his brainstorm to find his faithless wife dead at his feet, and would probably be so stunned by his own actions that he would be completely incapable of concealing his guilt.

Rafferty turned to the third of the trio and found himself considering Hilary Shore with rather more interest than he had hitherto taken in her. If, out of that entire household, Charles Shore was the member most capable of murder, his wife ran him a very close second. She could easily be taken for a man on a telephone. She hated Barbara, feared Charles's obsession with her, and she had a lot to lose. If she had suspected that Charles hoped to divorce her in order to marry Barbara, she would presumably get a generous settlement. But Rafferty suspected that whatever she received it wouldn't be enough for her. She liked the prominence she had as Charles's wife. She liked rubbing shoulders with politicians and society people, knowing the women envied her and the men wanted her. Without Charles, she was nothing out of the ordinary. Her looks, like her personality, were of the shallow variety that were dependent on youth. Without Charles, she was a nobody, a failed actress of little talent and fast-fading looks. He had been the important one, the one it would pay their friends and acquaintances to keep in with. If he demanded his ex-wife be shunned, then shunned she would be. She would receive no more elegantly designed invitations to chic dinner parties, no more first nights, or weekends at the stately piles of aristocrats, and Rafferty was sure such things were very important to Hilary.

Even if Charles wasn't vindictive enough to insist she be cold-shouldered, Rafferty suspected that Hilary had merely been tolerated because of her husband. She was a selfish, shallow woman, whom maturity had failed to improve. If she lost Charles, she would fall back into that obscurity from which he had plucked her.

From what Charles had said, Barbara had knocked him sideways. He had never experienced such a depth of love for anyone. In dying, Barbara had taken away the hope that she would change her mind. Without that hope, the longed-for reward of her love, would he have bothered to put himself and his children through the upheaval of a divorce? If he hadn't overheard his wife's lies about Barbara, he might easily have left things as they were and simply thrown himself even more into his business life.

Rafferty suspected Hilary Shore would have been willing to risk a great deal to ensure the status quo, to avoid a life where she could expect to be either shunned or patronized. How ironic if in order to keep her husband and her position she had killed Barbara but had then lost it all, anyway.

Rafferty glanced up from his musings to discover that Llewellyn was staring into space, a more morose expression than usual on his face. He deduced that his sergeant's thought processes had followed a similar line to his own and had also failed to come up with a conclusive reason for pinning a murder on any one of them.

'Cheer up, Dafyd. It could be worse. We nearly had another theory on the murder to add to the growing pile, but I managed to work out, all by myself, that it was a non-starter.' He explained the theory about the marigold that his ma had sparked off and how he had at first believed it could put Thomson more firmly in the frame. He kept to himself the message about Llewellyn's choice of roses—he might be glad of that little pearl the next time Llewellyn got uppity.

'No one can say I'm not prepared to consider all the angles,' Rafferty grinned. 'But I think that one's a little off the wall, as our American cousins say. Can you imagine a man like Thomson saying anything with flowers? The Poet Laureate he's not. Though, to clear his name off the list once and for all, I'll get on to the Ministry of Agriculture and find out exactly where Thomson stood with regard to that meadow. I want to see if he received any compensation for not being able to use it. If he did, he had no axe to grind, and therefore, no reason for murdering that particular victim.'

'Still, it's an interesting idea,' Llewellyn remarked, as if anxious that Rafferty's least likely theory shouldn't have *too* easy a death. 'And a countryman would be more likely to be familiar with the language of flowers. Learned at his mother's knee, perhaps?'

'Have you *seen* his mother?'

Llewellyn shook his head. 'She was out when I called to question Thomson, if you remember.'

'Terrible old woman. If she'd lived a few hundred years ago, she'd have been burnt as a witch. Even so, I doubt she'd have much knowledge of something like the language of flowers.' He snorted. 'She seemed to find the English language difficult enough. The only use *either* of them are likely to have for flowers would be to poison someone with 'em. A dose of deadly nightshade would be more in their line.'

'Mm.' Llewellyn stroked his jaw, gazed thoughtfully into space, and proceeded, to Rafferty's dismay, to launch into another lecture. 'Bit obvious perhaps? Especially when there are other, more seemingly innocuous plants she could use. It's surprising how many ordinary plants and flowers *are* poisonous. For instance, did you know that the leaves of tomatoes and rhubarb are dangerous when eaten? Even the superfluous parts of the common old potato can do unpleasant things to the stomach.'

Was there a subject Llewellyn *didn't* know something about? Rafferty wondered irritably. Better still, one that he wasn't prepared to lecture *him* on? So much for his attempt to inject a bit of cheer into the proceedings. Conscious that they were no further forward in catching the murderer than they had been from day one, and that both Superintendent Bradley and the media were becoming daily more critical of his handling of the case, Rafferty had no qualms about pricking the Welshman's knowledge bubble. 'As the victim was smothered, not poisoned, I don't see that it much matters, do you?'

Llewellyn chose to ignore Rafferty's sarcasm. 'Charles Shore's portable phone went missing *before* the murder,' he began. 'I know his wife took it for granted that the au pair had borrowed it, as it was found in her room, but it could just as easily have been taken by another member of the household and put in the Italian girl's room to hide the fact. It might be worth checking what numbers were called on it the day of the murder.' Damn it, thought Rafferty, he'd meant to do that. It was annoying that he'd forgotten all about it. 'It's certainly a coincidence that it went missing the day before the murder,' Llewellyn went on. 'I'll have a chat with the au pair and...' Rafferty grinned as his sergeant's voice petered out.

'Have you just remembered that our Carlotta eats innocent young Welshmen for breakfast? Perhaps Mrs Griffiths will agree to chaperone you? Go on,' he teased. 'You'll be safe enough. After all,' he added, mischievously, 'you're practically engaged to Maureen.' At this, Llewellyn's lugubrious countenance looked even more worried, and Rafferty exploded, 'Oh, for Christ's sake! All right, *I'll* speak to the wretched girl. While I'm doing that, and in order to clear Thomson off the suspects list once and for all, *you* can contact the Ministry of Agriculture. I want you to ask about the EC set-aside policy. See if Thomson lost out financially by being unable to plant crops in that meadow.'

He'd intended to ring them himself, but the prospect of playing pass the parcel—*him* being the parcel—with a lot of bureaucrats was more than he could stomach. Anyway, Llewellyn probably had a contact there from his university days. 'If you're right and she *didn't* borrow the phone, then whoever did could have been the person who left the message for Barbara Longman.'

'That possibility had occurred to me, sir,' said Llewellyn. 'And apart from Mrs Griffiths, who was the only person who would know where to find her when she left the house?'

'The person who left the message,' Rafferty replied obligingly. 'It's worth looking into, as we haven't been able to trace this so-called chap from the Conservation Society who was *supposed* to have left the message. All their members and their friends and relations deny phoning here that afternoon.'

He took the car keys from Llewellyn. 'Seeing as you're going to be idling at the office while I've got the unenviable task of chatting up the lovely Carlotta, when you've persuaded the servants at Whitehall to be civil, you can also find out which company Charles rented his portable phone from. Get on to them and ask them to check their records for the numbers rung on it last Thursday. It'll be interesting if the Shore's home number *does* show up.'

Before Llewellyn had a chance to even open his mouth, Rafferty decided to pass on his ma's grievance now rather than later. He thought it was about time he got *some* satisfaction out of this blasted case. 'By the way, what on earth possessed you to buy Maureen *yellow* roses for her birthday?' he asked. 'Surely, with all that useless knowledge you've got stuffed in your head, you know they symbolize the waning of love?'

Llewellyn's jaw dropped. Happy that he'd had the final word for a change, Rafferty turned and closed the office door firmly behind him before the Welshman managed to find his voice.

FIFTEEN

'I RANG the ministry of Agriculture,' said Llewellyn, later that day, when Rafferty had returned to the office. 'And according to the chap I spoke to, the set-aside regulations can be abused. Farmers are supposed to leave fields fallow on a rotation basis, but some set aside their least fertile land permanently— land that would be unproductive and unlikely to be used for crops anyway.'

'And were you able to find out if friend Thomson claims this compensation?'

Llewellyn nodded. 'The chap at the Ministry checked and got back to me just before you returned. Thomson's received compensation since the regulations were implemented. And, according to one of his neighbours, it's for the same piece of land— Tiffey Meadow. He boasts about it, apparently.'

'I bet it amused him to make an issue out of it with the Conservation Society, when he didn't want to plant in it anyway.' Rafferty frowned. 'I wonder—as the meadow is protected under the Wildlife and Countryside Act—whether he's *entitled* to claim compensation under the set-aside rules?'

'Do you want me to get back on to the Ministry and find out?' queried Llewellyn.

Rafferty shook his head. 'No. It's not important. He might be an unpleasant bugger, but I'm not going to bring myself down to his level by grassing on him to the bureaucrats. Let them do their own dirty work. You've found out what I wanted to know. Namely, that whether he's entitled to the compensation or not Thomson hasn't been losing out financially from being unable to use that meadow. Rather takes away any strong motive for being more than gratuitously unpleasant to Mrs Longman, doesn't it? By the way, I had a word with little Carlotta. She was adamant that she *hadn't* taken the mobile phone. Became quite passionate about it, with lots of heaving bosom, lyrical Italian and enough tears to raise the water table. Amazing sight. Did you manage to find out if anyone used the mobile phone to dial the Shores' home number that day?'

Llewellyn nodded. 'They did. And I found out something else as well.'

'Oh yes?' He looked remarkably pleased with himself, Rafferty noticed. As far as he was aware, they had no reasons to be cheerful; their discoveries so far were hardly earthshattering, as the super had already told him, at considerable length. But then, the Welshman was naturally contrary. He was probably only looking forward to breaking more bad news, Rafferty told himself grimly, painfully aware that he was running out of ideas and short on proof for the ones he did have. None of the family cars had been seen near the meadow. No one had seen anything.

'You know you were interested in the language of flowers, sir—Joseph?' Llewellyn went on.

'*Was* interested, you mean. I told you that little idea was a dead duck.' And he would prefer to give it a decent burial. To stop Llewellyn harping on about it, he observed sharply, 'As you discovered Thomson was compensated for not planting in that meadow, the flower theory is nothing more than a red herring.' Another one—if he went on like this, he consoled himself, he could always start a fish farm with the bloody things. 'I suggest we forget that damn marigold. We've got plenty of other things to occupy us. I doubt if we'll ever discover what it was doing in the victim's hands, anyway.'

Undiscouraged, Llewellyn persisted. 'Actually, I think I may have done just that.'

Warily, Rafferty raised his head. 'Oh?'

As if attempting to peer over a lecture hall lectern, Llewellyn raised himself to his full height of 5′ 9″ before he continued. 'As we know, that particular variety of marigold doesn't grow in Tiffey Meadow. It's a cultivated not a wild variety, which means that Barbara Longman couldn't have pulled it up as she struggled with her killer. It's obvious that *someone* brought it to the meadow, but why would the victim do such a thing? She was only stopping by there on her way to the rehearsal of the play. She was presumably in a hurry, so was hardly likely to pick flowers from her garden. The only feasible explanation, as far as I can see, is that her *murderer* must have picked it, brought it to the scene and deliberately put it between her fingers.'

Rafferty frowned. 'But who? *Why?* Tell me that and I might be prepared to listen. We've discounted Thomson. Can you suggest anyone else in this case to whom flowers hold such great significance?'

'Who else but the victim herself?'

The Welshman's usually sallow cheeks were flushed. Rafferty had seldom seen him so keyed up and he began to catch a little of his sergeant's enthusiasm himself. 'Go on, then,' he encouraged. 'Tell me the rest of this great discovery of yours. If I don't get some definite answers soon, I think I'll burst.'

But Llewellyn wasn't to be rushed. He apparently intended to savour his moment of triumph. 'As to the why—I've got an acquaintance at Essex University who's an expert on sixteenth-century romantic poetry as well as the Victorian flower language,' he explained. 'According to him, in the language of flowers, the marigold that Barbara clutched signified *grief.*' He met Rafferty's eyes and they gazed at one another for some seconds before Llewellyn added softly, 'My studies of psychology tend me to the belief that the murderer, knowing how important flowers were to Mrs Longman, used the symbolism of the flower in order to seek her absolution for his crime.'

Slowly, Rafferty nodded. 'Could be. And who's the person most likely to suffer grief from her murder? The one most likely to seek absolution?' he asked faintly.

'Henry. He *was* an artist, remember, so it seems the sort of thing he would be likely to do. I really can't see Charles Shore doing such a thing, however much he might have loved her. It simply wouldn't be his style.'

Rafferty's heart began to thump. He forgot his previous doubts in the excitement of Llewellyn's discovery. Slowly, he nodded. 'And it certainly isn't Hilary's style, either. Whether or not there *was* anything going on between Barbara and Shore, Henry believed there was. When you think about it, even the method of murder fits. Suffocation—when you compare it with our previous case and the victim's battered, destroyed face—seems a pretty gentle murder method.'

Llewellyn nodded. 'He loved her. He would have wanted her to suffer as little as possible, even if he thought she'd been unfaithful. He probably held a cushion over her face; that way, he wouldn't even have to look at her while he killed her.'

'It fits. And it certainly explains that flower away very neatly. And to think I swallowed his story. He fooled us both, Dafyd. He must have taken the housekeeper's keys from her bag after all, and driven off in her car.' Hadn't Llewellyn said the inquisitive Mrs Watson couldn't hear traffic noises from her kitchen? He was generous enough to congratulate his sergeant on his thoroughness. 'Well done, Dafyd. If it hadn't been for you...'

Llewellyn was equally generous. 'But if you hadn't thought of the significance of the flower *first...*'

Rafferty grinned sheepishly, aware that he had been ready enough to dismiss it. 'So we're both clever buggers,' he exclaimed, as he clapped his sergeant happily on the back. Unblushingly, he declared, 'I always knew we'd make a damn good team, Taff, and that's a fact.'

His self-satisfaction flattened out a few seconds later. If it was true, how the hell did they prove it? But they mightn't need to, he realized, as he picked up the phone and began to dial. Henry was weak. Surely with a little pressure he could be made to crack? For whatever reason he'd killed his wife, Rafferty suspected that, in his heart of hearts, Henry would long to confess. To gain the absolution he apparently craved.

IT WAS STRANGE how history repeated itself, Rafferty reflected as Mrs Griffiths let them in and left them to wait in the library. This had been one of those cases where it had happened frequently; even Charles Shore had commented on it, he remembered. Rafferty had the eerie sensation that a malevolent and ghostly brain had been guiding its path.

Once again, they waited in the library for Henry to appear. Or rather, not just Henry, for Rafferty had made it clear to the housekeeper that he expected to see the entire household: family, staff, the lot. He wanted plenty of witnesses when Henry confessed, enough to make a later retraction impossible. He was determined that no one would have cause to accuse them of police brutality when Henry finally admitted the truth.

Fleetingly, as the minutes ticked by and still no one came, Rafferty wondered if Mrs Griffiths had chosen not to pass on his message. But then, he reflected, even though she might wish to defy him, she wouldn't dare. Besides, he'd taken the precaution of passing the phone to Llewellyn so he could relay his request and he didn't think she'd want to get her compatriot in trouble with his boss.

They shared their waiting time with Charles Shore's young son, Edward. Far more self-possessed than his cousin, he knelt on the floor sticking together a broken computer joystick and studiously ignored them.

After attempting several friendly overtures, all of which were rebuffed, Rafferty, made irritable by the anxious waiting, gave up, sat back and watched as the excess glue congealed on the ruinously expensive rug. Nose clenched against the overpowering stench, he sourly hoped that when Shore eventually deigned to turn up he would deliver a painful punishment. All he needed to make the waiting time perfect was for Llewellyn to start grumbling again about his sinuses. Being more concerned himself with suffering imminent brain damage, he got up and flung open a window.

To Rafferty's surprise, when Edward squirted yet another long sausage of glue from the tube, the Welshman not only made no complaint about the smell, but actually began to enthuse about the damned stuff to such an extent that Rafferty wondered if he ought to notify medical science of its curative powers.

'Marvellous, you know, this modern glue. It'll stick anything. I remember last year, I broke my mother's favourite fountain-pen. She didn't think it would ever work again and nor did I, but we were both wrong, it was as good as new. I was talking to a chemist friend of mine about it and he explained . . .'

Rafferty groaned and tried to tune out the drone of Llewellyn's voice. Even if he *had* solved the case, Rafferty wasn't sure he wouldn't prefer to hear about Llewellyn's sinus trouble rather than endure another of his lectures. Where the devil was Henry Longman and the rest? he wondered uneasily. He had primed himself up for the confrontation, and the longer the delay the more doubts began crowding in. They made him feel guilty as this had been Llewellyn's triumph. You're jealous, Rafferty, his Catholic conscience pricked, that's all that's the matter with you. You're trying to pull holes in Llewellyn's deductions just so you can feel superior. The trouble was, there was still one tiny point that Llewellyn's explanation didn't cover.

Denying his conscience's unfair conclusion, Rafferty took a deep glue-coated breath and persuaded his mind to stop dwelling on his doubts about the case, by letting his eyes flicker from Edward and his growing river of glue over to Maximillian Shore's portrait and the egotistical Latin quotation beneath. The arrogance of the wording still irritated him. Wasn't it typical of a man like Maximillian Shore to choose such a motto?

Rafferty had been staring intently into the painted eyes of old Maximillian's portrait for several minutes, still hoping to clear up the lingering doubts, when suddenly he saw what should have been obvious to him virtually from the start. How could he have been so blind? Relieved that his doubts had some substance and were not, after all, based on jealousy, he glanced guiltily at Llewellyn. He just hoped Dafyd didn't take it too badly.

In more ways than one, the glue had given his brain a much-needed buzz, for now he realized just how much he had been affected by tunnel vision. Breathing shallowly, taking in a cautious top-up of brain lubricant, he withdrew his eyes from those of the portrait and let them flicker once again over the boy and his joystick before ranging along the room. So deeply was he sunk in his thoughts, that he jumped as the door was suddenly thrust open and Charles Shore appeared. He led a crocodile of family and staff behind him.

'I hope this won't take long, Inspector,' said Shore, as he glanced impatiently at his watch. 'I'm due at a meeting in forty minutes and—'

Rafferty held up his hand. 'I wouldn't worry too much about your meeting, sir,' he told him. 'You may find you wish to cancel it after you've heard what I have to say.'

'The devil I will,' Shore contradicted. 'Edward.' He addressed his young son. 'If you haven't removed that disgusting mess from my library in ten seconds, I can promise you'll be very sorry.'

Although his voice was quiet enough, it was evident that Edward knew his father didn't make idle threats. To Rafferty's quiet satisfaction, the boy hurriedly put the top back on the tube, picked up the glue and his damaged joystick and made himself scarce.

'Henry, open the rest of the windows,' Charles ordered, before he sat heavily in one of the leather chairs. 'I take it you've got some news for us at last, Inspector?'

Rafferty nodded distractedly, his mind still busily working out the whys and wherefores of his latest and—he hoped—his final theory.

'Perhaps you'd better get on with it, then,' Shore suggested sharply as Rafferty, deep in thought, continued to sit frowning at them all. 'If it turns out you're right and it is necessary for me to cancel this meeting, I'll need to do it before my fellow board members leave for the venue.'

Apparently, Shore had now got over the worst of his grief, and it was business first, as usual. Rafferty nodded again and leaned forward. He didn't take offence at Shore's peremptory tone. Why should he? He reasoned, as he took another quick glance at the portrait. He had reason to be grateful to Shore. He recognized that if the man had arrived on time, he would have made a grave mistake.

He studied the little tableau spread around the room before turning to the tall figure standing by the window. His voice was grave as he announced, 'Maximillian Shore, I hereby arrest you for the murder of Barbara Longman. You do not have to say anything unless you wish to do so, but what you say may be given in evidence.'

FOR ABOUT ten seconds, Rafferty's words shocked everyone into silence, but then a noisy clamour broke out. Charles Shore's authoritative bellow easily drowned the rest as he demanded, 'What the hell are you saying, man? Why should the boy kill Barbara? It doesn't make any kind of sense.'

'Oh, but it does,' Rafferty contradicted, raising his voice above the continuing hubbub. 'It makes the only kind of sense there is.' In the sudden resumption of silence after he had spoken, he was able to add softly, 'Doesn't it, Maxie?'

Maxie stared at him, with eyes that held more than a touch of his grandfather's arrogance, but none of the old man's strength of character. His mouth fell open as if he was about to defend himself, but his uncle told him to keep quiet.

Shore didn't believe Rafferty's assertion, that much was obvious. His eyes were alight with the inner fire that every boardroom battle probably produced. He seemed to have forgotten how much the dead woman had meant to him, and he immediately began to issue orders with all his natural pugnacity. 'Henry, get on to Hadcliffe.' He consulted his watch. 'He should be in his chambers. Tell him I want him here urgently.'

Rawley Hadcliffe, Rafferty guessed he meant—one of the smartest briefs in London. And—with good reason—the most expensive. He gave one despairing glance at Llewellyn, but the Welshman was staring at him, a dazed expression on his face, too shocked by Rafferty's accusation to share his anxiety.

Of course, Rafferty reminded himself uncomfortably, as far as Llewellyn was aware, they had come to accuse Maxie's father of the murder. And so they would have done, Rafferty conceded grimly—until about thirty seconds ago, when his growing doubts, the smell of the glue and the vision it conjured up as it flowed out of the tube had made everything gel in his mind. And now, if the boy kept quiet till Hadcliffe got here, as Charles Shore had sensibly advised, his case would probably be destroyed. Hadcliffe knew every legal trick in the book, he would take a matter of minutes to discover that Rafferty's proof was all circumstantial evidence and seat of pants guesswork.

But Rafferty was sure he was right. He *knew* it, was as certain of it as he was of his own name. It explained so much, including the marigold clutched in the dead woman's hand, and the other rare meadow flowers scattered all around her. One glance at Maxie was enough to convince him his assumption was correct. The boy's defiance was beginning to crumble, the fear of retribution was there in his eyes. Hadn't he virtually told Rafferty that day, after he had poured out his grief to his grandfather's portrait, that, far from changing his life for the better as he had expected, his murder of his stepmother hadn't made any difference to his life at all?

Rafferty was surprised to see that Henry hadn't moved to obey Charles's orders. Instead, he continued to stare from his son to Rafferty, until finally his bemused gaze settled on the inspector.

'You think Maxie murdered Barbara?' he asked faintly. 'But—but why? I could understand it if you were accusing him of murdering his real mother. God knows, her drunken outbursts have humiliated him in front of his friends almost as frequently as they have me. But he had no grudge against Barbara, he loved her, for God's sake. We all know he loved her.'

Rafferty nodded. 'I don't doubt it.' He glanced uneasily at the boy's ghastly pallor and suggested his father get him a chair. But Henry didn't seem to have heard him. He ignored him as he had ignored Charles, and it was Llewellyn who fetched the chair and pressed Maxie into it. Rafferty turned his attention back to the boy. 'That's what first made you think of killing her, wasn't it, Maxie?'

'Don't call me that.' The boy's voice was intense, his body jerky and nervous, like a horse ready to bolt. 'I told you, my name's Maximillian.'

'Very well—Maximillian. Isn't it true that it was your love for your stepmother that first made you think of killing her?' Rafferty repeated. The boy didn't answer, but his rapidly blinking eyelids provided answer enough.

'I don't understand,' said Henry. He ran his hand over his thinning brown hair distractedly. 'What is he talking about?' he asked his son. He shook off Llewellyn's restraining hand and pulled the boy out of the chair. 'You loved her as much as I did. I *know* that. Why should he think you killed her? Why?'

Llewellyn managed to loosen Henry's grip on his son and Maxie collapsed back in his seat, but still he remained silent.

Rafferty provided the answer. 'His grandfather's theories suggested it to him.' Briefly, he interrupted his explanation to give his sergeant a few orders. 'Llewellyn, get on the phone. We'll need a search warrant. And get Hanks and WPC Green out here. I think a woman's touch is called for.'

'A search warrant?' Charles protested. 'What the hell do you need a search warrant for?'

While Llewellyn got busy on the phone, Rafferty turned to Shore. 'I think if we search your nephew's room, we'll find your father's collection of theories.' He didn't tell him that Maxie had probably taken them from his mother's flat. 'It's my guess that your father hit upon the central idea behind his theory on success years ago, and his library backs up his ideas to the hilt, as young Maxie realized. His own autobiography, his youthful experiences and your own, Mr Shore, all say the same thing. If you want to be successful, first you must suffer a little. The suffering provides the necessary fuel, as it were.'

He walked around the room, allowing his fingers to run along the spines of the books. 'If you look at the books in this library, they're all about successful or famous people, people who suffered a particular tragedy when young. Adolf Hitler lost his father when he was fifteen, Abraham Lincoln lost his mother at nine, Henry Ford lost his mother at thirteen, Lloyd George lost his father before he was two, Tolstoy, Twain, Bertrand Russell, you name them, they all suffered parental loss at a young age. This

whole library is a testament to your father's favourite theory: that to suffer parental loss when young increased your chances of becoming successful.'

'But that's preposterous,' Shore protested. 'There
must be any number of successful people who didn't
suffer any such loss.'

'Oh, undoubtedly.' Drily, Rafferty agreed with
him. And any number of unsuccessful people who
had, he added to himself. 'But is it so preposterous?
Especially to an impressionable teenager? Especially
to one who not only felt he had unfairly lost his inheritance, but who had to suffer the humiliation of
being a poor relation in the bargain, a poor relation
that everyone seemed to despise. Think about it. Your
father himself lost both his parents at fifteen, so did
you and, as I understand it, you're even more successful than your father was. Maxie's fifteen too, in
case you've forgotten. I think he probably felt that,
for this family at least, fifteen was a significant age.
That's why...'

'I know how old he is,' Shore retorted sharply.
'And I still don't believe a word of it. He hasn't the
brains, for one thing.'

'He didn't need brains—his grandfather supplied
those in his writings.' Rafferty could see that in spite
of his arguments Shore's vehemence was weakening.
As his glance settled on his nephew, it held a curiously cold light and Rafferty quickly took advantage
of it. It might be the only chance he got. 'But perhaps I'd better give you some more evidence? I'm
pretty sure it convinced Maxie, maybe it'll do the
same for you?'

Rafferty took a few paces forward, till he was in the centre of the room. He looked silently round at the sea of faces and went on. 'It was my sergeant here who made me realize how strangely the law of averages worked in favour of such a theory. Of course, I made no connection at the time,' he admitted, with an apologetic glance at Llewellyn. 'He told me, right here in this room, just how many British Prime Ministers had suffered a similar loss. What was it, Dafyd? Up to the Second World War, about sixty-three per cent of our Prime Ministers had lost one or both parents while still children or teenagers. I seem to remember your telling me you'd read an article about it.' Pity he hadn't listened at the time, he thought. Another lesson for the future.

Slowly Llewellyn nodded. 'That's right, sir. It mentioned a book published several years ago, called *Parental Loss and Achievement.* I believe I saw a copy on the shelves here. It suggested that bereaved children overcame their feelings of rage at being abandoned—as they saw it—by directing that anger in a purposeful way. It was a—now how did they put it? It was a "springboard of immense compensatory energy".'

'Exactly,' agreed Rafferty. 'Robert Maxwell had it, Lord Weinstock, Anita Roddick, Sir Phil Harris, and so on. And you'll find books about all these people on your shelves. Who bought them?' Although Maximillian Shore senior had undoubtedly bought the older books, he couldn't have bought the later ones, as he had died years before they were published.

His previous bellowing voice strangely subdued, Shore told him, 'Maxie, Maxie bought them.'

'That's right,' Henry whispered. 'And I gave him the money. He told me he thought learning of their early struggles would encourage him to persevere with his school-work. Now you're saying that his real reason for wanting them was to increase his proof of his grandfather's success theory.' Shock had drained his face of colour as he turned and stared at his son. 'So he could bring himself to kill Barbara.'

It seemed he had succeeded in convincing Henry, at least, thought Rafferty, but instead of triumph, all it brought was a feeling of sadness.

'But these people suffered a *natural* loss of their parents,' Charles Shore protested, his desire to wait for Hadcliffe evidently forgotten. 'They didn't murder them. Why should Maxie think that by killing Barbara he could also become successful?'

'I'm afraid you'll have to ask your nephew that, but it's my guess that he craved success so desperately, he was willing to take the chance.' Because he had no proof, he didn't add that he now believed Maxie had attempted another murder—that of his friend Tom Shepherd, and that Barbara had suspected it. His friend had pushed him out of the tree at Easter, deliberately, Maxie believed. He had a grudge against him, maybe he even wanted to test himself, to see if he was capable of murder, before he tried the important one, the one that would, as he believed, guarantee his successful future.

Rafferty could imagine that a strongly moral woman like Barbara would have confronted him over his wicked behaviour; she hadn't hesitated to take the powerful Charles Shore on. Suddenly, something else occurred to him. Barbara had been pregnant; Henry had said that no one else in the family knew, but he couldn't be sure of that. According to Mrs Griffiths, Maxie had been at home the day Barbara received the results of the test. What if he had overheard her ring Henry to tell him the news? What would Maxie's reaction have been? Would he have felt pushed out, rejected, *angry* at the news?

Mindful of his promise to Henry, Rafferty said nothing about this latest conjecture, but he was certain that Barbara's pregnancy, the uncertainty of what she intended to do about his murderous behaviour towards his friend, plus the humiliation of the failure of that violence would, together, provide the extra push he would need to put his grandfather's theories into practice. Even if she had decided to keep his wickedness quiet, she would have surely persuaded Henry to send Maxie away to school to learn some discipline—hadn't Henry said she had, in fact, suggested such a course on the morning she died? Maxie would have hated that. The teasing he endured from his cousins would be as nothing compared to the cruelty he would suffer as a boarder from the other boys. In many ways he was a natural victim, and he knew it.

Of course, Maxie had never been a bright youngster. It was possible that he had completely missed the whole point of his grandfather's theory; that it was the *grief,* the sense of bereavement that was the essential factor. Though it was possible the boy had reasoned that his grief would be no less real for being self-administered. Of course, the fractured skull he had suffered when he had fallen from the tree could have caused unsuspected damage to his brain. It was well known that head injuries could cause problems months, even years, later.

'You know,' he went on, 'I didn't connect Maxie with Barbara's death until Charles's son, Edward, helped me to see how he could have killed her. After that, the *why* just fell into place.'

Charles Shore stared at him. 'Edward—Edward helped you? How?'

'I'm sure it was quite unintentional,' Rafferty observed drily. 'But when he used that glue in here just now, it not only reminded me of the river as it came out of the tube, but it also came to me where else I'd smelt such an odour before. It was in your shed. The small outhouse by the Tiffey.'

He turned to Maxie, who sat with unfocused, staring eyes. 'I thought then it was just from an old Airfix Spitfire that was abandoned there, but you used it to stick the broken paddle of the canoe, didn't you, Maximillian?'

Still the boy said nothing; he seemed to have retreated into some kind of catatonic state, and Rafferty continued. 'You repaired the paddle with the glue so you could use it to canoe up the river to reach the meadow ahead of your stepmother and kill her. You could have reached there easily in five minutes—half the time it would have taken to get there by car. Then, when you had returned, you broke the paddle again in case anyone should suspect you. How could you use the canoe, you must have reasoned. The paddle was broken. You even reminded your father, in my presence, that he hadn't replaced it, so I would know how long it had been broken and that, in the unlikely event I would suspect you of her murder, you would have your alibi ready.

'It's funny,' Rafferty added almost to himself, 'but I remember noticing the day we found her body how straight the river was once it left Elmhurst, and I never considered it as a possible means of reaching the meadow. All I thought of was the road, and how long it would take to get to the meadow through those winding roads from here or Elmhurst. To reach the meadow via the river would have taken only half the time, but, because I never took that into account, I dismissed you as a possible suspect almost straight away. You obviously cared a lot for your stepmother and you couldn't drive, wouldn't have been able to reach the meadow in time—or so I thought. But I was wrong, wasn't I, Maximillian? At least about the second aspect, though I agree with your father that you were genuinely fond of her. There would have been no point in killing her if her death caused you no grief. And then, of course, there were the flowers that were scattered under and around your stepmother's body. They puzzled me.

'Mrs Longman would never have ripped up the rare flowers that meant so much to her. So who had? It finally dawned on me who, and why. Firstly, you needed a reason to encourage her to come into the meadow, because as soon as she saw Thomson's tractor *wasn't* there, she would leave. So you waved a bunch of the wild flowers you had just picked, to gain her attention, and when she challenged you, you carried on picking them. You weren't sure you would be able to overpower her, which was why you wanted her partly over-balanced leaning over, trying to stop you picking more flowers.'

Maxie raised his head. He made no attempt to deny Rafferty's accusation, instead, his gaze fixed on his grandfather's portrait. It was as if some communication passed between them. It appeared to give the boy strength. He turned to his father, his face expressionless, but his voice was filled with contempt. 'Mother's right, you're a failure, a nobody, a nothing. I wanted to be a success like Grandfather.' He frowned and after gazing thoughtfully at his grandfather as if for reassurance, he added softly, to himself, 'Perhaps I still can. Maybe it takes longer than I thought for the grief to work its magic?'

Rafferty felt the atmosphere in the room change. The tension was now a physical thing. Shore's powerful hands had begun to flex and unflex, as if he had Maxie's neck between them, his face was a colour kaleidoscope of deep emotions and Rafferty, worried Shore's impressive self-control would fail him, wanted to get the boy out before it did.

Quietly, in a voice that was as calming and emotionless as he could make it, Rafferty told the boy, 'You're over fourteen, Maximillian. Over the age of criminal responsibility. You know right from wrong. The murder of your stepmother was carefully planned, premeditated, and I think the courts will agree with me. I must ask you to accompany me to the police station.' He glanced at Hilary Shore. 'Perhaps your aunt will help you gather a few things together.'

'No!' Maxie's scream made him falter. Until now, Maxie had remained very quiet, whether from shock or disbelief of what was happening, Rafferty didn't know. But now, his matter-of-fact mention of practicalities seemed to get through to the boy where the previous dramatic retelling of the murder had failed, and, as grim reality swamped the theories that had obsessed him for so long, he ran across the room to the portrait of Maximillian Shore screaming hysterically, 'Grandfather,' he begged. 'Help me. You've got to help me. It was your idea. I'd never have thought of it on my own. Make them see that I had to kill her.'

Appalled at the ghastly spectacle of the shrieking boy scrambling over the table to reach his grandfather's portrait, Rafferty could only stare helplessly at him.

It was Llewellyn who pulled the sobbing boy away. 'He won't help you, lad,' he soothed. 'Come with me now and get whatever you think you'll need.'

Docile now, as though stunned by the speed of events and the disproving of his omnipotent grandfather's theories, Maxie began to follow the sergeant. But as he passed his father, he clutched his arm in a pleading gesture, as if he had forgotten just who it was he had murdered. 'Father?'

If Maxie had forgotten whom he had killed, Henry hadn't. He stared, with a kind of horrified fascination, at the monster he had spawned, before, quite deliberately, he wrenched his arm from the boy's grasp and stepped back, leaving him utterly alone.

Blinking rapidly, Maxie swallowed hard, before turning to Charles Shore. 'Uncle?' he whispered. 'Tell him he can't do this to me. I'm a Shore. The rich always evade the law. You taught me that.'

'But you're not rich, are you, boy?' Shore may have managed to control his urge to physical violence, but his capacity to wound verbally was given full rein. His despised nephew had deprived him of his desire, and it made him cruel. 'You've not even a Shore,' he taunted him. 'Your name's Longman and a Longman you'll remain. You gambled Barbara's life on a long shot and lost. Get out of my sight, you mindless cretin, before I forget how much I have left to lose, and kill you myself.'

Maxie backed away, his face with its still childish curves looked even more stunned at this latest rejection. He might be a murderer, but now he looked simply a pathetic child, a child seduced by dreams of wealth and success and power. As the family who had helped to twist his personality abandoned him, Rafferty experienced a twinge of pity for the boy. He managed to force it down and told him, 'As I said, you'll be taken from here to the police station.' He glanced at Henry, but couldn't bring himself to remind the man that Maxie was still his son and needed him. Henry had plainly had as much as he could take for one day. 'The state will provide you with legal representation, if necessary.'

He saw through the library window that WPC Green and Constable Hanks had arrived, and he gestured to Llewellyn to take the lad out to the waiting police car. Perhaps the housekeeper would be willing to bring along a few things for the boy later?

The gravel crunched and as the police car moved away, Rafferty caught a glimpse of Maxie's white face staring back at them. He looked frightened, bewildered and alone, his body curled into a foetal posi-

tion in the far corner. Rafferty sighed and was
relieved when the car turned on to the main road and
the boy's face, with its look of desperation, was
whisked out of sight.

SEVENTEEN

THE SEARCH FOR Maximillian Shore's theoretical manuscript had been successfully concluded. As Rafferty had guessed, Maxie had hidden it in his room. Once he had been brought to the police station, Maxie had ignored all advice to keep quiet, whether from his appointed legal representative or anyone else, and had insisted on telling them the details. As Rafferty had guessed, Maxie *had* known of his stepmother's pregnancy and his reaction had been a predictable fury. He had thought she loved him, he had told them, loved him *best.* She had made so much of him that he had thought he was enough for her. But the discovery that he wasn't, that Barbara was to have a child of her own, made his love turn temporarily to hatred and he had decided that he wasn't going to compete for her love with a baby. If he couldn't have her love for himself, then no one would have it.

Rafferty believed the shock of his arrest had tipped him over the edge of sanity. The boy appeared to have forgotten the earlier grief he had felt; he had seemed proud of his own cleverness and boasted of how easy it had been to borrow his uncle's mobile phone, how he had used a handkerchief over the mouthpiece and cotton wool in his cheeks to disguise his voice. As he had gone on to explain how he had punched Barbara in the temple to stun her, before smothering her with one of the pretty cushions he had brought with him specially for the purpose, Rafferty had experienced a growing horror that was still with him several hours after the interview finished.

'Success was everything to the Shore family,' said Rafferty, to Llewellyn later, as they sat over comforting mugs of tea in his office. 'Henry told us as much, if you recall? Young Maxie felt he had been deprived of his rightful inheritance. His grandfather didn't approve of Anne's marriage to Henry, and had removed her from his will. And, although they were reconciled when Maxie was born, the old man was unfortunately murdered before he could change his will back again. Consequently, Maxie was a poor relation, with little prospect of ever being anything more. He and his father lived on sufferance in his grandfather's house.

'I think, as he got older, that fact twisted his mind, which was never very strong to begin with—you've only got to look at his mother to see there's instability in the family. I think he inherited that, as well as his grandfather's self-will, and I doubt if his mother, with the drunken accusations she must have poured into his ears, helped the situation. She was very bitter about being dependent on her brother's charity. She hated Henry for that and she hated Barbara for the loss of her son. You know, thinking back to some of the things she said, I get the impression she had guessed months earlier about the strength of her brother's feelings for Barbara, and was hoping for some family confrontation from which she could benefit. I bet she didn't anticipate this result, though.'

Llewellyn sighed. 'I wonder how many times Maxie watched his father belittled by his mother and uncle for his lack of achievement?'

'Enough, it would seem. Neither Maxie nor his father were bright enough to make their pile from using their brains. Didn't we hear his cousins tell him as much when we arrived at the house just after Barbara's body had been found? Remember his cousins were taunting him and he retaliated?' Llewellyn nodded. 'Remember how astonished the younger boy seemed that Maxie had stood up for himself?' Llewellyn nodded again.

'I get the impression he had never done that before. Of course he'd killed his stepmother less than twenty-four hours earlier. I imagine he felt filled with power just then and it gave him the courage to stand up for himself that he had lacked before. He was presumably convinced that his life would start to become more successful. It was only later that he began to realize it wasn't going to happen, and that he had killed the only person who had truly cared for him for nothing. I imagine it was a bitter discovery.

'Of course, Henry was happy enough to potter along. He might have resented being beholden to the Shores, but he was enough of a realist to know his life would be a whole lot chillier in the outside world. Even when Hilary convinced him that Barbara and Charles were conducting a passionate affair under his nose, it wasn't enough to force him to do something. The difference was that Charles was wrong about the boy—Maxie *was* a Shore, whatever his actual name, with enough of his grandfather in him to make him ambitious. And he was young; fifteen's a very vulnerable age, and he was more vulnerable than most to the powerful influence of his grandfather—didn't I tell you he was at the root of this case?

'Added to that, he felt his own and his father's failure acutely. His mother tried to imply that Charles had turned the boy against her, but I imagine she did that pretty effectively herself. She had probably humiliated him countless times with her drunken exhibitions. He would hate her for that. Luckily for her, his grandfather's theories on success demanded that the stepmother he loved, rather than the mother he hated, was the appropriate victim.'

He drained his mug of tea and went on. 'Of course, he'd inherited that ruthless streak from his grandfather and had apparently managed to convince himself that the murder would make him not only invulnerable but secure, with success guaranteed. It's a pity for him and his victim that he didn't also inherit his grandfather's sharp mind. If he had he might have realized that even with the chips all stacked in your favour life's still a chancy business. By the way,' he broke off. 'Did you get on to the hospital as I asked?'

Llewellyn nodded again, and began tidying the reports that still littered Rafferty's desk. 'You were right. They found yew berries mixed in with the jam that boy Tom Shepherd ate. Dangerous shrubs to have around with children about the place.'

'Especially when one of them was Maxie. Of course, unless he confesses, we'll never be able to prove that he tried to poison his friend—it's just possible those berries got in the jam by accident. But it doesn't really matter. One successful murder is enough to ensure he's put in a secure place for a very long time.'

He sighed. The whole case had depressed him and now, as he made a conscious effort to cheer up, he thought he knew the very thing to do. Was there anything quite so satisfying, he asked himself, as rubbing the ultra-efficient Welshman's nose in one of his own mistakes? And it wasn't often he got the chance.

'You know,' he said, with a sly glance at Llewellyn. 'It's funny when you think of it, but if that lad had met us before he embarked on his murderous career, he might have reconsidered his grandfather's theory.'

'Oh?' Llewellyn's eyes narrowed. 'What do you mean?'

'Well, we both lost our fathers young, and we're neither of us noticeably successful, are we? He got it wrong—just like you when you sent those ill-chosen flowers to Maureen. You know Ma thinks you're playing fast and loose with the girl?'

'As it happens, I *didn't* get it wrong.' Loftily, Llewellyn corrected him. 'I asked the shop to send a dozen *red* roses, and they made a mistake. Perhaps you'll both be happy to know that, to make up for it, she's going to receive *two* dozen red roses. Red roses for love's waxing.' He got up and opened the door. 'If you want me I'll be in the canteen placing the order.'

The office door slammed shut behind him, before Rafferty could come back with a suitable riposte. Llewellyn had got the better of him—again. But this time Rafferty didn't mind. He even smiled. After all, it wasn't every day that he managed to bring a murder case and a budding romance to a successful conclusion. His ma *would* be pleased.

ALASKA GRAY

SUSAN FROETSCHEL

A Jane McBride Mystery

First Time in Paperback

NEW BEGINNINGS, DEADLY ENDINGS

Jane McBride is a woman with secrets and sadness—and Alaska seems just about as far away as she can get from her past.

Her big welcome comes in the form of an anonymous phone call telling her to leave. Then Jane learns that the finance job she left Boston for has been eliminated. But the beauty of Sitka lures her, and she is determined to stay—even after she surprises an intruder ransacking her room.

The death of a young local woman has no connection to her…or does it? Soon Jane is trapped in the middle of a very sophisticated evil in the small town….

"A page-turner…"—*Pittsburgh Advertiser*

Available in July at your favorite retail stores.

To order your copy, please send your name, address, zip or postal code, along with a check or money order (please do not send cash) for $4.99 for each book ordered ($5.99 in Canada), plus 75¢ postage and handling ($1.00 in Canada) payable to Worldwide Mystery, to:

In the U.S.	In Canada
Worldwide Mystery	Worldwide Mystery
3010 Walden Avenue	P. O. Box 609
P. O. Box 1325	Fort Erie, Ontario
Buffalo, NY 14269-1325	L2A 5X3

Please specify book title(s) with your order.
Canadian residents add applicable federal and provincial taxes.

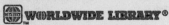 **WORLDWIDE LIBRARY** ®

ALASKA

Die Dreaming
Terence Faherty

First Time in Paperback

An Owen Keane Mystery

ALMA MURDER

Ex-seminarian turned seeker of lost souls—especially
his own—Owen Keane attends his tenth high school reunion
and finds himself the butt of a practical joke by the old gang.
Vengeance being the operative mood in his "morning after"
state, he starts asking sticky questions about a decade-old
secret that has shadowed the lives of everyone involved.

What he discovers is shocking, but pieces are missing.
Not until the twentieth reunion do they fit together. One of
the gang has been murdered, and Owen is determined to
unravel the tangle of lies that cost a man his life—and now
may cost Owen his own.

"Rich and surprising..."—*Publishers Weekly*

Available in July at your favorite retail stores.

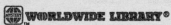

WORLDWIDE LIBRARY®

DREAMING

REGINALD HILL
BLOOD SYMPATHY

A Joe Sixsmith Mystery

ALL THIS AND A MATCHMAKING AUNT, TOO...

It is feast or famine for ex-machinist turned private investigator Joe Sixsmith. One minute he's dozing in his office, the next he's been hired by a self-proclaimed dabbler in the dark arts to retrieve a stolen locket. There's also a man who dreams he has murdered his entire family and two thugs who seem to think Joe's in possession of several kilos of heroin. Add to that a meddlesome aunt who wants to fix him up with marriage candidates.

Things are sticky at best. But for a private eye with admittedly more wits than guts, and an alcoholic cat as partner, a bit of luck may just keep him single— and alive.

"Sumptuously plotted..."—*Kirkus Reviews*

Available in August at your favorite retail stores.

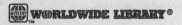

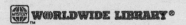

CRIMINALS ALWAYS HAVE SOMETHING TO HIDE—BUT THE ENJOYMENT YOU'LL GET OUT OF A WORLDWIDE MYSTERY NOVEL IS NO SECRET....

With Worldwide Mystery on the case, we've taken the mystery out of finding something good to read every month.

Worldwide Mystery is guaranteed to have suspense buffs and chill seekers of all persuasions in eager pursuit of each new exciting title!

Worldwide Mystery novels—crimes worth investigating...

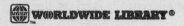 **WORLDWIDE LIBRARY®**